BLACK DONNELLY, RATS AND PIGS

Fergus P Egan

BLACK DONNELLY, RATS AND PIGS

Copyright © 2018 Fergus P Egan
All Rights Reserved

Author and Publisher: Fergus P Egan

ISBN: 978-1-9993941-1-0 (Electronic Book Edition)
ISBN: 978-1-9993941-2-7 (Hardcover Edition)
ISBN: 978-1-9993941-0-3 (Paperback Edition)

Email: FergusEganPublishing@gmail.com

Editor: Andrew Niall Egan
Proofreader: Aisling Egan
Cover design and photographs of the
Irish coastline and landscape: Andrew Niall Egan

ISBN: 978-1-9993941-0-3

On Tuesday 05 August 1947, nine-year-old Murty Muldoon's idyllic summer holiday at his uncle's farm in the West of Ireland is shattered by the killing of a recluse, 'Black Donnelly'. The killing is believed to be an execution by the mythical 'Black Pig' – in local folklore, a phantom harbinger of death.

Detective Inspector John Patrick Murphy, 'Murf', does not believe in ghosts. He sets out to unravel the mystery. His inquiry uncovers bitter motives stretching back to the trenches of World War I at the Somme in 1918 and to the Anglo-Irish War of 1919-1922 and the subsequent civil war.

The story is in answer to "Grandad! Tell us a story! But don't make it too long!" It is a work of fiction. The location and setting of the crime are purely imaginary.

....

Written for Mitchell, Malcolm, Madeline,
Rebecca, Sophie and Noah Egan.

The 'mystery' is to find the true story
hidden within the make-believe.

LIST OF CHIEF CHARACTERS

<u>Murtagh (Murty) Muldoon</u>:
Nine-year-old boy in 1947; witness to a frightening incident

<u>Detective Inspector John Patrick Murphy (Murf)</u>:
Unconventional police detective

<u>District Officer Superintendent David Fox</u>:
Sergeant in the Royal Irish Constabulary; later, District Officer 'Foxy' of Garda Síochána (Irish Police) in Killbawn, Mayo; Murf's superior officer

<u>Daithi Mac a'tSionnaigh</u>:
David Fox's name while serving in the IRA

<u>Captain Daniel Edward Kennedy</u>:
Captain in the Royal Irish Fusiliers; explosives expert in the British Army; leader of a British Auxiliary Flying Column in the Irish War of Independence

<u>Terence (Tracy) Prior</u>:
Bomb engineer and dog handler in the British Army; republican communist during the Irish War of Independence; joins the Colonial Police Force

<u>Michael Carr (Mickey Go-Carr)</u>:
IRA runner and assassin;
antisocial and regarded as slow-witted

<u>Ben Muldoon</u>:
Murty Muldoon's uncle and friend of Mickey Carr

TABLE OF CONTENTS

PROLOGUE PART ONE

MURTY MULDOON'S CURIOSITY

Summer 1947

I want to get past Black Donnelly's horrible place; but not before my uncle is convinced of things there. Was it really a nightmare I had last night?

No! I am certain of what I saw.

Rounding the bend, there it is. Black Donnelly's place in the spent bog, as bleak and foreboding as ever. Parked in front is Mickey Motor's motor-car. And Mickey peering in through the front window, cupping his hands to his eyes against the glare of the dirty panes.

"I brought two pigs for Donnelly. He's not in the slaughterhouse where he ought to be at this time of day. And there's no answer from the house. He must be dead or something!"

Mickey goes around to the back, to enter the slaughterhouse by the trapdoor, the one used to haul the carcasses by the winch. There is an entrance to the house from the slaughterhouse. Mickey seems to know his way around the forbidding place. We wait for Mickey to reappear. My uncle hammers on the door with his fists.

He shouts, "Mickey! Mickey! Are you there? What's keeping you? For God's sake, Mickey, answer me!"

There is a sound from the house. Mickey, or someone, is falling about in there. Is he tripping or slipping or what? At last the sound of the front door being unlatched, and Mickey stumbles out holding on to the wall for support. His black boots and blue overall knees are wet, so he must have fallen on a wet floor. He moves away from the door, still leaning on the wall for support. Then he vomits and slides to the ground. He is shaken, pale and weak. Nevertheless he grips my uncle's wrist like an iron vice to prevent him from entering. I am still down at the road, but I can hear their lowered voices.

Mickey is still spluttering and coughing bits of vomit. "Donnelly – dead."

"Do you think the lads from Cork…?"

"No! Too gruesome. Not even the Tans at their worst would have done this."

"Done what?"

Mickey grips him with two hands to impress upon him not to enter. "His chest. His heart cut out."

"With his own knives?"

"I don't think so. It's too crude; many hacking cuts; more like he was gnawed."

Now my uncle slides to the ground. So bewildered am I that I almost laugh at the spectacle unfolding in front of me.

This is the evidence – what I saw last night was no dream.

I shut my eyes. How quickly things change.

....

Four Weeks Earlier

In the 'forties I noticed all sorts of anomalies resulting from 'the Troubles' (1919 – 1923). But no one spoke about 'the Troubles', so I could only speculate and, for the most part, remain unenlightened. I still know very little about 'the Troubles', and although this story is not about 'the Troubles', it has a lot to do with the fallout – the uneasiness left hanging unresolved.

I grew up in rural South Donegal near Lough Erne, in the 'Free State' (more correctly 'Éire', but the previous term was still commonly used). Standing at the spot where the Termon River enters the lough, I reflected. The river was in the 'Free State'; the lough was wholly in 'the North'. Eddies and miniature whirlpools appeared and disappeared where the current of the river thrust into the placid water of the lough – sometimes here, sometimes there, a few feet away. The actual point where the river became the lough changed second by second, and was influenced by the ever-changing flood of current in the river. Experts, politicians and surveyors were certain as to the exact location of the border – where the river ended – yet could not agree on which of the many 'certain' and 'exact' locations is the correct one. In all likelihood, they never will.

I swept my eyes around the wedge-shaped field to take in the ruined castle and the herd that grazed contentedly on the lush grass. The point of the wedge, where I stood, was at the lough. The ground here was soft, evidenced by the number of rabbit burrows dotting the bank. The riverbank was heavily wooded. And on the other side of the wedge, the forest of the estate came to the lough's edge. The smells were in perfect balance – the rich grass, the clean water, the woodiness of the trees. And as the breeze gently lifted and fell, the forest seemed to whisper from one side of the field to the other in conversation. How could there ever be turmoil in such a tranquil place?

I walked over to the slipway where a boat was moored. I looked into the boat at the pool of still water collected in the bottom, probably from the morning's rain. I studied my reflection – Murty (actually Murtagh) Muldoon, nine years old, reddish-fair hair and freckles, slighter than the boys who worked on farms, brown short-sleeved shirt over brown dotted tweed knee-length trousers.

The wedge of the field protruded into 'the North' –
Looking out over the lough, I faced 'the North';
To the right was also 'the North';
And to the left, 'the North' yet again.

Lough Erne was actually south of where I stood. The only visible place here that was not 'the North' was north. 'The North' was also called the 'Six Counties', which made sense. I could name all six – Derry, Antrim, Down, Armagh and Tyrone that touched Lough Neagh (the largest lake in Ireland or Britain) and Fermanagh with Lough Erne. The house here beside the slipway, where I stood, was also in the 'Free State', unoccupied (as in 'not lived in'). It was previously occupied by the British when it was in 'the North'. And then the border had been redrawn. Perhaps it was never in 'the North', but the British just held on to it after the treaty.

That's the way it was then, 24 years after the 'the Troubles' ended – the border unresolved, houses vacant, owners absent, and reclusive people hidden away silent in remote houses. 'The Troubles' were still the source of a lot of unexplained anomalies, and I wanted to find out more and uncover their secrets. In the summer, the summer of 1947, I planned to do just that.

My paternal grandparents live in Mayo. I spent summer holidays with them there in Killbawn. And it was that summer that I went to work on my Uncle Ben's farm in Ballycorry, ten miles outside Killbawn. Nine-year-old boys do a lot of responsible work on farms. Most of the boys in my class are involved in sheep farming or cattle farming, and they all do a man's work. I spend a lot of time on farms, even helping out with the sheep dipping. I was never responsible for any farm work of my own, just helping out whenever I chose. It was more like a game. But that is about to change.

My uncle, Ben Muldoon, lives alone on the farm. To say he lives 'alone' is misleading. There are farm workers constantly in and out of all the farms in the area. Work is shared. Each helps each other with the work – here today cutting the corn, and the next day over on Magee's farm working on the hay – and Mrs. Slattery brings lunch out to them. They hang about in the evening drinking porter.

My favourite animal on the farm is a jennet. My uncle calls it a 'jinnit' because that's how they talk in Mayo. She is smaller than a horse but does the work of a horse. She has no name other than 'the jinnit'.

I don't like the sow. She is my least favourite animal. She is fat and greedy and would dunt you out of her way in her quest for food, which is almost anything, anytime. The jennet doesn't like the sow either, and will not venture near the apple trees if the sow is about. And if the sow ambles in, the jennet gets spooked.

There is a lot to do on the farm – honeycomb to collect from the beehives, butter to churn – but that concerns me less now that my uncle has a really responsible job for me. Tomorrow I would drive the jennet and cart to the market, and later bring her back. But first we need to repair the cartwheel.

The cartwheel is lying on the ground within two stone circles, each shaped to the design and size of the wheel. The wooden part, comprised of the rim and the spokes, is lying in one circle; and the iron ring for the outer rim is lying in the second circle. This second circle also contains burning turf coals, so that the iron rim is hot, really hot. With tongs, my uncle lifts the iron rim and carefully places it over the first circle so that it encircles the wooden wheel. Then he pours water on it. The iron rim hisses and steams and contracts to grip the wooden wheel. Ah! So that's how the cartwheel is held together. Some generous lathering with goose grease and placing it on the cart axle with a secure pin, and the cart is in good shape for the morrow. Next we apply Dubbin to the harness, massaging the leather straps between thumb and forefinger. Dubbin consists of wax, oil and tallow. It keeps the leather supple and soft, and prevents it from stiffening and cracking. It has a pleasant leather smell, like newly-polished boots, but it does not impart a shine.

Tomorrow would be Tuesday, the first Tuesday of the month. According to Old Moore's Almanac, the first Tuesday of the month is pig-market day in Killbawn. The sow had given birth to a litter of 'banbhs', and it is time to sell them. There is no harm in that. The greedy sow has no interest in minding her own banbhs. They would be much better off on another farm.

On the morrow, Tuesday, I hitch the jennet to the cart, a red cart with blue painted shafts, and set to padding the crate with straw for the banbhs. My uncle told me to use straw, not hay. Of course I know the difference between hay and straw; I know the difference between hay-for-fodder and bedding-hay. Straw does not feel as dry as hay, and has a neutral smell, not like the rich smell of hay. The crate, well-lined with straw is put in the box of the cart. My job is to hold the jennet easy while the squealing banbhs are placed in the crate one by one – all ten of them. The jennet needs a lot of calming. She is snorting and flicking her ears and tapping the ground skittishly. She sure is nervous around pigs. Stroking her nose calms her, and with the banbhs now quiet, she is anxious to get away from them. With blinkers on, she does not realise that they are in the cart and coming with us.

My uncle, 5'6'', dressed in a grey cloth cap, a striped blue collarless shirt, dungaree overalls, and black hobnail boots, sits down in the cart with one eye on the banbhs and consults his 'Old Moore's Almanac' in the section under the heading 'Agricultural Fairs, Markets, and Livestock Auctions', jotting some figures with a pencil.

I, for my part, stand in the front of the cart and make all those tsking and clicking noises with my tongue that horses and jennets understand. Down the lane we pass Slattery's. Slattery's is the farm next to us, and Noreen Slattery told me that I could use her bicycle anytime. Noreen Slattery is also nine years old. Unlike other girls her age, she has her brown hair cut short and favours primrose yellow frocks and bare feet. That way she is able to run shortcut through the stream beside the house to access the fields. She had left her bike against the gable of the house for me, but I don't want to ride it. It is a girl's bike with a basket on the front. Still, it is nice of her. The whole Slattery family is nice.

I see Mrs. Slattery cooling her morning batch of bread on the window sills. Mrs. Slattery is short and plump, and waddles as she walks. She always wears a flower-patterned wrap-around apron that totally conceals everything else she wears, even her shoes.

"It's a fine day! Mrs. Slattery!" my uncle shouts in greeting.

"A fine fair day, Ben!"

"A fine pig-fair day!" I say.

"So you're off to the market with the sow and banbhs, then?"

"Just the banbhs!"

"All right then. I'll have the twins keep an eye on things while you're in town!"

Pat and Joe Slattery, the twins, are two years older than

me, and at eleven years old, are already doing a man's work. They always work together as a team and often help Uncle Ben on the farm.

The jennet kept a steady pace throughout this exchange and, having passed by the house, I guide her left onto the boreen that would take us to the main road, and thence to Killbawn. The whole journey would take a couple of hours.

"So, what's in Oul' Moore's Almanac?" I ask.

"Well, that depends on whether it's the Irish one or the English one. They're not the same, at all, at all. This one's the Irish one," says he, waving it at me. Maybe that's the reason it has a green cover. "Everything you need to know is in here – the market days for every town and village in Ireland, what weather to expect, the number of daylight hours in any day of the year, sunrise and sunsets, the tides, and lots more. This is what I consult to determine if I should go to the bog on such-and-such a day to cut turf, or mow the meadow, or whatever. It tells you all you need to know."

"Well then, does it tell you about 'the Troubles'?"

"No! It doesn't tell you about 'the Troubles'. Nothing tells you about 'the Troubles'."

"You said that it tells you all you need to know, and I need to know about 'the Troubles'."

"Ah, cub," he says softly, and I am aware that he says 'cub' in the warm Donegal fashion rather than the local more dismissive term 'gossoon'. "You don't need to know about 'the Troubles'."

To change the subject, he says aloud, "Pay attention to the road; there might be a car!" I knew he was pulling my leg because he says "kyar" to mock my accent.

I sing back at him in cuckoo-call fashion "kay-ir! kay-ir!" – which is how they say it in Mayo. And we take to laughing. I laugh so hard, I get dust up my nose and I sneeze.

"Dia linn!" (God be with us!), he exclaims.

"What did you say?"

"'Dia linn!' That's what we say in Mayo when you sneeze. What do you say up in Donegal when you sneeze?"

"Up in Donegal when we sneeze, we say 'Ah tisshew!'" And we take to laughing again.

The roadside hedge is thick with brambles filled with blackberries. The berries are not yet ripe; they are red, which is the colour of a blackberry when it is green. Coltsfoot and nettles compete with the brambles for space at the roadside. Bees and dragonflies buzz and dart about. After some distance the hedges peter out to be replaced by whin (gorse) and mountain ash. The whins are just coming into bloom. Whin flowers are a pretty yellow, like daffodil-yellow, and have a distinctive coconut scent that attracts bees and insects. But they are a bane to farmers due to their invasiveness. Where whins are abundant, farmland is sparse. Their presence signals our departure from the farmlands.

PROLOGUE PART TWO

BLACK DONNELLY AND
THE BLACK PIG

Suddenly all is quiet. The jennet's ears are twitching; her nostrils are sensing the air as we round a bend to view a bleak landscape. The boreen crosses an area of bogland. It is bleak because the bog has been worked out and there is no more turf to be had there. Treeless. Not even a hedge at the side of the road. Lifeless. It is without colour and is dark even with the morning sun beating down full. Not fit for man or beast. At the bend ahead, the road swings sharp left at a right angle, and then straight as a rush for a mile across the flat bogland to where the welcoming farmland takes up again. All three of us stare ahead; even the jennet has forgotten to blink. There is a stone house at the bend. It will be on our right as we pass. We are approaching it from the gable side. Its frontage is at right angles to the long bog road. It's as if the straight road is built as an approach to this house, and then just before it reaches the front door, it suddenly changes direction and turns sharp right.

The jennet's shoes are clicking a rhythm of iron on stone; the iron-rimmed wheels are making that peculiar crunching sound on the black stone chips that surface the road. As we near the bend we can make out the front door of the house, black and lifeless, even though it is facing east and is taking the full light of the morning sun. The whole house appears even bleaker than the bogscape, and we can make out the surrounding low buildings almost hidden by the bogland sloping upwards behind the property. Not fit for man or beast.

And now a whiff of pig, disturbingly different from the

smell I am familiar with on the farm. It brings to mind manure and rot – and something dead. The jennet is getting skittish. I do my clicking thing to soothe her, and she settles back to her rhythm. As we round the bend I notice the front door nudge open a fraction. Is someone peering at us from out of the dark interior? Through the partly open door I hear the 'bong, bong, bong' of striking clocks. Just then I am startled by the unexpected added sound of alarm clocks, all ringing at the same time, and the door closes with an audible clunk. How strange that there should be so many loud clocks in a lifeless house out here in a dead bog.

My uncle mutters, "Black Donnelly's."

The dark sinister house is now behind us, and a mile of straight road lies ahead. I had heard of Black Donnelly. But I thought it was just a story to frighten children. Like my granny in Killbawn would say, "If you don't behave yourself, Black Donnelly will get you!"

As we travel further from the house, the smell of pig diminishes. The banbhs in the cart do not smell of 'pig'; they smell clean like oatmeal. There is no other smell except for the flintiness in the air that blows incessantly from the exposed bedrock of the worked-out bog. It would be some time before we reach the market, enough time to learn something about Black Donnelly and maybe gain some insight into 'the Troubles' – surely only 'the Troubles' could drive one to live in such a forbidding abode. Donnelly was not from around here, at least no family admitted to being related to him. He is dour, friendless, reclusive. He runs a pig-slaughtering operation which supplies the local butchers with sausages and black puddings. If it were not for the high quality of his sausages, he would have no contact with humanity. I remember seeing butcher shops with the slogan 'Donnelly's Sausages are the best...' and then give all the current reasons why they are so. Donnelly's only interest, outside of pigs, is with clocks. He repairs clocks, he makes clocks, he collects clocks – but not from anyone around here. They say that he has hundreds of clocks, but what I heard today sounded like a million. My uncle does not enlighten me beyond this, because it goes back to 'the Troubles'; and no one talks about that. I wonder what Donnelly might have done during 'the Troubles' to render him an outcast.

Where did he come from?

Why is he called 'Black'?

Is it by his own choice that he is friendless?

Perhaps Donnelly was a bombmaker or an executioner.

Or an informer. No one likes an informer.

Maybe he is lying low and there is a price on his head.

What if his real name isn't Donnelly at all?

Here we are at Killbawn. Second street on the left, down the hill and beside the river, is the pig market. I don't remember turning off the boreen onto the main road to town, distracted by my wild imaginings of deeds and misdeeds that Black Donnelly might have committed during 'the Troubles'. We set up our crate in the market. There are other farmers with pigs, and all have crates or roped-off sections for their pigs. Some are selling pigs and some are buying pigs. All the pigs here smell clean, like the banbhs. There is a noticeable smell of pipe tobacco in the air. Smoking and talking go hand in hand, and there is a lot of talking as everyone is intent on catching up on the news. No one is in any hurry, and I see from all the socialising that this is going to take all day.

I see Uncle Ben strike up a conversation with Mickey Motor. His real name is Michael Carr. He is called Mickey Motor on account of converting a motor-car into a transport van. From what I could see, he had removed the back seat and installed a wooden cage. Still, it is better than a cart, and he is proud of it.

During all the wheeling and dealing I am left in charge of the jennet. She needed water, some oats and a turnip. She is munching the grass on the green and I am happy with myself. I observe Uncle Ben and Mickey spit on their hands and then clasp them in a handshake. This indicates that the deal was struck, and they go into the pub for the ceremonial drink to good health. It's time for me to hitch up the jennet to the cart and be ready for the trip back to the farm.

Most of the farmers are drinking 'good health' by this time; there are more pigs than farmers visible in the market square. Next to us is a makeshift pen, unattended and not very secure, with a pig in it. This piggy sees his chance to freedom, and runs through the ropes – right toward the jennet and through her front legs. I am standing in the cart holding the reins when the jennet rears up and takes off at a gallop. Vegetable stands are knocked over as the jennet races in panic through the market, and straight for the river. Keeping my balance I steer the jennet around and to a slower gait. She is still skittish, but slow enough for Uncle Ben and Mickey to run from the pub and catch her. We manage to soothe her. My uncle is proud of the way I handled the situation in saving the jennet from certain drowning, and it earns me a few back slaps from the onlookers.

Mickey remarks that I speak with a northern accent, "You don't sound like you're from the 26 Counties, do you now?"

"He's from Donegal…" says my uncle.

"…where they ate the spuds, skins and all," laughs Mickey.

I understood 'Free State', and 'Six Counties', a bit

confused about 'The North', and now here in Mayo they speak of the '26 Counties'. I suppose that has to do with 'the Troubles' too. But I say nothing, and Mickey did not expect an answer. He is eager for an excuse – which my jennet-handling skills provided – to order another round of drinks – oh, and a lemonade "for the gossoon."

The pub is a low limestone building with a slate roof. The windows are small. Inside it is dark, made even darker by the tobacco smoke hovering throughout the saloon. The floor is spread with fresh-smelling sawdust but is unable to compete with the smell of pipe tobacco and cigarettes and the sweet-sour smell of spilt porter. There are no chairs. Along the wall, benches surround the room, but no one is sitting. Everyone is shouting at the same time and laughing and slapping each other in camaraderie. Mickey and Uncle Ben make their way to a square wooden table in the corner where they indicate that I could sit on the bench. Uncle Ben brings me a bowl of soup and a wedge of cheese from the bar, and two pints for himself and Mickey, and then he remembers to return for the lemonade. I am unable to eat because of the invasion of competing smells – smoke and stout and sawdust – so I take my bowl of soup and plate of cheese with glass of lemonade balanced on top, and go out to the cart. I see Mickey leave the pub a few minutes later, but Uncle Ben remains socialising with his farmer-friends for an hour or so. It had been a good day, and now it is time to return to the farm.

On the way back, my uncle makes himself comfortable sitting in the cart, propped up in one corner. With the excitement over, and a few porters in him, he eventually rolls over onto the bed of the cart and falls sound asleep in the banbhs' straw. Standing in my position of driver, I urge the jennet to keep up a steady pace. Being tired, and since my uncle would not notice, I sit down and let the jennet choose her own pace. Shortly, she decides that it is time to go home. She ceases chomping the roadside grass and sets a steady pace with determination. I could tell that we are heading west into the evening sun. Sitting against the boards with my back to the jennet and the reins slack in my hands, I lazily observe the lengthening shadow of the cart on the road. The iron rims mark the road surface behind us, tracking our progress. We might still get to the farm before dark.

The lurching of the cart rocks me left and right with the rhythm of the jennet's steady pace. I am being lulled to sleep, too sleepy to light the lamps on the tailgate. The carbide is probably stale, I suppose, and would be unable to ignite. And I don't have matches.

The tracks of the wheels on the road are like the wake of a boat, drawing two white parallel lines all the way from Killbawn to the farm. Now and again I check our progress through half-closed eyes looking backwards at the road behind us, recognising a tree or a bend in the road, and now passing the creamery… all the while the two white lines are being scored into the black road surface. As the shadows lengthen, the black road surface gets blacker; the white tracks of the wheels get whiter. Our progress is being written in luminous white lines suspended in darkness.

The sweet smell of moist earth and grass diminishes as we leave the farmlands; the sylvan smells of leaves and ferns fade as we leave the fringe woodlands; and I feel the cold flinty breeze of the desolate mountainside brush the top of my head. We had turned onto the straight length of bog road that leads to Black Donnelly's. I am unperturbed, too elated and too content with myself to let thoughts of Donnelly ruin a perfect day. I am rehearsing in my mind how I would relate this day's event at school in Donegal next month. Most of the children would have tales to tell – the turf, the hay – but my story would take the biscuit. I am sure of that.

Something rounds the bend behind us. Probably a local dog. Dogs are common sights on country roads, and like the jennet, this dog is probably on his way home. A black dog on a black road. It is difficult to make out his features or determine the breed. But there he is, trotting up between the two luminous strips of white, as if he owned the road. Who does he think he is? De Valera en route to the airport? The setting sun illuminates his eyes. They glow red. This is the only discernible thing about him, indicating his size and proximity.

The lengthening shadows give over to twilight as the sun goes down. But the eyes still glow, even brighter, and ever closer. My eyes, which were half closed, come to full alertness, and my hair stands on end, as I strain to make out what manner of dog this is. I listen for his panting. What I hear alarms me. I hear the snorting breathing of a snout, and surmise that this may not be a dog at all. The jennet realises what this might be. She rears up and takes off as she did earlier at the market. Galloping up the road, I am aware that the cart is not designed for comfort or speed. It lurches and skids from side to side. I grip the side panel for fear of being thrown overboard. My uncle is lying in the bed of the cart, sound asleep. He is of no help. I am frightened and helpless.

Even with our increased speed, the glowing eyes still come closer and closer, until I lose sight of them under the tailboard. There is a thump on the tailboard, and I see a malevolent face piercing me with its eyes, a black pig with fiery eyes burning into my chest. I fear my heart would stop. The black pig attempts to clamber over the tailboard, but his crubeens fail to grip, and with a lurch from the cart he falls back onto the road. Now he is coming again. Snorting saliva and wheezing steamy breath, and staring with his demonic eyes.

A feeling of dread washes over me from my head downward, and I feel the warmth drain from my body, and I feel the blood drain from my veins, and my bladder fails. This is dying. I know this is dying. I feel my mind slipping away.

Thump! There he is again clambering over the tailboard. This time he might succeed. Death itself cannot be worse than the terror of dying, and I wished that he would get it done and over with. Another lurch. The cart tilts up on one wheel. Sparks are flying from the skidding wheel, red and blue. The cart is going to tip over and that will be the end. But the pig has lost his grip once again as the cart bumps and rights itself. I feel myself leaving my body, drawn to the malevolent beast of death. I cannot hold myself. In one quick glance, like a lightning flash that is instant but can be viewed over the succeeding few seconds, I see that we had rounded the bend and that the pig-beast had continued straight on to the front door of Black Donnelly's. I see him disappear through the black door; or is the door wide open with the entrance in black shadow? I cannot tell.

And I am gone... I see the cart; I see my uncle in the bed of the cart; I see myself sitting in the cart still gripping the sides. I see the jennet ease her pace, and though still spooked, get home. I see my uncle waken, not fully awake, but enough to perform the routine actions. I see him and me unharness the jennet and push the cart into the shed for the night. I see this from outside. But where am I, really?

And then I am back... I am sitting before the fire. I am cold, and I am afraid in the dark. I sit there poking the fire to produce higher flames and brighter sparks in an attempt to produce warmth and light. At daybreak I am still there poking the fire. My legs are measled with first degree burns from the fire, but I am still cold.

My uncle is shocked at my appearance when he comes for breakfast. He was not aware of it on the previous night. In answer to his puzzled look I say, "Black Donnelly is dead; the Black Pig got his heart." He tries to convince me that it is my imagination, stimulated by the excitement of the day. Understandable. Everyone had heard of the Black Pig, a popular piece of local folklore. No doubt I had fallen asleep on the journey back and had experienced a nightmare of sorts. And considering my uneasiness with the Donnelly place, very understandable. But something to get over. He tries, but fails to convince me.

I insist on leaving the farm in Ballycorry and going to my granny's in Killbawn. This annoys him. He is a day behind in his farm work and needs my help. But seeing that I am so distressed, he softens and says that he would get the Slattery twins to help out. He tells me to take his bicycle; it is the fastest way to get to town. But I do not want to pass by the Donnelly place alone and insist that he comes with me. Okay! He agrees to go as far as the Donnelly property, and thence I would continue on alone. Uncle Ben's bicycle is too high in the saddle, so I would have needed Noreen's bicycle regardless.

Down we go to Slattery's for Noreen's bicycle and to arrange for farm help. Uncle Ben goes into Slattery's; I remain outside and get Noreen's bicycle from the gable end. I am anxious to get going, and stand by the gate. From inside I hear Mrs. Slattery quizzing my uncle about the market and the banbhs.

"I suppose you sold them to that eejit, Mickey Motor; he has two pigs fattened up for slaughter, so he'll be needin' to start fattenin' the next lot."

Only Mrs. Slattery's voice carries through the walls. "So

you'll be wantin' the twins to help out today?

"Fine! Fine! They know the routine.

"A nightmare, you say? Well, I'll have to have a look-see at him." Out she comes and looks at me. My pants are stained and I must look a sight. "You haven't had breakfast!"

It wasn't a question, so I do not answer. She spits on the corner of her apron and rubs my cheek with it. As she turns back to the house she whispers admonishingly to my uncle, "Benedict Francis Muldoon!"

She returns almost instantly with a thick slice of soda bread, a farl sliced horizontally, still warm, and the butter melting on it. And she places another farl of the scone in the basket of Noreen's bicycle.

"And what do you say to Mrs. Slattery?" my uncle prompts me.

"Black Donnelly is dead; the Black Pig..." I begin.

"Stop!" she says holding up her hand. "There'll be no talk of the Black Pig here!" With that, she surprises my uncle as her upheld hand became a well-placed fist to his ear, sending his cap flying and knocking the almanac out of his pocket.

"In the name of God, man! Have you no sense, fillin' this gossoon's head with nonsense and frightenin' the wits outta him? Look at the state he's in!"

She attempts another fist; my uncle dodges this one. "You were drinkin' with that amadan Mickey Motor last night? And scarin' your own kin with banshees and ghosts?"

My uncle retrieves his cap and almanac, not too sure which one goes where.

"Come, a graw (love)," she says to me, "spend the day with us till you get settled." And then in the direction of the house, "Isn't that all right, Noreen? We'll look after him..." and turning to my uncle, "...where his own kin is doing such a poor job."

I am eager to leave as soon as possible and go to my granny's. I tell this to Mrs. Slattery.

"Very well, then." And to my uncle, "Take him directly to his granny. No pubs; and no Mickey Motor! I'll be callin' in to Maggie Muldoon tonight, and if that young gossoon is not cleaned up and settled down you'll get the other ear thickened. "D'ye hear?"

"Yes! Mrs. Slattery! Of course! Mrs. Slattery!"

I see the twins coming down from the upper field, attracted by the commotion. They are both dressed in blue shirts, blue dungaree overalls, and black Wellington boots. They are bare-headed, hair bleached by the sun, tall and broad-shouldered for eleven-year-olds. The whole townland would know inside the hour, but I don't care.

We make quick progress on the bicycles. I am anxious to get to Killbawn and then get back to Donegal. My uncle is anxious to get some distance from Mrs. Slattery, his left ear stinging red. I want to get past Black Donnelly's horrible place, but not before my uncle is convinced of things there. Was it really a nightmare, and my fear and dread unfounded? No! I am certain of what I saw and experienced, but I need someone to see the daylight evidence.

Rounding the bend, there it is. Black Donnelly's place in the spent bog, as bleak and foreboding as ever. Parked in front is Mickey Motor's motor-car. And Mickey peering in through the front window, cupping his hands to his eyes against the glare of the dirty panes.

Seeing us coming, he shouts, "This place is dead!"

Of course it's dead, I could have said. Everything here is dead – Donnelly, the clocks, the whole place.

And he continues shouting to us as we near; but I stay well back on the road as my uncle approaches the house. "I brought two pigs for Donnelly. He's not in the slaughterhouse, where he ought to be at this time of day. And there's no answer from the house. He must be dead or something!"

My uncle had reached him by now and gives him a dig in the ribs to shush him. Now both of them peer through the front windows.

"It's quiet, all right," says my uncle.

I shout from the road, "Of course it's quiet, the clocks are dead!"

They look at each other, and back at me, but say nothing. Mickey goes around to the back, to enter the slaughterhouse by the trapdoor, the one used to haul the carcasses by the winch. There is an entrance to the house from the slaughterhouse. Mickey seems to know his way around the forbidding place. We wait for Mickey to reappear.

I shout to my uncle, "Can you see any clocks?"

"A few."

"What time do they show?"

"Twenty past ten on that one, and twenty past ten on the other one," a pause. "It's twenty past ten on all of them."

"The time of sunset?"

"I don't know, and even..."

"Oul' Moore knows!"

He pulls out the almanac, and consults it. Puts it back in his pocket, but is a shade paler now. He hammers on the door with his fists, shouting, "Mickey! Mickey! Are you there? What's keeping you? For God's sake, Mickey, answer me!"

There is a sound from the house. Mickey, or someone, is falling about in there. Is he tripping or slipping or what? At last the sound of the front door being unlatched, and Mickey stumbles out holding on to the wall for support. His black boots and blue overall knees are wet, so he must have fallen on a wet floor. He moves away from the door, still leaning on the wall for support. Then vomits, and slides to the ground. He is shaken, pale and weak. Nevertheless he grips my uncle's wrist like an iron vice to prevent him from entering. I am still down at the road, but I can hear their lowered voices.

Mickey is still spluttering and coughing bits of vomit. "Donnelly – dead."

"Do you think the lads from Cork…?"

"No! Too gruesome. Not even the Tans at their worst would have done this."

"Done what?"

Mickey grips him with two hands to impress upon him not to enter. "His chest. His heart cut out."

"With his own knives?"

"I don't think so. It's too crude; many hacking cuts; more like he was gnawed."

Now my uncle slides to the ground. So bewildered am I that I almost laugh at the spectacle unfolding in front of me.

This is the evidence – what I saw last night was no dream.

Mickey puts a cigarette in his mouth but is unable to strike the match. "We'll have to get word to the guards."

"You go, Mickey, in your vehicle."

"Yes."

But neither one moves. Mickey tries to strike another match, but it breaks.

"Mickey! The guards!"

He stumbles up shakily and staggers down to his motor-car.

"And drop off the young lad at Muldoon's on the way to the barracks!" my uncle shouts after him.

He looks at me as he fumbles with the matches. "Are you comin' or stayin'?" he asks with little interest.

"Home!"

"Home to the Six Counties, is it?"

He tries again to light his cigarette, but his hands are shaking badly. He breaks another match. I get into the car; he is not going to invite me. The two pigs are still in the back, the unlit cigarette is still in his mouth. It begins to rain. He starts the car. The wipers don't work, so he has to drive with his head out the window. Now his cigarette is wet.

Mrs. Slattery was right. Mickey is an amadan. He never learned my name, and thinks I am from 'the Six Counties'. And his car is a wreck. And it smells of pig stink, and of Mickey-vomit, and of wet cigarettes.

I shut my eyes.

In the 'forties I noticed all sorts of anomalies that were a result of 'the Troubles'. But no one spoke about 'the Troubles', so I could only speculate and, for the most part, remain unenlightened. I still know very little about 'the Troubles'. But I don't wish to know any more.

I never hitched a jennet to a cart ever again.

CHAPTER ONE

THURSDAY 07 AUGUST 1947 –
KILLBAWN GARDA STATION

08:00 hours, District Officer (Superintendent) David Fox is standing at his desk. His office is spotless. David Fox is 6'0'', 56 years old, with thinning hair neatly trimmed in a short-back-and-sides. Fox himself is spotless, albeit a little portly, dressed in Superintendent's uniform of the former style, with the high military-style stiff collar. Dark-blue is the current police colour. He misses the smartness of the old dark-green uniform, so dark it was usually regarded as black. He favours steel tips on the toes and heels of his highly-polished shoes – being a superintendent he wears shoes rather than boots; the clip of his step adds to his military bearing and serves as a warning of his approach. Neatness and smartness are marks of a good policeman.

There is one file on his desk, 'Donnelly – Homicide'. It contains two sheets of paper. Other than time and date of the incident, there is nothing on page one. There is nothing at all on page two. Twenty-one hours after the incident was reported, there is nothing solid to report. He sits down, hands to his head, and ponders the blank sheets. He presses the knuckles of his right hand against his forehead, and thinks aloud, "Who is Donnelly? What is his full name? He is known as Black Donnelly due to his anonymity. No one has ever seen him. Some frightened locals claim to have seen a dark shadow in the doorway of his bleak cold house. It is incredulous that we have a homicide victim on our doorstep, one who has lived here for 20-odd years, and we know nothing of him. There is no known family connection, no baptismal records, nothing on Donnelly. It is as if Donnelly himself were a ghost. Except for the brutal reality that there is a very real homicide victim out there at the edge of the bog. And locals are saying that a phantom pig is the killer." Fox knocks his knuckles against his brow and sighs, "Oh, God!"

To get a grip, Fox reverts to his daily routine in the hope that this restores some order to his mind. He cannot start the day without his copy of the 'Irish Independent' and his cup of tea – and two of those goldgrain biscuits he has hidden in his drawer. He hates to be caught off-guard not knowing what important events are happening. As the D.O., he ought to be as well-informed as any other reader of the newspaper. He hopes that there would be nothing reported about 'Murder in Quiet Town in Mayo'. At least, no reporter has contacted him so far. But soon, very soon, he will need to make some public announcement. He twirls in his hand a jar of hydrocortisone in clotrimazole. His crotch itch flares up when he is stressed.

08:01, and where in hell is his tea and newspaper? "Garda O'Reilly!" he shouts.

Garda O'Reilly is the most junior member of the staff, lanky and quiet. He even walks quietly in his standard-issue police boots. Quiet O'Reilly is probably confused over how much milk to pour, or how many lumps…

His office door opens, and O'Reilly says, "Superintendent O'Brien to see you, sir."

Superintendent Kevin O'Brien is the district officer of the neighbouring division. O'Brien had been a boxer. He represented Ireland in Amsterdam in 1928, the first Olympics for the newly-independent country. He did not succeed in winning a medal but is regarded as a hero nonetheless. It is people like O'Brien who get preferential treatment. He is fit, witty, popular and ambitious. He does not hide his aspiration for the position of chief superintendent. O'Brien always has some smart remark, and Foxy is always at a loss for a comeback. Fox quickly hides the jar of medicinal cream in the top drawer alongside his biscuits. "Hi! Kevin!"

"Hi! Foxy!" taking it all in with a glance. "Neat office. Only one file? You know, you should spend less time on your arse. You wouldn't get the itch."

Damn! He had seen the jar. "It's for athlete's foot."

"Ah. You're an athlete now? Good." taking a few annoying mock jabs at Foxy's chin, enough to force a blink.

"I'm here to see Murf for a few minutes. A case I'm working on. You don't mind if I run it by him?"

"He's in his office. I'll grab my tea and follow you down."

O'Brien pops off down the hallway, and steps inside Murf's office. "Hi, Murf."

"Hi, Slugger." And shuts the door.

Fox still has not had his tea. "O'Reilly!"

O'Reilly comes in with Fox's 08:00 tea at 08:04. Fox has time for a quick dunk of a goldgrain before joining O'Brien in Murf's office. Damn! The biscuit breaks and leaves a section swimming in the cup. Fox is attempting to fish it out with his spoon as he arrives at Murf's door. Unexpectedly, O'Brien bursts out of Murf's office all smiles. Fox drops the biscuit section back into the cup with an audible plop as O'Brien whizzes past.

"Thanks, Foxy. I owe you one."

Fox would like to respond "You owe me TEN!" But as always with O'Brien, he is one step too late.

The entire local D.O.s drop in on Murf for help in solving cases. His reputation is quite vast. O'Brien is the most frequent. And Fox can never land a witty punch.

Fox goes in to Murf's office, curious to know what the visit was about, and why it was so brief. Inside, Detective Inspector John Patrick Murphy is sitting with his feet up on the desk, or to be more accurate, his feet cushioned on a folded newspaper on the desk; he is wearing Wellington boots that are caked in dirt, some of which is smearing the newspaper. His trousers are a light-grey flannel with no crease – actually his trousers have multiple creases from frequently crushing the ends into his socks and thus into his boots. Is there any other policeman who wears his pant ends inside his socks? His socks, which Fox cannot see, are the thick woollen multi-dotted socks worn by county council work crews. His shirt is pinstriped with a detachable collar – which is missing – and Fox suspects that the buttons on the shirt probably don't line up. He is afraid to look. Murf, when upright, is 6'2". A funny thing about Murf, he is unnoticed in a room until he makes himself seen; and in spite of his choice of farming boots, he is silent until he wants to be heard. Like a conjurer's rabbit – 'now you see him, now you don't'. A lot of the time Fox doesn't know if Murf is in or out.

"Good God! Murf! Did O'Brien see you like this, with cow dung on your boots?"

"It's not cow dung, Foxy. It's a mixture of pig manure and peat from the bog. I'm watching it dry."

"Why are you watching muck dry? Have you nothing to do?"

"It's the case I'm working on. I'm studying how the bog clings to the treads in the heels."

"Of course, Murf, you're on a case right now," and sighing, "but how does this help with the case?"

Murphy looks at his boots and seems to address them rather than Fox. "Each patch of bog is unique; the composition of the peat contains traces of the fauna from which it formed. Here you have bog stains containing root traces of bog plants and meadow plants. It's the result of the bog encroaching on manure-rich soil, pig manure in this case. These stains can only come from the perimeter of a pig farm in the boglands. And there is only one such place. Unmistakable. I could recognise this unique pig-and-bog stain anytime..."

"No. Don't explain. Tell me about O'Brien."

"Oh, O'Brien just solved his case."

"How?"

"Well, I had him look at this picture," pointing to the front page of the Irish Independent. It is a picture of Éamon de Valera in top hat, riding a horse at the RDS (Royal Dublin Society) Horse Show.

"You showed him a picture of Dev on a horse – and he solved his case?"

"Yes," says Murf, twirling a magnifying glass.

"You did the 'white dot' thing with O'Brien – right?"

Murf uses this technique to demonstrate how the brain files and retrieves, and ultimately understands data. This is how he explains it:

Look at a picture in a newspaper through a magnifying glass. You see many dots, some white, some black, of varying sizes – there are many more white dots than black dots. The picture is indiscernible until you remove the magnifying glass, and then you can 'see' it. Your eyes can see it all along, but the brain does not comprehend it at first. Now take the facts of a case. The more information you have, the better; even if you think it is not pertinent. Picture in your mind each fact as a white dot; fill in the black dots (by logic and inference) and stand back. The picture becomes clear.

"And you did this with O'Brien?" asks Fox.

"O'Brien closed his eyes, and punched his finger as if writing on an imaginary chalkboard; he hmmed and hawed, stepped back and opened his eyes and exclaimed 'I got the answer, Murf! I have it! You are right; it was there all along, but I couldn't put the elements in perspective until I looked at the full picture.'"

"And what was the answer? What was his case?"

"I haven't the foggiest idea."

"But you helped solve his case by showing him a picture of de Valera on a horse? And how come you have my Irish Independent?" and shouting down the corridor "O'Reilly!"

Murf tears out a middle section and hands a bog-and-manure-stained paper to Fox. "Here you are, Foxy; I only need the farming section. Oh, and tell O'Reilly it's a mare."

Foxy storms down to the front desk, to O'Reilly. "O'Reilly! The newspaper! On my desk at 08:00, not on Murf's desk!" slapping the newspaper down in front of a frightened O'Reilly. And pointing to the front page with its picture of Éamon de Valera on horseback, "and what does Murf mean 'It's a mare'?"

O'Reilly, red-faced stammers, and Reynolds and Caldwell busy themselves within earshot at the wanted posters, stifling laughter.

"Out with it, O'Reilly, I'm going to find out anyway!"

"Sir! I just said 'Look at the bollocks on the horse!'"

Reynolds and Caldwell are unable to contain their laughter.

"O'Reilly! The next time you have something smart to say, let me know BEFORE Superintendent O'Brien arrives."

Fox goes back to his office, sits down with his newspaper, and realises that he has left his teacup in Murf's office. "O'Reilly!" he shouts. "Get me my tea from Murf's!" And stands up again with his legs apart looking out his window. His jock itch is flaring up. He hears the door open and the sound of the teacup being placed on his desk, and says, "And send in Murf!" Turning around he sees that it is Murf. "Where's O'Reilly?"

"O'Reilly's busy at the front desk. He's going through the sports section. You know he's on the county team."

Fox returns to looking out the window, his back to Murf.

Murf speaks, "Nasty business there, yesterday." An understatement, but no response from Fox. "And you had a tiff with the Mrs."

Fox picks up on that, in preference to addressing the pressing police business. "A tiff? Why do you say that?"

"I saw Mary buy a sun hat in Casey's General Store for 7/11."

"So?"

"She didn't ask for her 5% discount – the garda discount."

"How…?"

"And you have invited me to dinner on Sunday."

"What's that…?"

"And the grandchildren too."

"Fuf-fuf-fuf…"

"Looks to me like you are mustering support…"

"Sit down, Murf! My head hurts!"

"I AM sitting down! And stop scratching, Foxy."

Fox sits down. He looks at the empty file-folder on his desk. It looks even emptier when compared to the bulky folder on Murf's lap. "Murf, you were there yesterday. What do you make of it? I can't file a report that a 'ghost-pig' or the 'devil' committed a murder. That's what everyone believes – 'The 'Black Pig' – the devil come to claim his own'. The whole townland of Ballycorry is afraid to go out at night."

Murf waits for him to pause.

Fox holds up the file and reads aloud, "'Homicide – victim Donnelly'. That's all I can write."

Murf interjects. "Kennedy!"

"Forget 'Kennedy'. I have to deal with 'Donnelly'. And who is 'Kennedy'?"

Murf thumps his folder, his big thick file-folder, on Fox's desk. "The victim, I believe, is 'Kennedy – Daniel Edward Kennedy'. Here is his picture," selecting a page from his folder and sliding it to Fox. It is a beaten-up old 'wanted poster'. "This, Foxy, is a wanted poster from 1919, from the Manchester Police."

"It's a pretty poor picture. Are you sure this Kennedy is the same man?" Suddenly Fox jolts to alertness. "Hold on there, Murf. How come you have such a thick file on an incident that is just a day old?"

"Foxy, I have been looking into 'Black Donnelly' for over a year, connecting dots and trying to get a handle on him. And I have come up with a picture, pardon the pun, of a troubled and terrified man."

"Troubled? And terrified?"

"Yes. He was murdered, but not by the devil."

"He was murdered by a human being? Not by a mythical devil-pig? Well, that's a relief! No! It's not a relief; I mean, it is something we can deal with."

Fox reaches for the phone and connects to the front desk. "O'Reilly, put me through to Castlebar!"

Murf asks, "You haven't informed forensics yet?"

"Oh, they are already on the way. They should be here inside the hour; Garda Quigley is taking them to the crime scene at 09:00. I reported a 'death by unusual circumstances'. I did not want to get into 'devils' and 'pigs' and 'ghosts'. They would not take me seriously. By describing it as 'unusual', forensics is responsible for determining the cause of death and hence if it should be classified as 'homicide'."

Murf queries, "So why do you need Castlebar now if

they are already on the way?"

"Because, Murf, it's protocol in a homicide case. Castlebar needs to be informed."

"Why?"

"Because they decide who leads the investigation, either take it over or assign it locally. What's wrong with you, Murf? We are going to need help with this. That's why."

"And banjax the case!" Murf interjects. "Foxy, I have a list of suspects, people with motive enough to harm Donnelly-Kennedy. I am narrowing that down to those with means and opportunity. I am looking at a few particularly strong suspects."

"How did you establish that even before the investigation has commenced? Oh, your 'dots' I suppose."

"If Donnelly is the Kennedy I believe him to be, it is surprising that he wasn't knocked off a long time ago. So why now? Why not twenty/thirty years ago? What happened to change things? Foxy, what I need is the forensic report and to confirm some information locally. What I DON'T need is long-nose O'Neill and his flat feet stifling the flow of information. You know how people clam up with outsiders…"

"I wouldn't call O'Neill and his Castlebar Gardaí 'outsiders'."

"No, Foxy? What about Mickey Motor?"

Fox instantly realises that Mickey 'Motor' Carr, the first person on the scene, the one who reported the incident, would only confide in three or four people in the whole world. Mickey Carr had a very troubled childhood and is emotionally scarred. He is distrustful of everyone. There are a few exceptions. He is talkative with his farming neighbour Ben Muldoon. They had been schoolmates together a long time ago. He is trustful of Superintendent Fox whom he addresses as 'Sergeant Fox'. And he is quietly cautious with Murf. Apart from that, he is withdrawn, or talks nonsensically. And so people regard him as the local idiot 'amadan', making fun of him and playing hurtful pranks on him. If Mickey 'Motor' Carr gets a whiff of a hint that

Castlebar is investigating, he will withdraw into his own lonely non-communicative world.

Murf raises his voice to emphasise, "Foxy, I already know who the most-likely murderers are. And it is murderers, plural! I need the proof before I can pin it on them, and I don't want to expose my hand prematurely."

O'Reilly shouts from the front, "D.O.! Castlebar on the line!"

Murf leans forward. "Tell Castlebar that it is a homicide, yes; tell them that the investigation is progressing swiftly; suspects are under surveillance; arrest is imminent; blah, blah, blah."

Fox is doubtful. "Are you sure?"

Murf assures him. "Yes! I need something more than dots to lay a charge. Just keep Castlebar out of the investigation!"

Fox, into the phone, "Chief Superintendent? Yes! I'll hold." Fox covers the mouthpiece, "Murf, you better be right on this!"

"When have I ever not been right?"

"Never. Not so far. But don't start..." and into the phone, "Chief Superintendent..."

CHAPTER TWO

DAVID FOX COULD
WRITE A BOOK ON MURF

Foxy had just completed his telephone conversation with Chief Superintendent Ultan O'Neill. O'Neill has 'complete faith in Inspector Murphy'. That's what he said. 'The best damn detective in the county!' That's what O'Neill said. Foxy is standing looking out the window at the rain, sipping his tea. "You know, District Officer Fox," talking aloud to his reflection in the window, "O'Neill is wrong. Murf is the best detective EVER! Foxy, you could write a book on him."

TEN YEARS EARLIER
THEIR FIRST MEETING –
FOX INTERVIEWS
SGT. JOHN PATRICK MURPHY IN 1937

"Sergeant Murphy, please sit down." Superintendent Fox is seated at his desk, dressed in his favoured high-collared old-fashioned superintendent's uniform. The station's personnel files are neatly stacked on the corner of his desk. One file is open in the centre. Fox looks from the file to Sergeant Murphy. Murphy is already sitting, not having waited for the invitation, cheeky blaggard. And a bit too lax in his dress. His dark-brown hair is a shade too long; his shirt is the blue garda shirt to be worn with the uniform, rather than a white shirt appropriate to plain clothes; his navy-blue tie is askew revealing a missing button on his shirt; he is not wearing a jacket, which is required to conceal any sidearm or handcuffs, but then he isn't wearing any of those either; his grey flannel trousers are tucked into his socks; his socks are work socks, and his shoes are black rubber-soled farm boots. Perhaps in Killbawn this is regarded as 'plain clothes'. Good God! "I believe that to run a police barracks efficiently…"

"Garda station," interrupts Sergeant Murphy.

Fox thinks quickly. Rude bastard, no respect for rank. He glances at the personnel folder open on his desk and reads again the comments of his predecessor –

> *'Best detective ever*
> *Take full advantage of his skills*
> *Will not disappoint'*

Damn! The wrong personnel sheet must be in Murphy's file. No. The sheet is entitled 'Murphy, John Patrick, Garda Detective-Sergeant'. "Excuse me! Sergeant Murphy!" Fox uses his full authoritative tone to silence Murphy.

But Murphy takes it as a cue to continue. "In Mayo we don't say 'police', ever; we also avoid the term 'barracks'; bitter memories from former times – it upsets the people."

Fox notices that Murphy's speech is rude and local, yet it is not 'culchie'. And Murphy was perfectly correct. Fox was well-aware of this, but Fox's former Royal Irish Constabulary training slipped out in his speech. Murphy was correct in what he said, but totally out of line by saying it. Fox attempts to recover by recommencing his introductory speech. "I believe that to run a garda station efficiently, the district officer should know the men, and vice-versa. I have the advantage of you, Sergeant Murphy, having access to your personnel file, but I feel that is my duty to fully introduce myself …"

Again, Murphy interrupts as casually as at the bar of a local pub. "You are Superintendent David Fox, newly-appointed District Officer of Killbawn Garda Station…"

"Good God!" thinks Fox. "Does this man not have any inkling as to his rudeness and impropriety and insubordination? I'll start the paperwork today to have this man removed. He may have got around my predecessor; Oh-ho! But I'll stamp on him before he gets too big for his boots in my station."

Murphy is still reaming off Fox's career "… married to Mary Fox (nee Wilson)… formerly in RIC with the rank of sergeant… joined 'The Civic Guards' in 1922 after a three-month stint with the Irregulars…"

Fox has his hand up and is about to bark a command at Murphy when the words hit him – 'stint with the Irregulars'. Fox pales and tries to sit down, only to realise that he is already sitting, and tries to sit further down. Two people know of his brief membership in the anti-treaty IRA – Maura Rua O'Hara, the firebrand matriarch of the local republicans; and Mickey Go-Carr, an IRA assassin during 'the Troubles'. No one else knows – not even his wife Mary knows. Fox had concealed this piece of damning information when applying to join the Garda Síochána.

Murphy is still speaking, "...where you went by the alias 'Daithi Mac a'tSionnaigh, Oglach', your Irish volunteer name and title when you served with the North Cork Brigade."

"I was never part of the anti-treaty IRA," Fox croaks unconvincingly. Fox knows quite well that what Murphy says is true. He remembers too, that while serving in the North Cork Brigade of the Irregular IRA, he took an active part in the assassination of a government minister in 1922. Fox is only half-listening to Murphy now. How could Murphy know? Maura Rua would never reveal his secret. Neither would Mickey Go-Carr. Then how could Murphy know? Fox is troubled. If Murphy knows, then who else knows? He has visions of his career coming to a sudden crashing end. He laments aloud, "Finished! Disgraced! No pension!"

Murphy consoles him. "Your career is far from over, Foxy. First, no one knows, or will ever need to know. Secondly, even if it should leak, be assured that you are among republican sympathisers here. Even the regional chief superintendent would regard it as a mark in your favour. And for all you know maybe Dublin already has that on file. You're not the only garda in Ireland to have made the transition from RIC via IRA."

"But how did you unearth this information?"

"Connecting dots."

"Connecting dots?"

It's not a big jump. 'Fox' disappears for a brief spell; and 'Mac a'tSionnaigh' – 'Son of the Fox' – makes a brief appearance. The dots connect. "And let me say, Foxy, your actions in 1921/22 trained you better than any RIC or garda training. I believe you'll make an excellent district officer – and you have the stuff for regional command."

"Thanks, Murf." How did he know to call him 'Murf', and did Murf just call him 'Foxy'?

Fox blinks at his reflection in the window and returns to the present. He sighs in relief at how things worked out. Murf was not booted out. Ten years later, Murf is still here, and still not wearing a sidearm.

Murf's reluctance to wearing a sidearm is not due to sloppiness, but to his conviction that an 'unarmed police force' should be unarmed and be seen as unarmed. The RIC prior to 1922 was visibly armed, and its successor, the RUC, is visibly armed. The RIC/IRA conflict during the struggle for independence resulted in a popular distrust of a visibly armed police force. The negative connotation of firearms in the context of the previous policing practices of the RIC is not in keeping with the current concept of 'Guardians of the Peace'. The Gardaí from its inception is primarily an unarmed police force. However, detectives and certain units are commissioned to carry firearms. Murf chooses not to do so.

And Murf was right about Fox, too. Fox had performed well here and is now being considered for a position of regional chief superintendent.

CHAPTER THREE

If David Fox could write a book, so too could Fate.
Unlike David Fox, Fate does not rely on memory.
With Fate, all time coexists.
The future is already in the past;
The past lives in the present;
The present is ever-present, but is seldom fully revealed.
When Fate writes, she merely unveils.

SEPTEMBER 1918 –
THE SECOND BATTLE
OF THE SOMME

"Pigs! Pigs! Daniel E will make sausages out of you!"

By 02 September 1918, in the Second Battle of the Somme, the Germans had been forced back to the Hindenburg Line, from which they had launched their offensive in the spring. Heavy German casualties were inflicted; Canadian Corps seized control of the Drocourt-Quéant line. The Canadians also captured more than 6,000 unwounded prisoners. Canada's losses amounted to 5,600.

A fortnight later, British, Australian and American forces are preparing for a major assault. Demoralising the Germans in order to weaken their resolve is one of their objectives in preparation for the assault. This assault, if successful, would force a German surrender. The employment of tanks raised the morale of the Allied soldiers. It was tank support that turned the tide in favour of the Allies two weeks previously. Each advance necessitated the construction of more trenches and previously-abandoned sections were returned to service. Some sections had once served the British Empire, then the German Empire, and now back again to the British.

On 26 September, Captain Daniel Edward Kennedy of The Royal Irish Fusiliers is waving his pistol at the German lines. "Pigs! Pigs! Come on you pigs! Daniel E will make sausages out of you German pigs!" Captain Kennedy is 5'10", fair-haired, with dark-blue eyes. At 21, he looks like he should be on a recruitment poster. His uniform is clean and well-fitting, winning admiration and respect for him amid the mud and filth of the trenches. His bravado is uplifting to the men in the trenches who respond with the RIF battle-cry *"Fág a' Bealach!"* meaning "Clear the Way!" Few, if any, understand the words of the Faughs' battle-cry, but shout it anyway in the context of "We're coming to get you!" They shout across to the German lines "Fog-a-balla!" in a decent approximate rendering of the cry *"Fág a' Bealach!"*

The Kennedy family are wealthy landowners in Tipperary's Golden Vale. Daniel E. Kennedy is the third generation Kennedy to serve in the Faughs. Grandfather, Colour Sergeant Dan (Daniel) Kennedy of the 87th (Royal Irish Fusiliers) Regiment of Foot, served in the Crimean War (1854) and the Indian Mutiny (1857). Father, Sergeant Donal (Daniel) Kennedy of the Royal Irish Fusiliers, saw active service in the Boer War (1899 – 1902).

Because of his rank, Captain Daniel E. Kennedy is unlikely to lead a bayonet charge, or man the vanguard of an infantry advance; so Captain Kennedy's bravado is unlikely to be tested in the field. Of course he could follow in the footsteps of Lieutenant Geoffrey St George Shillington Cather, 9th Battalion Royal Irish Fusiliers, who was awarded the Victoria Cross for gallantry at the first Battle of the Somme, in 1916. Yes. He could, but he wouldn't. His bravado is at the outer perimeter of enemy sniper range, at the third line of trenches.

Kennedy makes his way to the second line of trenches, and then on to the front line. En route he uplifts the spirits of the fatigued soldiers. They salute him and smile at his threats to engage and defeat the Germans. One soldier, however, does not acknowledge him. Sapper Terence (Tracy) Prior sits in the mud. Prior is 5'5'', squat and broad – built like a beast. He is as fast as a trap when in action; otherwise he sleeps close to a state of alertness. His brown hair is short and stubbly which makes him appear older than his 19 years. Tracy Prior looks up at Daniel E, and then down again. He does not join in the cheering. He just sits in the mud – mud with urine and faeces mixed in an unhealthy cocktail almost as lethal as the bombs he plants – careful not to get a scratch. Prior could not get any dirtier than he already is, so he just sits there, fatigued from the previous night's foray close to the German lines. Beside him, equally dirty, is Prior's battle companion, Rex, a black-brindled English mastiff that understands only German. He lays his hand on the mastiff's head. *"Guter Hund! Braver Hund!"* The mastiff responds by lifting his head a fraction, and then, with chin on paws, releases a tired snort.

Tracy Prior is from London's East End, with a passion for, and understanding of, dogs. He joined the army as a combat engineer, required to perform a variety of military engineering duties such as laying or clearing minefields, demolitions, and field defences. His present work is primarily tunnelling under the German lines to plant explosives. He is anti-social and does not associate with his fellow soldiers. He is permitted, on a volunteer basis, to work as a mine and bomb planter at the German lines. Whenever he can be released from tunnelling duties, he devotes his entire time to his volunteer duties alone with his dog.

The object of the war, Prior is convinced, is for the realignment of wealth among the privileged classes. There could be no positive outcome for the likes of Tracy Prior. He listens to Daniel E's ranting and considers how useless this privileged Irish loudmouth will be to society when the war ends. Humanity would be better off without him.

Daniel E is quite aware of Prior sitting in the mud like a rat. Rats scurry all over the place, but chiefly in no-man's-land where they feast on the dead and the dying. It is a rat-heaven. Prior is a rat. He too crawls through the mud and filth of no-man's-land at night – to plant mines and bombs at the

German lines. Ah. Yes. It sure as hell demoralises the Hun. But after the war, what possible benefit would Prior be to society? Humanity would be better off without him.

They have one thing in common – the Webley Mk VI, with which they are both extremely proficient. Daniel E now points his Webley at the rats in no-man's-land and imagines shooting them. He has sufficient skill to pick them off with ease, but reins in his temptation to fire. He envies the firing squads back behind the lines. He turns around to better hear the 'pop-popping' of their guns as more deserters are executed. As many as 20 in one hour are executed. Most of those executed are just shell-shocked boys that had frozen in fear when the order to 'Advance!' had been given. Disobeying an officer in wartime is treated as 'desertion'. The arrested soldier would have the charge read to him, usually on the following morning, to which he would plead "Guilty!" or "Not guilty!" It wouldn't matter; he would be found guilty in any event and shot. The whole trial and execution would take only a few minutes, so as not to interrupt the monotonously slow rhythm of the war.

Daniel E returns his attention to the rats. To discharge a shot in the direction of the German lines would provoke unauthorised gunfire – not something an officer should engage in. So he just lines up his shots and 'pops' his tongue as he 'shoots' the rats – including Tracy and that abomination of an 'English' dog that is German-bred and trained.

It had been a number of weeks, during a shelling assault, since Rex and his German handler fell into a water-logged bomb crater in no-man's-land. His handler, severely wounded, drowned in the water. The dog was unable to clamber out of the hole. He was unsettled by the shelling and his dead handler could no longer soothe him. Two days later, Prior was on one of his night forays when shelling again occurred. Coincidently, he too sought shelter in the same bomb crater. The dog by now was near dead, frightened by the shelling and fatigued from vainly trying to climb out. Against his training to trust only his designated sole handler, the weakened dog surrendered to Prior's care. Prior dragged the weak dog back to the British lines, and over the next few weeks nursed him back to health. The dog's collar identified him as 'Rex' and his military role *'Bombendetektor'*. Both dog and man found protection in each other and formed a bond. Prior's protection was in Rex's ability to navigate safely through German minefields, and thus encroach deeper into German-held territory.

By 26 September 1918, Prior's bomb and mine planting is at its peak. His bravery so impressed his C.O. that he earned a mention in dispatches. He requests, and is assigned, two sapper assistants. In effect this elevates Prior to the rank of Lance Corporal, but no formal promotion was conducted.

Daniel E. Kennedy's skills are valuable in the current campaign. He is a bomb-development expert who works closely with the engineers. Ironically, a good working relationship between Prior and Daniel E is essential to this operation, notwithstanding their mutual contempt. Daniel E modifies bombs for specific purposes to ensure that each bomb functions to its desired end. His bombs are rugged, reliable, and his timing devices are accurate. Daniel E works at delivering deadly bombs; Tracy Prior works at delivering the devastation.

In order to see the mastiff during the night-time forays, Tracy has placed two small circular dots above the dog's eyes and two small triangular dots behind his ears. These dots are dark red and are phosphorescent. With night vision Tracy can determine the location and proximity of the mastiff and the direction he is facing. In the unlikely event that the dots are observed from the trenches, they would appear as insects hovering over the mud. Tracy and Rex deliver death and destruction like a plague. German demoralisation increases.

Tracy, even in his sleep, is alerted by the silence. There is no ranting to be heard. The shouting *"Fág a' Bealach!"* had ceased. It is peculiar how one can sleep amidst the noise of battle, but is awakened by silence.

"I'm addressing YOU, soldier!"

Tracy half opens one fatigued eye to observe Captain Daniel E. Kennedy standing over him, still brandishing his service revolver.

"Is this a sapper, or a rat? How can one tell? A soldier stands in the presence of an officer, and salutes!"

Tracy opens the other eye, but does not move.

"A RAT slithers into the filth."

The silence along the line is solid and frozen. Every sniper and guard-sentry turn to see how this is going to play out. Had it been any ordinary soldier, he would have jumped to his feet and saluted, regardless of injury or fatigue. But Tracy is not ANY ORDINARY soldier. Tracy is an angel-of-death soldier – one to be feared (except by the stupid or arrogant). Daniel E is very arrogant and is behaving stupidly. He realises it now but it is too late to back out. He has to see this through, but fears that Tracy might be holding his Webley Mk VI in his hand concealed inside his overcoat. Daniel E realises what peril he is in. But the men are looking at him – some apprehensively, some in amusement, but all with interest. He needs to act like an officer and save face.

Tracy bores a look into him that pierces him cold.

Daniel E feels a cold sweat on his face and concentrates hard, attempting to will a thought into Tracy's head – "For the love of God, Tracy. Stand up! And let this be over!"

Tracy doesn't hear the thought; Tracy does not want to hear the thought.

Daniel E shouts loud enough for all to hear. "Stand up, soldier!" and kicks Tracy on the sole of his boot.

Tracy gives him the look that says "That's a mistake!"

The on-looking soldiers exchange looks with each other that say "That's a mistake!"

But more than anyone, Rex looks at Daniel E with a look that says "That's a mistake!" Rex is a lot more expressive. Bared fangs, a snarl and a pounce convey a clear message to Daniel E. Kennedy. Rex claims the space between the two men to protect his handler.

Captain Kennedy jumps backwards in a reflexive movement. And lands knee-deep in a bog of muck. Out of this humiliation, Daniel E sees a way to save face – shoot the damn dog. The sound of the shot would be subdued down here in the trench, and the death of the dog would be viewed as apt punishment for Tracy's insubordination. He would come out unscathed and with the upper hand – unscathed, but not untarnished. Daniel E thinks fast, but does not act fast enough. Before he can discharge the shot he feels a thud on his face; he hears a sound from inside his head, but the inside of his head feels like it is 20 meters away – it is the sound of his own nose being broken; he is falling; he is drowning. Now struggling to stand, to breathe, to see. Agh! The pain hits him and he screams. To the onlookers it is much more graceful and satisfying. Faster than most could register, the inert Tracy had catapulted himself at Daniel E with a shattering blow to the nose, rendering him flat on his back and submerging him under a half meter of muck. Some soldiers fish him out before he drowns. His military uniform is entirely soaked in muck, he is blinded by filth, his nose is pouring blood, and he is howling in pain and spitting mud.

Rex takes off into no-man's-land at Tracy's command. Tracy is arrested for striking an officer, to be tried by court-martial and executed, inescapably, the following morning.

CHAPTER FOUR

DISTRICT OFFICER FOX
AT DIVISIONAL HQ, CASTLEBAR

Wednesday 25 June 1947

All district officers had been summoned to Divisional HQ to receive instructions regarding de Valera's forthcoming visit to Mayo scheduled for the weekend of 27/28 September. Éamon de Valera was then Taoiseach (Head of Government) and was bolstering his support to face the threat of a new party, Fine Gael (Tribe of the Irish) that was increasing in popularity.

Fox was put in command of security for the route and for the venues. Dev's personal bodyguard would be responsible for his personal safety. Castlebar and Dublin would work together on this. For the month of September, Fox would be posted in Castlebar and would be on call 24/7, answerable directly to O'Neill. Fox is in his element here, straightening his collar, using his serious face and speaking with his old formal 'correct' RIC accent. He is relieved that he had not been overlooked. He was dreading the meeting with O'Neill in the light of the ruckus over Murf's recent court incident. He was expecting the worst for Murf – dismissal from the force – and had prepared to argue in his defence. Or, if necessary, resign from the force.

At the end of the meeting all are dismissed. Fox is exiting the door when O'Neill says, "Fox, a moment of your time. And shut the door." O'Neill has a very official-looking form in his hand.

Ultan O' Neil, at 55 and bald, is an old warrior, standing

just short of 6'0". He was once a member of the Irish Republican Police (IRP) that operated under IRA brigades from June 1920 to February 1922 in defiance of the British. He is as tough as nails and takes no nonsense from anyone. He is also on first-name terms with the leaders of the 'Old IRA', many of whom are ministers in the current government. "Have a seat, Fox. Do you know what I am holding here?" brandishing the form.

Fox swallows. It is bad news.

O'Neill continues. "This!" waving the form for emphasis "is Inspector Murphy's suspension. One month's suspension from active duty. We have one month to come up with a credible defence for Murphy. If we fail, Murphy is dismissed from the force."

Fox swallows and says, "Murf had a row with Justice Daly, the circuit court judge."

"It must have been a helluva row. The Ministry of Justice has demanded the garda commissioner treat this expeditiously. The commissioner is rankled that Justice is dictating to him about disciplinary matters; he is supposed to have autonomy in that; but he was reminded that he IS appointed by Justice, and he is answerable to Justice." O'Neill regards the Department of Justice as too closely modelled after the British system – it is not as 'Irish' as An Garda Síochána.

Fox continues, "Murf was in court…"

"Why in hell WAS Murf in court? He's not allowed in court for the very reason that he argues with judges."

"He was not meant to be in court. He had escorted a prisoner to another division, and they asked him to deliver the prisoner to the court. He obliged."

O'Neill leans both elbows on his desk and places his hands over the pate of his bent head. "Go on. I'm listening."

"It was a case of sheep-stealing. The defendant pleaded 'guilty' and the state had a signed voluntary confession. The case should have been over in minutes. But Judge Daly likes to be theatrical, and because he's a judge he is humoured. He said something like 'Well, who can argue against a signed voluntary confession?' It was a rhetorical question, but Murf took him literally. Murf raised his hand for attention. The judge was about to strike his gavel and declare 'Guilty!' when he noticed Murf standing there with his hand raised.

"Daly looked at him over the rim of his glasses and asked enquiringly 'Yes?'

"'I can, Your Honour.'

"'You can 'what'? Hm...hm...and who are YOU?'

"'Inspector Murphy, John Patrick Murphy, but you can call me 'Murf'.'

"'Can I now, MURF? And what is it that you can do?'

"'I can argue against a signed voluntary confession.'

"Daly expected to humiliate Murf by agreeing to have the confession read aloud, and thus put him on the spot. At the judge's instruction the clerk of the court read the confession. Murf then pointed out that the accused, being fully familiar with sheep, would refer to the animals in precise colloquial terms. The confession was worded too literate for one who could only express himself in colloquial language. For example he would not say 'sheep and lamb', as was in the confession, he would refer to them as 'yeo and lamb' – he gave the colloquial pronunciation as 'yeo' rather than 'ewe'. Daly then made fun of Murf's use of the word 'yeo', and corrected him –'You mean EWE and lamb, surely!' and laughed. The room laughed also, humouring him.

"'No, your Honour! I mean 'YEO'.' Murphy then attempts to educate the judge on terms such as hoggets, gimmers and theaves. '...these are all 'EWES' but none of them are 'YEOS'.'

"His point was to expose the confession as a contrived confession, possibly a forced confession, and hence its unreliability in evidence. Unfortunately, the judge regarded Murphy's opinion of the confession as a criticism of the judge himself. By this time the judge was red-faced and salivating in anger. The judge shouted 'An idiot can see that this man is guilty!'

"To which Murf shouts back, 'Yes, Your Honour!'

"Now there is wholesale laughter. The judge storms out, then turns back and orders Murf arrested and detained for contempt of court.

"To which Murf shouts 'I'm the only garda present. Am I to arrest myself?' More laughter."

O'Neill remains still for a few moments. He knows that Murf is a great detective – all the divisions in Mayo lean on him for help. He also knows that Murf rubs authoritative figures – judges and chief superintendents – the wrong way. O'Neill empathises with Murf, having been tempted himself in similar circumstances with pompous judges. Only O'Neill always bit his tongue in time. He comes to a decision. Murf is too good to lose. He lifts his head and says, "Fox! For now, assign Murf to non-policing duties – filing papers or counting sheep. Bury Murf in Blacksod Bay! He is not to come east of, or south of, Killbawn." He notices an envelope placed on his desk, presumably from Fox. "What's this, Fox?" pointing to the envelope.

"It's my resignation. In the event that Murf goes, so do I."

O'Neill takes the envelope, and without opening it, tears it in pieces and drops it in the trash basket. He lifts his phone. "Get me the chief commissioner's office, and ask for Chief Administrative Officer Chris Fagan." Fox gets up to leave.

"Sit down, Fox, you need to hear this."

His phone rings. He lifts the receiver. "Chief Superintendent O'Neill, Castlebar." He is drumming his fingers. Then he shifts in his chair. "Fagan!" he shouts into the phone. "I'm looking at a piece of paper here, and I don't know which trash bin to shove it in!

(Pause) "Murphy's suspension and threat of dismissal is what I'm talking about! Whose idea is this? And whose arse did it come from?

(Pause) "It came from 'Justice'? Did it now?

(Pause) "Hold it, Fagan! If Murf is dismissed, you'll have half the guards in Mayo out for your blood – and you will undoubtedly have some resignations too.

(Pause) "Oh-ho! No! You've got it wrong there, Fagan!

(Pause) "No! I won't apologise! The only apology is for the commissioner to recognise the positive work of Murf and members of the Garda, how they have earned the trust of the people. It has taken us over 20 years to shake off the distrust we inherited from the police image in 'the Troubles'. And you're undoing it all now?

(Short pause) "Keep it quiet, you say? Too late! The 'Connaught Telegraph' and the 'Western People' are already on the story.

(Pause) "Revoke this asinine suspension!

(Long pause) "You're such a shoite, Fagan!

(Short pause) "Oh! de Valera is going to love this one! He's comin' to Mayo next month. And will he answer why the Fianna Fáil Justice Minister is putting the heavy on the guards? – unlikely to happen if Fine Gael gets in!"

O'Neill shifts the phone receiver away from his face and holds it out with both hands. He shouts at it. "Fagan! Fagan!" He looks at it with surprise. "The shoite hung up on me," and slams the receiver down with such force that the phone is propelled off his desk and it shatters on the floor. He goes to the door and shouts out, "McCann! The phone is broken again! Get me one that works properly!" He turns back to face Fox. "Fox! NOW you can go! And bury Murf in Blacksod Bay! If the suspension is not revoked, he is off the force in 30 days!"

As Fox is leaving, the phone rings at the front desk. He delays his departure to listen.

"Chief Superintendent. It's the garda commissioner himself on the phone."

O'Neill, whose office phone is broken, takes the call in the general office. The entire office is hushed, including a few of the divisional D.O.s from the morning's briefing. "Commissioner! This is Chief Superintendent O'Neill here.

"Yes, sir.

"It was a bad line, sir. We got cut off.

"No, sir. 'Imprudent' might be a better word.

"Well, maybe, 'ill-founded'.

"Yes, sir. …Yes, sir. …Yes, sir. …Thanks for your understanding." and hangs up.

They all exchange looks and raise eyebrows. The commissioner was 'understanding'? O'Neill looks around at everyone faking busyness. He then returns to his office.

CHAPTER FIVE

27 SEPTEMBER 1918 –
COURT-MARTIAL AND THE
SECOND BATTLE OF THE SOMME

27 September 1918, at 06:00 hours, the C.O., Lieutenant-Colonel Browning, is clearing his paperwork. Browning is dressed in battle fatigues. He is in his 60s, thinning grey hair to his 6'2'' – now more like 6'0'' due to the droop of fatigue. His cheeks are hollow and there are dark circles under his eyes. The strain of the war is taking a toll on his health. He hates paperwork. He is a soldier fighting a war. Paper just gets in the way. He usually dispenses with it as quickly as possible, trusting his aide to draw his attention to important matters. His 'office' is actually a root cellar at an abandoned farm. It is the most comfortable, driest and quietest place this close to the front lines. The darkness is dispelled by the light emitted from an oil lamp on a wooden bench, which also serves as his desk. The air is thick with the smoke from the lamp and smoke from his cigarettes. Through the haze and gloom, one can make out the few shelves that once held potatoes and turnips. Now they contain a few files and some of his personal belongings. Compared to the smells at the front lines, this place smells clean – just the smell of burning oil mixed with stale cigarettes, potatoes and turnips. The other farm buildings here are unsuitable. The farmhouse itself is unsafe due to the collapsing roof; the barn is large and dry, but very draughty due to the air currents whistling through the slats and planks; the pigsty is structurally strong, but is low and cramped. So Lieutenant-Colonel Browning is here in the root cellar.

His aide, Corporal George Smithson, 24, looks more like a bookworm than a soldier. In a uniform that is one size too big, he looks smaller than his 5'8'', his ginger hair plastered down with hair oil, and glasses that continually slip down the bridge of his nose. He is an excellent aide and Browning relies heavily on him. Smithson places two files on Browning's desk. "We have a problem, sir."

With a major offensive about to occur, what could be the problem that his aide couldn't handle?

File-1 Recommendation for a medal of honour and promotion for Sapper Terence Prior.

He could not see any problem with that – Tracy Prior exhibited great courage and bravery in the exercise of his volunteer duties.

File-2 Court-martial; Striking an officer; Punishment by firing squad – Sapper Terence Prior.

"Oh, God. Corporal Smithson!"

"Yessur!"

"Make this go away!"

"Sir. Which one?"

"All of this!" handing both files to his aide.

"Sir...."

"That's an order. Just do it!"

"Yes, SIR!"

Saluting and exiting the office, Smithson enters the outer office. This is a tent erected at the entrance to the cellar. From the outside it all looks like a small tent erected up against a small hillock. The tent conceals the entrance to, and evidence of, the root cellar within the hillock. This is currently the command centre, since they could be on the move any day. Smithson slaps the file down on a card table, nearly collapsing it, and exits the tent. He looks up at the sky and shouts "Bollocks!" Corporal Smithson needs to work fast. He has no significant rank, at least not in relation to Captain Kennedy.

Captain Kennedy is in sickbay. He is preparing for the court-martial at 08:00, and is fussing with his uniform. Smithson convinces the medical-officer-in-charge to delay the release of Captain Kennedy until noon – "the wishes of the C.O., and all that..." And to enforce it with M.P.s if necessary. It makes no sense to the medical-officer-in-charge who clears non-serious injuries out of the way as early as possible. But the C.O. has his reasons. Smithson says a private prayer. "Thank God he didn't ask for a written copy of the order."

The M.O. goes to Captain Kennedy. "Captain. You are under observation for six hours. If you are considered out of danger at that time, you will be discharged." And to the two M.P.s, "See that Captain Kennedy remains safely here until then." And spins around and leaves before anyone can reply.

The Court-Martial – 27 September 1918

The court-martial is held in the barn, the dry but draughty barn, one of the four structures in the rectangle of the farmyard. It is diagonally opposite the farmhouse and at right angles to the pigsty on the right, and the root cellar on the left.

The first poor chap to be tried has the charge read. He mumbles something incoherently; he is found guilty and is led out to execution. All under five minutes.

The next prisoner is Sapper Terence Prior. "Lance Corporal Terence Prior! You are charged with striking an officer! How do you plead?"

"NOT GUILTY!" shouts Corporal Smithson, sliding his glasses up the bridge of his nose. (And when was he made 'lance corporal'? Did he not 'kill' the paperwork this morning, rescinding the promotion?) This interruption is a surprise and brings a sudden stop to the proceedings. "Corporal George Smithson, if it pleases the Court, counsel for the accused."

Smithson is uncertain if this makes sense. He is unfamiliar with court-martial procedure. He feels that the presiding officer is about to order him to cease, and maybe even court-martial him, when a gentle cough from the back of the room attracts the attention of the presiding officer.

There is a hesitation. Then "Present your case, counsellor."

Smithson addresses the court. "Is it not for the

prosecution to present the case? Please instruct the prosecution to present the case, and present evidence for cross-examination."

Another gentle cough from the back of the barn. Unprepared for this interruption, papers are shuffled to and fro. Eventually an aide finds what is required and places a paper on the judge's desk. He calls for "Captain Daniel Edward Kennedy!"

The clerk/aide calls, "Captain Daniel Edward Kennedy to the stand!" But Captain Kennedy is not here.

Smithson speaks. "If it pleases the Court, since no evidence is presented against my client, there is no case!"

The officer-in-charge queries, "Is there ANY evidence to present in this case? Anyone?"

Another gentle cough from the back.

"Case dismissed for lack of evidence. The prisoner is free to rejoin his duties."

Smithson has time to briefly glimpse the C.O. exit from the back of the barn. Smithson, with the helping coughs of the C.O., has pulled it off.

Tracy, who had remained silent throughout the proceedings, exhales loudly. Smithson, who has a mountain of urgent paperwork to cope with, exits promptly. Tracy does not get to thank him. He is ordered back to his unit and leaves as quickly as possible, relieved that he has dodged a bullet – literally.

There is a lot of activity in his unit. The current tunnelling and bomb placing has been at an urgent pace. But suddenly the engineers are withdrawn from the tunnels, all except a few key explosive experts. Tracy is not one of them. The sudden inactivity is more tense than the previous high activity and many of the sappers are unable to relax notwithstanding their fatigue. Tracy requests, and is granted, permission to make one of his forays into no-man's-land. This time he is given coordinates restricting the area of his venture, and he is issued a time limit within which he must return. He enlists the help of two sappers eager to remain active and he requests explosives to his specification.

On the night of the 27/28, Prior makes his last foray to the German Western Front. Captain Daniel Edward Kennedy does not appear. No shouting to the Germans and threatening to make sausages out of them. No ranting with gun in hand. With his nose bandaged and the memory of his encounter with Tracy still fresh, he is a laughing-stock for the moment. The incident, however, will lose interest as soon as the next military engagement commences. It will be forgotten by all except by the two antagonists. For Kennedy and Prior it is not just an incident – it is a demonstration of their contemptuous disregard for each other.

For Tracy Prior, this night is a priority. Allied Command wants to weaken the German defence line in preparation for an assault. Prior is required to plant a series of connected explosives to collapse an entire section of German fortification.

As Tracy and the two sappers crawl through no-man's-land, he is troubled by a nagging thought. Is it his conscience? He takes comfort in no-man's-land. He is, after all, a no-man himself. He is more at home here than with his regiment. Why, he wonders, does he take satisfaction in killing Germans? He doesn't hate them. If he were to set about killing those he hates, he would put the Butcher Haig on top of his list. Field Marshal Douglas Haig, commander of the British Expeditionary Force on the Western Front – now that's the enemy. Halfway across no-man's-land his thoughts are interrupted. He sees the floating fireflies that are Rex's identifying spots. Rex runs to him. He struggles to have Rex remain focused and calm, but the mastiff is too overjoyed at the reunion. *"Sitz, Rex! Platz!"* He cannot risk a frisky dog so close to the German line, so he holds back while the two sappers place the explosives as they had been instructed.

The two sappers are well-trained in setting explosives. With the explosives planted strategically in place, they set and activate the timers. Ten minutes should be enough time to clear out. It is delicate due to the nature of the multiple bombs that are interlinked for simultaneous detonation. Prior draws back toward the Allied line, lest the sound of the dog's excited panting and snorting should carry to the German trenches. *"Hier! Braver Hund!"*

Then an explosion fills the air and one sapper flies into pieces; the other sapper stands up in panic, is silhouetted against the flash, and is ripped apart by gunfire. Tracy and Rex hug the dirt beneath a ridge as a barrage of bullets flies inches above them. After the last bullet has sounded, they lie for another three hours. Then crawl slowly, very slowly, back to the British trenches. The timers tripped prematurely? Not likely. Kennedy's timers are accurate.

On 29 September 1918, British, Australian and American forces spearhead an attack in a single combined force against the German Siegfried Stellung of the Hindenburg Line. Under the command of Australian General Sir John Monash, the assault achieves all its objectives, resulting in the first full breach of the Hindenburg Line. The Great Offensive along the length of the line convinces the German high command that the writing is on the wall regarding any hope of German victory.

Tracy has Daniel E in his sights; just as Daniel E has had Tracy in his sights. They now have their own private war. Tracy and Daniel never cross paths again in the Somme. But there is life after the Somme – and death.

CHAPTER SIX

AT THE GARDA COLLEGE

June 1947

Matthew (Matt) Slevin, TD (Teachta Dála – Member of Parliament) for Galway South, more importantly, Parliamentary Secretary to the Minister of Justice, pays a surprise visit – unofficial, of course – to the Garda Headquarters in the Phoenix Park. Someone from 'Justice' visiting Garda HQ is not unusual. Notwithstanding its autonomous administration, the national police service is answerable to the Department of Justice.

Matt Slevin is one of the 'hot boys' in Fianna Fáil. In his early 40s, he is of average height with a trim active body. He is one who is going places – and fast. He talks fast, thinks fast, walks fast, drives fast. He even dresses fast in a snappy well-fitting blue suit, red-blue regimental style striped tie, and well-polished black oxford (Irish made) shoes. His black hair is well-groomed, even to the point of a few locks deliberately out of place to give a boyish active appearance. His eyes, a rich hazel, are always alert and twinkling through slightly closed eyelids – 'smiling eyes'. His teeth and mouth are naturally well-designed to present a pleasant smile. That same smile, without any physical change whatever, can be equally threatening. He never forgets a face or a name, and always knows where he is going – as he does now.

"Good Morning, Deputy Slevin. May I help you?"

"No thanks, Garda. I know my way around," he replies in his warm western tone. Matt makes his way to the Garda College.

The minister was concerned about some tiff between Justice and An Garda Síochána – an internecine dispute – and Matt was trying to ferret out information. The name 'Inspector John Patrick Murphy', known as 'Murf', came up. How many times has this name come up? He could not remember, but this is not the first time. Murf is currently under suspension, and is on the chopping block, likely to be booted off the force.

Problem: Murf is efficient and is popular with the rank and file, and any squabble within the department would reflect poorly on the government – not a good time for this to happen. Fine Gael were making serious inroads, and Fianna Fáil are in danger of losing the 1948 election. At present, the Taoiseach, Éamon de Valera, is touring the country to bolster support. He is due in Mayo next month – in Mayo, the flash-point of the quarrel.

Matt, who could read his boss very well, sensed that he was looking for a way to save Murf rather than nail his coffin – it might very well be the minister's own coffin that is in question. But like so much in politics, nothing was said lest it comes back to bite.

Ah. Here is the training room. The instructor is Sergeant Joseph Dunleavy, a known 'Murfite'. Matt slips into the room, observed by Sergeant Dunleavy, who immediately calls the class to attention. "Aire! An Teachta Ó Sléibhín! Chuirtéis!" The entire class of 20 cadets rise to attention and adopt the formal salute.

"It's all right, Sergeant. This is not an official visit – no need to be formal. I'll just sit here at the back. Just carry on."

"Shocracht! Suighigí síos!" And the class resumes. English is the common administrative language, but proficiency in Irish is a requirement, and a number of formal duties – including some training classes – are conducted in this medium.

Sergeant Dunleavy, who is lanky and tall at 6'6'', and speaks with a mid-Ulster accent, reverts to English. "Today's case study should be of interest to Deputy Slevin, who is sitting in with us today." As he passes out the case study papers, he comments, "There is a popular perception that it is good policing to apprehend robbers; ...arrest them; ...bring them to justice; ...punish them with fines or imprisonment. Today we will examine that." He finishes by giving a copy to Deputy Slevin. "You are given a case – a real case with the names changed, but a real case nonetheless. Once you hear this case you will break into four groups of five. On your papers you will find 20 questions. Each of the four groups will present their answers to the class. The class will challenge your findings, and you will be required to argue your case convincingly."

Matt thinks to himself, "Dunleavy is a step ahead of me. This is for my benefit. Okay, go ahead Sergeant."

Dunleavy, to the class: "Garda John Patrick Murphy was instructed to deliver a summons to Mrs. 'Shop' for littering – a fine of 5/- (five shillings). Mrs. 'Shop' had recently moved from County Tyrone for the sake of her husband's health, and ran a fruit-and-vegetable shop in a Donegal fishing town. The sidewalk outside her shop was frequently littered with bits of fruit and vegetable pieces.

"Some minutes before Garda Murphy's arrival at the shop, it had been robbed by two youths who played out a scene from a motion picture of the previous night. They asked Mrs. 'Shop' for a packet of Aspro, for a headache, and requested a cup of water. When Mrs. 'Shop' returned with the cup of water from her kitchen, she discovered her till had been emptied and the two youths had left. When Garda Murphy arrived she asked for his help. She did not know the names of the two youths, but she was sure she could identify them if she saw them again.

"Garda Murphy approached 'Paddy the Fish' who was sitting on a window ledge at a pub a few doors away. Paddy was a retired fisherman and local inebriate. Garda Murphy feared that a direct question to Paddy would elicit the response 'I didn't see anything.' He engaged Paddy with comments about the poor state of the fishing industry and the poor state of the economy. Paddy lamented that there was no money anymore, but strange that some young ones had enough money to go drinking in the morning. Paddy inclined his head to indicate to which pub he referred.

"Garda Murphy entered the pub and escorted two youths from there to Mrs. 'Shop', who immediately identified them. The youths confessed and Garda Murphy induced them to return the money, which Mrs. 'Shop' found to be short by 5/-. Garda Murphy directed the two youths to clean up the sidewalk, and to clean the shop. He convinced Mrs. 'Shop' that it was worth the expense of 5/- to have her place tidy and her goods neatly displayed. He got a further assurance from the youths that they would assist her with stacking and packing and tidying the shop every day for half-a-crown a week, to which Mrs. 'Shop' agreed.

"Garda Murphy did not deliver the summons to Mrs. 'Shop'. Garda Murphy did not arrest the two youths.

"Break into teams. You now have 30 minutes to answer the questions and present your arguments." Sergeant Dunleavy walks to the back of the room and sits facing TD Slevin.

Slevin flashes his trademark smile, "That case study was for me, wasn't it?"

"I can guess why you're here."

"Can you now? And what happened to Mrs. 'Shop' and

the two youths? If it's true."

"Mrs. Brannigan returned to County Tyrone two years later, after her husband's death. One of the youths, 'Chucky' – his nickname – got a full-time job in her shop up until she left. 'Big Joe' – his nickname – joined the guards and is now an instructor in the Garda College." Joseph Dunleavy pats the case study paper lying on the table and slides it toward Slevin. "Here. Take the case study back to your boss, and have him answer the 20 questions."

"Sergeant, you may have answered the one question the minister wants to know."

"And what question is that?"

"Oh, the minister didn't ask; neither did I. But you have answered it all the same." Matt stands up and places the copy of the case study in his pocket. He pauses at the doorway. "Thanks! Big Joe!"

CHAPTER SEVEN

AFTER THE SOMME 1918 –
BACK IN ENGLAND

The euphoria of victory is short-lived. Unemployment and strikes are common. Worker discontent is running high. The police force experiences two strikes in 1918 and 1919. Terence Prior joins the Communist Party.

Kennedy, on the other hand, prolongs the illusion of euphoria with wine, women and song – three engagements in which he excels.

In January 1919, Prior visits Germany. He greatly admires the German military/police-dog training, and he works closely with a *Hundezwinger*, a relationship that would endure for twenty-eight years notwithstanding British/German hostilities.

He easily secures a job in a government quarantine station, and he is able to kennel Rex there during his six months quarantine for rabies. He also obtains two more dogs from Germany and engages in developing skills – both Tracy's own skills and the dogs' skills. In July 1919, Tracy's dogs clear quarantine.

Prior's political activities bring him into contact with the London Irish members of the Connolly Club. The club is named in honour of James Connolly (*Séamas Ó Conghaile),* one of the leading Marxist theorists of his day. In Dublin, Connolly established the Irish Citizen Army with Jack White, both former British Army. In 1916 the Irish Citizen Army joined with the Republican Brotherhood and Sinn Féin to occupy the General Post Office on O'Connell Street (previously Sackville Street), Dublin. Connolly was the commandant of the Dublin Brigade and was de facto commander-in-chief. The revolt was successfully crushed, due in large part to the Royal Irish Fusiliers who had been sent to quell the rebels. For his part, Connolly was executed by British firing squad. Tracy remembers that Captain Daniel E. Kennedy is RIF. Connolly's vision of a 'Gaelic Socialist Republic' intrigues Prior. The Irish situation warrants close attention.

In January 1919 Ireland declares an independent Irish Republic. They also declare the Irish Republican Army (IRA) the official army of the state.

In the same month, the Irish Republican Army begins the Irish War of Independence. Tracy Prior is convinced that this is a class war. In August 1919 Tracy and his dogs travel to Dublin. The Connolly Club in Dublin is expecting him and receives him well. English Tracy Prior and his German dogs join the IRA.

Daniel Edward Kennedy's high living is about to come crashing down. Wine, women and song have drained his available cash. The Stoat brothers' nightclubs had provided him with all the pleasures that the Manchester underworld could provide – nightclub life with 'extras'.

His most recent 'extra' is gambling, which Bob and Tony Stoat run in back rooms. The Stoat operation is run by 'Ma' Stoat, the tough old matriarch of the family. Ma works from home, delegating on-site management to her two sons.

Daniel E had taken to gambling in an attempt to raise enough money to pay off his overdue nightclub account. But, alas! He falls still deeper into debt, so deep that by January 1920 he is faced with selling assets in Ireland as the only way out. He is not so naïve as to expect his father, Donal Kennedy, to welcome back the prodigal and bail him out. What to do? On 02 January, after running up further expenses due to New Year's celebrations, on Friday night/Saturday morning, two of Stoats' debt collectors engage Daniel E at the club. They extract 'interest payment' from him by removing the tip of his finger from the upper knuckle – the little finger on the left. Tomorrow, Sunday, they would extract more 'interest payments', and every succeeding day until Kennedy comes up with full payment. Sunday's deadline is 3:00pm. In the Stoats' experience, the first 'interest payment' is enough inducement to extract instant payment in full.

On Sunday, Ma, Bob and Tony Stoat are at home waiting for news of Kennedy's anticipated payment. They are joking as to how they had shaken up the 'T'ick Mick' with a little finger-snipping. What they fail to take into account is that Daniel E, who had his wound treated, had gone to the chemist shop to obtain fresh bandages. He had also purchased some other supplies from the chemist and has obtained a few more things from the hardware shop next door – things that he can skilfully apply to wipe out his debt and clean the slate. The Manchester Corporation Gas Undertaking unknowingly provides the final ingredient.

Currently, the British Government is seeking men willing to 'face a rough and dangerous task', to boost the ranks of the Royal Irish Constabulary (RIC) in policing an increasingly anti-British Ireland. There is no shortage of recruits, many of them from unemployed army veterans. On the Saturday afternoon, 03 January, following his purchase at the chemist shop, 'Edward Daniel' signs up to join the Temporary Constables of the RIC, a group made up of ex-army officers. In the urgent rush to rapidly post the men, background checks are waived, relying on the honour of the recruits to accurately state their previous rank and experience. Actually, any man with a 'past' would be preferred to a 'gentleman' in this campaign. He is instructed to report for duty on Monday 05 January. This gives Daniel E enough time to settle his financial affairs.

Sunday 04 January is a quiet Sunday afternoon in Manchester. At the Stoat's dining table, Ma Stoat and her two sons are jokingly speculating on Kennedy's debt repayment. They detect the odour of gas. Ma goes to the kitchen to check the oven. Suddenly the Stoat house is wrecked by an explosion.

"Die you rats! Ma-Ma Stoat-rat! Baby Stoat-rats!" Here is Captain Daniel E. Kennedy, dressed in RIF army uniform and shaking his service revolver at the burning house. An acrid smell from the blast permeates the street, followed by the odour of burning flesh – a smell familiar and satisfying to Kennedy. No one survives the explosion; the entire crime family is wiped out in a single foul-smelling blast as repulsive as their corrupt criminal operation. Kennedy calmly walks away before any of the shocked citizens are fully aware of what has occurred.

And Captain Daniel E is not finished. The two 'debt collectors' are engulfed in flaming petrol when their car explodes. The driver is trapped against the steering wheel and is killed almost instantly. The second occupant stumbles from the burning car and runs blindly into a wall before collapsing in a fiery heap on the ground. The final death toll is five. The three nightclubs are set ablaze by petrol bombs igniting and exploding simultaneously. No one suffers directly from these three explosions, but five people, employees and patrons of the clubs, sustain minor injuries in the ensuing panic to evacuate the burning buildings. All three buildings are extensively damaged rendering them unsafe and unusable.

The results are immediate and widespread. Not only is the Stoat crime family wiped out, but other underworld operators are struck with fear. Hundreds of poor denizens of Manchester, in attempting to circumvent the severe rationing, had been ensnared into debt by criminal elements that provided black-market goods on credit. These poor people, hitherto trapped in unattainable loan repayments due to punitive interest, are suddenly freed from the Stoats' debt. Thanks to Captain Daniel E. Kennedy, Stoats' loans are rendered uncollectible. People are newly-emboldened. They resist loan sharks and black marketers and cooperate with police. Organised crime loses its grip and Manchester sighs with relief.

Unlike trench warfare, killing in Manchester results in a police investigation. It takes some time, but the Manchester Police piece together enough information to seek the arrest of the prime suspect, the man observed leaving the crime scene in RIF uniform. They endeavour to apprehend Daniel Edward

Kennedy.

There are many Manchester citizens who would gladly clap him on the back, rather than clap him in gaol, for cleaning up the Stoat blight that for years had been beyond the reach of the police.

Daniel E is no 'T'ick Mick'. His exit plan works. On 09 January 1920, four days after reporting for duty, Second Lieutenant Daniel, Edward (having dropped 'Kennedy' from his name in favour of 'Daniel' as his newly-altered surname) commences training in the Temporary Constables of the RIC, and on 25 March, he arrives in Ireland. He is not the only member of the unit to have a chequered past or dubious name. The overriding requirement is to ruthlessly crush the IRA.

The Manchester Police are stymied in their attempts to locate Daniel E. Kennedy. Clearly, he had left the local area. The regiment in Armagh could provide no clue either. He had failed to rejoin his regiment after a post-war furlough and is currently listed as AWOL. In the hopes of locating him in Tipperary, where he might have reconnected with family or past friends, the Royal Irish Constabulary is co-opted into the investigation. That too fails to locate him. Police forces in England, Wales, Scotland and Ireland are advised to be on the lookout for him. On 01 April 1920, wanted posters are issued to all police stations. Daniel E. Kennedy's picture appears in wanted posters in police stations everywhere, and a reward is offered for 'information leading to an arrest' – £1,000

Daniel E has found a job well-suited to his talents and temperament – a battle-hardened killer-Irishman in the Black & Tans.

CHAPTER EIGHT

TD SLEVIN MEETS WITH MURF

June 1947

Matt Slevin, TD for Galway South, Parliamentary Secretary to the Minister of Justice, pulls his car to the side of the road. The road is so narrow that his black MG 1½-litre Y-type car takes up half the width of the road. Across the stone wall he could see two men and a border collie at a tin shed in a field. No. He couldn't call it a field – it is a small fenced area with an undersized tin shed against the stone wall. There are no fields around here, just rolling treeless countryside at the Atlantic coast. The fenced area contains a small flock of sheep. The two men, in Wellington boots, are foot-bathing sheep – walking them through a trough of 10% zinc sulphate solution; after which they jam wads of cotton wool, soaked in pitch and 10% zinc sulphate solution, into the cleft of the hooves of each sheep before releasing them out of the pen. What a smelly disgusting job.

"Excuse me!" he shouts across to them. They don't appear to have heard him. He shouts louder. "Excuse me! I'm looking for…"

"…Murf." one of the men interrupts. "You're looking for Murf. Right, Matt?" The man, almost totally splattered in dirt, climbs over the stone wall. He is shouldering a short snub-bladed spade.

By contrast, Matt is dressed in light-tan cavalry twill slacks, dark-tan sports coat over a brown narrow-striped shirt with a well-fitted collar (custom made) and a moss-green soft tie; his shoes are light-brown and spotless; a dark-brown

Stetson tops off his wardrobe. This would be Matt's 'rural attire'. "Yes. I'm looking for Inspector Murphy. I was told I could find him with John-Joe McCafferty at the sheep shed on the road to Dundon. And how do you know me as 'Matt'?"

"Yon is John-Joe." and turning back to the shed, "Give Deputy Slevin a wave, John-Joe." and back again to Matt Slevin "and here we pronounce it 'Dún Duinne'." He extends a hand smelling of sheep foot-bathing solution. "I'm Inspector Murphy. Everyone calls me 'Murf'."

Matt reluctantly steps forward and shakes his hand, and to make small talk, asks, "Why do you use the local Irish pronunciation?"

"Well, investigation requires local knowledge. Local word usage identifies the character of a place; the anglicised form may hide it."

"Ah," says Matt. "'Dún Duinne' – the 'Fort of… Brown'."

"That's right."

"So you're investigating?"

"I'm under suspension. And you're standing in mud."

Matt looks down at his shoes, and steps back onto the dry road. He looks at the ring of mud that has collected around the side of his soles. He goes to brush the mud from his shoes on a clump of grass.

Murf catches his arm. "No. Don't brush the mud. You'll brush it in and stain your shoes. It's just 'blue till'. It will quickly dry to a light-grey powder that you can blow off." Murf leads him back to the centre of the road. "I thought you were not due in Mayo until Dev's visit to Castlebar in September. So you're stirring up support for the party in advance?"

"Just making sure that the 'Long Fellow' is still loved

by the people. We can't be having any discontent..."

"...between the guards and the circuit court judges?"

"...distracting the people from the path of achieving a republic. Right, Murf? Anyway, the minister asked me to drop by to say 'hello'."

"Ah. For the sake of the Republic – on your way home, like." Murf had started to walk down the road in the direction of the ocean, the spade balanced on his shoulder. "Walk with me, Matt. You want to talk with me?"

"Where are we going? We can take the car."

"You won't see anything of interest from the car. You'll miss a lot unless you step into the place – the smells, the feel... Just consider what a place like this could reveal. Or what could it hide?"

"Hah. So you're on a case, are you?"

"I gather you were talking to the lads at the station. What did they tell you?"

Matt falls into step with Murf. He should be annoyed, but there is something about Murf that tugs at his curiosity – and it is truly a pleasant July day for a walk by the sea. "The guards at the station say that there is a case of a runaway girl. She ran off to Dublin with some boys that were holidaying in Achill. Her parents are upset. The guards in Dublin are following up with the boys; they got their names from the hostel in Achill where they were staying. You don't agree?"

"The dots connect, but that is not the picture that emerges."

"Sergeant Joe Dunleavy says that you connect dots. Is that what you were doing with the sheep? Connecting dots?"

"Not exactly. I was gathering information from the sheep, and from John-Joe. Both have excellent local knowledge. But you, Matt, are going to help me connect the dots."

"To solve a crime that may not be a crime at all?"

Murf does not answer. Instead he says, "Teresa McDaid was a pleasant girl (Matt noted that he said 'was', not 'is'), but she was easily swayed by flattery. The Dublin boys flattered her. It thrilled her to be with 'bad boys'. But, no, she was not so foolish as to run off with them." Murf looks down at Matt's shoes. "Your shoes are dry now. Give them a whack with your hanky." Sure enough, there is a powdery dusting on his shoes that blows right off without leaving a stain.

Murf continues, "Her parents came into the station yesterday to report her missing. They gave us a recent photograph of her and a description of her clothes – last seen in a blue wool coat and red beret. Charlie Mulligan was with them. He was the one who took the photograph just a week earlier when they were gathering dillisk. At the interview, Charlie Mulligan was quite talkative. He was clearly distraught and offered all kinds of suggestions to the guards, mostly pointing to the Dublin lads. There was talk that Charlie and Teresa might get married next year. The talk seemed to come more from Charlie than from Teresa. The girls at Casey's General Store think otherwise – they update me on all the news."

"That would be Mrs. Casey's local intelligence services," Matt comments, thinking aloud.

"Teresa, known as 'Tee' to her friends, is a cousin to Tessie who works in the store."

"Two 'Teresas'?"

"Three. There is a grandmother too. Anyway, Tessie is of the opinion that Tee likes to lark about a bit and is not yet ready to settle down. The story, as best I can put together at this point, is this. A couple of nights ago, Tee and her cousin Tessie, and Tessie's twin sister Bessie, met up with three Dublin lads, and the six of them went off to hear the 'Flyin'

Fiddler'..."

"The 'Flyin' Fiddler' who plays at 'The Hovel' in Westport?"

"So you know it, Matt?"

"The best céili music and come-all-ye singing in the West."

"Well, afterwards Tessie, Bessie and Tee return from Westport before midnight and, according to Tessie, she and Bessie were dropped off at The Cross."

"And Tee went off with the lads?"

"At that point, yes. But we don't know if she went the whole way to Dublin with them. Or did they drop her off further down the road, like at the mill at the corner of her laneway?"

"But you, Inspector Murphy, don't think she went to Dublin?"

Murf declines to answer. They continue to walk further out the headland, and Matt holds the brim of his hat because of the sea breeze.

Matt turns to Murf attempting to get more information. "What about the interview, Murf? At the interview, did Charlie give you any important information?"

"Yes."

"What did he tell you?"

"Not so much what Charlie said, so much as what was revealed by the photo and his shoes. There was a ring stain crusted on the edge of his soles – not blue till, not bog peat, not any of the farm soils from around Killbawn – a dun colour like brick."

"And the photo?"

"The background was the wild Atlantic."

"So you came out here to consult with sheep?"

"Sheep wander over a wide area, but they have favourite

spots while the grazing is good. Do you know that you can predict the weather by observing where they graze? Their hooves can tell you a lot. And John-Joe knows sheep, and he knows the whole area around here intimately. He knows where there is peculiar brown mud."

"Where is this taking us, Murf?"

"Dúndon. We're almost there – a mile from where you parked your car."

Matt looks back in disbelief, and admits to himself that he could not make out the location of where he parked the car.

Murf just continues to walk and talk. "The sheep told me to come here. Actually the high incidence of hoof rot in this grazing area tells me that drainage is so bad that there is no soil. No other place in the sheep-grazing area is as bad as this, not even the bog."

Murf hands the spade to Matt. "Here, Matt. Step off the road and try jamming the spade into the ground."

Matt tries it and it feels like hitting solid rubber. He tries harder, and gets the same result.

"See, Matt. There is a thin film of dirt, just a fraction of an inch. The grass – you can't really call it grass – is stunted here. In lots of places the subsoil is visible."

They had reached the loop at the end of the road, guarded by a solitary trash bin. Beyond the road, the sea is crashing against the rocky cliff face, and overlooking it all is the ruin of an old fort. The smell of sea spray and wrack fills their nostrils, and Matt wipes his wet nose with his white handkerchief and jams his hat more firmly on his head. It is a lonely spot.

Matt asks, "Does anyone come here?" looking at the trash bin.

"Yes. The Boscos (Don Bosco Athletic Club) have their

weekly ten-mile race from Maggie's cross to here and back –
and don't always manage to put their trash in the bin; in
spring, the farmers harvest kelp for fertiliser; when weather
and tides are favourable, people harvest dillisk. At night the
area is dark, except for the white glow of the crashing surf –
very romantic."

"Romantic? For Charlie and Tee, perhaps? Murf, I'm
picking up on where you are going, on what you are
connecting."

"See here, Matt. Here is an area – from here to the ruins
– where the dun-coloured subsoil is exposed. See how slimy
and slippery it is?"

Matt agrees.

"Matt. You need to get down and feel it. If you slowly
rub the ground with your hand pressed flat, the slimy subsoil
curls like butter."

Matt does so, and is surprised at how easy it is to curl up
a portion of the surface, yet it is so resistant to a jab from the
spade.

"This stuff, Matt, clings to your shoes, building an
encrusted ring around the soles. It can be moulded like putty.
When dry, it hardens to brick; but when damp, it gets slimy
and rubbery again. It is totally useless. See how they used it
for the walls of the fort, and how it all collapsed."

They are approaching the ruined fort. Matt makes out
the building stones in the mud and imagines how this was
once a fortress. "Murf, did you know this all along?"

"Somewhat. But I'm still filling in as we go along. Keep
focused on gathering information."

Matt realises that he is still carrying the spade. "Hey,
Murf! Do you want your spade back?"

"No. You'll need it inside the ruin."

"I'm going inside the ruin?"

"Yes, Matt."

"Why?"

"Have a look and have a poke around. See if you can find something of interest. That's why we came here."

"So what am I supposed to do?"

"See if you can dig a hole two feet deep in fifteen minutes."

"That's impossible."

"You're a politician, a 'Soldier of Destiny', Matt. You'll find a way I'm sure."

"Are you not coming to help?"

Murf is walking away. "No. You go ahead. I'll be hoking through the trash down here."

Matt looks around, talking to himself. "How could anyone dig in here? If it isn't the rubbery mud, it is the stone slabs. Ah – the stone slabs. By moving some stone slabs I could dislodge enough to have a hole in no time. I can use the spade as a lever to move them. Now there is a likely pile. No need to tell Murf that I found an easy way to dig a hole in this place." He levers off the top slab and lets it slide off the mound. Then sets to moving a few more. His spade strikes something soft, like a piece of cloth. He lifts another slab to get a better look and sees blue wool fabric.

"Murf! Murf!" he shouts. His body is immobile at the expectation of seeing something untoward. "Murf! Murf!"

Murf comes to him. "Steady on, Matt! Here, hold this!" placing a shattered Kodak in an evidence bag and passing it to him.

Murf continues to move rocks and dirt until the body of Teresa McDaid is revealed. They assume it is her. The description fits, and she is wearing a blue wool coat. No sign of her red beret. Murf pats her pockets and finds a roll of film.

Matt asks, "How did you know that she would be here?"

"I didn't know – not for sure. I needed someone who thinks like a killer, someone smart and dishonest, to chose the right spot. You were perfect for it, Matt."

"God, Murf. Now I know what Fox means when he says 'You'll hate him, but you'll love him'." Matt is slapping his hands together to dislodge residue of brown slimy mud. He gives up, resigned to an overall browner hue than his wardrobe warrants.

"Matt, I'll stay here. Run back to your car and fetch the lads. They'll need to tell Castlebar to get forensics out here. Give them the shattered camera and roll of film. It may be the evidence needed to nail this one down."

The body is positively identified as Teresa McDaid. Charlie Mulligan is arrested. The muddied shoes and the prints on the broken camera and the pictures from the developed film all put him at the scene. He confesses, is tried, and is convicted of manslaughter – the result of a fit of jealous rage.

As to Murf's suspension – it is revoked the day following TD Slevin's visit.

Fianna Fáil – The Republican Party, the 'Warriors of Destiny' – however, suffered a drop in popularity. They failed to obtain a majority in the election held on 04 February 1948. Even with 46% of the seats, they were unable to form a coalition. Six minority parties and 11 independents, united only in their common distaste of Fianna Fáil, formed Ireland's first inter-party government. This lasted three years, at which point Fianna Fáil swooped back into power.

CHAPTER NINE

TRACY PRIOR IN IRELAND

In August 1919, Tracy Prior has no trouble connecting with his socialist comrades in Dublin. An English communist former British Army soldier is no great stretch for party members who admire James Connolly, who himself was born in Scotland and who had also served in the British Army. Joining a flying column of the IRA might prove to be a greater leap. Tracy's go-between is Finnegan. Finnegan is highly-educated, but is not hesitant about getting his hands dirty. He is portly, in his 40s, and of a pleasant disposition. For three days he prepares Tracy by moving him around to sample the many faces of the party.

Under Finnegan's guidance Tracy observes that in rural Ireland there are regional idiosyncrasies of speech; and within each region are four (or more) segments – 'Country Speech', 'County Speech', 'Town Speech' and 'School Speech' – much the same as in England. Finnegan, who is from Tipperary, slips in and out of dialects and accents with ease, sometimes changing mid-sentence (as in 'things' and 't'ings') to render a different import. This is a common linguistic tool. By juggling literalisms and euphemisms with irony, and by employing homophonic words, an outsider (as Tracy would be) might take a meaning quite different from what is communicated between insiders. It is essential to fit in right from the beginning, and Finnegan is preparing him.

Tracy is to meet the IRA where they are most active, in County Cork. They set out from Dublin in a 1919 Ford Model T Pickup, built in Cork, according to Finnegan. There are no front doors, but being August, Tracy doesn't mind. The window/hatch at the back opens onto the flatbed and is ideal for the three mastiffs that accompany him. Tracy is dressed in working-class army-issue trousers and jacket with non-regulation brown cloth cap, brown shirt and black 'daisy-roots' boots, the clothes one buys cheaply at any Army & Navy Surplus Store. His merchant seaman's donkey coat is thrown in the back with his duffle bag and the black-brindled mastiffs.

Finnegan is wearing a dark-blue pinstriped three-piece suit, over a white pinstriped shirt with detachable collar – the collar he changes every day, the shirt not quite as often. His tie is burgundy, tied in a simple sling knot. He wears black laced cap-toe oxfords and grey wool socks. As always, rain or shine, a dark-grey felt Stetson is jammed on his head. Because it is a hot day, Finnegan has removed his jacket, revealing a waistcoat with watch-and-chain that is struggling at the buttons, some of which are not fastened. He smokes Players Medium Navy Cut cigarettes, one of which is always dangling from the corner of his mouth, and permits the ash to drop on his chest. At most villages he passes through, he stops for a 'half-one'. He is so quick at this that one must assume that the whiskeys are already set up and waiting for him at each stop.

Tracy, picking up on Finnegan's instructions, "How? 'Homophonic' words?"

"Well, words like 'Jew' and 'dew' are pronounced the same; 'mourning' and 'morning'…

You'll likely meet 'Joker' or 'Choker' Kelly." And Finnegan demonstrates the homophonic words.

"So should I address him as 'Joker' or 'Choker'?"

"Tracy, you have a bit of a problem there. Try 'Choker' on the job and 'Joker' off the job. He's a good soldier, but his mouth can be a pain in the arse."

Ten hours after leaving Dublin, Finnegan shouts, "Ah! Here we are!" as they round a corner, and turn up a laneway to a farmhouse. The sentry gossoon recognises Finnegan and greets him, waving him through. Approaching the farmhouse, Tracy hears loud voices from inside.

"My God. They're all singing."

"Ah no, Tracy. That's the way they talk here."

"Do they always sing like that when they talk?"

Finnegan turns off the engine, slaps him on the back and

says, "No. Sometimes they actually sing."

At the door Finnegan hesitates. "Tracy, prepare to meet the 'Byes from Cark'" slipping into yet another vernacular. He knocks the prearranged code, and the door opens.

"Hey! It's Mr. Finnegan himself!"

"And jaepers if it isn't that English communist fella that's with him..."

"And three big German-speakin' killer-dags!"

"Say something in German to the dags!"

Finnegan holds up his hands and hushes the crowd of 30 or so. They are all in their teens, farm boys mostly. If there was any suspicion of Tracy Prior, it disappears with the presence of the dogs. All these lads know work dogs. They are all comfortable around dogs, and acknowledge a dog's space.

Tracy says *"Sitz!"* and the dogs sit.

All the lads are intrigued and curious, looking over each other's shoulders.

Finnegan has them well in hand, and says to Tracy "Time to meet the North Cork Flying Column 22!"

"Is this not them?"

"No. Not the flying column. They're in the back room..." waving him onward, "...waiting to meet you. Go on! The dogs are fine here. I'll explain to the byes."

"Bleib." and *"Braver Hund."* Tracy speaks to each dog in turn with an added gentle nudge. Sounds of approval and admiration from the lads.

Tracy Prior enters the back room and meets the North Cork Flying Column 22. Now this is a different atmosphere from the outer room. There is no sing-song jollity in this room. Tracy inhales, holds his breath, and exhales slowly. So this is a flying column, Tracy reckons, as he sizes up the company.

Their leader is Taigh Mór O'Toole – leader most of the time. At 24, three years older than Tracy, he is the oldest. They have no formal ranking. Taigh Mór is their acknowledged leader due to his bravery and prudence, and they admire the skills he exhibits. They are one of the elite

IRA 'Flying Columns', which means that they operate anywhere in the country as required. There are eight in the squad. That is small, but not unusually so. Flying columns are highly mobile at short notice. This squad moves around the country in two cars to complement local units in engagements, usually comprised of 20 to 30 local men. They had just lost a member, and are in no mood for niceties.

Taigh Mór sizes up Tracy. He looks right – in his army-issue battle gear. His three monster dogs sitting outside the doorway give him an ominous aura – like a dark angel with hellhounds. Rather than interview Prior, Taigh Mór decides to put him to a test.

"We have a raid in five minutes! Are 'ou ready?" He looks at the other six and communicates by eye contact that Prior would either pass the test or die. He winks at Joker Kelly, who he appoints to have a gun ready at Prior's back at the first hint of instability. There was no immediate raid planned. Taigh Mór decided this on the spur of the moment – but there is always an RIC barracks worth hitting.

Taigh Mór tosses a Lee-Enfield at Prior. "Five minutes!"

Prior immediately starts to dismantle the rifle.

"Don't you understand 'five minutes'? Now four minutes!" swinging his pocket watch.

Prior ignores him. He dismantles the rifle and reassembles it in 90 seconds and tosses it back at Taigh. "This gun is dirty; it's inaccurate. At best it will miss target; at worst it will blow up in my face! I prefer to use this." displaying his Webley Mk VI.

From the back, Joker Kelly says to his comrades "Now isn't he smart." – pronouncing it 'shmay-irt' to denote a 'know-all'. The others snigger in agreement. "…going into battle with a handgun."

Leaving the dogs behind at the safe-house, not needed in this engagement, they drive for half an hour and then walk through fields for ten minutes. The drivers stay with the cars and the remaining six go on ahead. The RIC barracks is a solid stone building. Its doors and windows are sand-bagged with coils of barbed wire draped over the entrance. Tracy moves his position to take advantage of a few gaps in the fortifications. He could make out the face of one policeman and the back of another's head through the doorway.

Taigh Mór cries "Fire!" and Tracy nails both his targets in two rapid shots. There is a lot of gunfire. The Flying 22s shoot at the stone building causing no damage. And the police fire wildly in the direction of their shooting. Taigh Mór cries "Withdraw!" and they run along the hedge to the cars – a three-minute fast pace. They are gone.

Back at the safe-house, the Flying 22s are celebrant with their success. There was no purpose in the engagement – not to occupy the building, not to capture munitions – other than to test Prior. Now, however, Prior's killing of two constables is an unexpected bonus. Finnegan and the 'byes' are gone, and the dogs appear not to have moved since they had left. Tracy greets the dogs. Eight fighting men and three fighting dogs have the house to themselves. They compliment Prior. "Well done! Two dead! Good job!"

Taigh Mór says. "Congratulations, Prior! You passed the test!"

Prior's response is unexpected. "But YOU didn't pass MY test...not one of you." He continues. "What is the police compliment for that barracks? How many were present at the raid? What is their strength and chances of retaliation?"

"Hey. Hold on there, Prior. It was just an RIC barracks."

"And you're a bunch of country boys shooting at a stone wall!"

Everyone is shouting now; the dogs agitated and snarling.

Taigh Mór cries, "Stop! Enough!" to bring calm.

And continues, "This Prior fellow just demonstrated that he can handle a gun. We were informed about him before he came, about how experienced he is." And then addresses Prior. "All right, Prior. Talk to us."

"Number one: Clean your guns and align the sights; Number two: Never engage a target until you have assessed his strength and have worked out a strategy; Number three:

The enemy is not the police force; the RIC are Irishmen like yourselves. The enemy is the British administration – the advantaged people who influence the government, the British Army, the British Auxiliary Forces."

"Is that all?"

"No. But it's a start."

Shouting starts up again, but Taigh Mór subdues it. "First your number three: We have determined what our legitimate targets are, and the RIC as supporters of the British administration ARE on our list. Your number two: Tonight's raid was just your introduction into our squad; we did not expect any casualties; the barracks is known to be severely under strength, that is until the Black & Tans arrive. Your number one: And here you are correct. Our guns are in poor shape. Are 'ou able to show us how to fix them?"

"Fair enough. Let's start with the guns."

"All right, Byes. All guns on the table. Let's start taking them apart."

Prior sets about showing them the proper procedure to clean and maintain a gun. While the seven men rub and polish and clean, he sits down on the floor to nap with his dogs.

Joker Kelly is complaining. "How come an Englishman is telling us what to do. Aren't we supposed to be killing the bastards? And Lord, look at him now resting comfortable while we work." The rest of the squad ignores Joker – he is always on about something, and they do not take him seriously.

Joker goes over to Tracy and dangles his polishing rag in his face. "Tickle. Tickle. Englishman – wake up. Tickle. Tic…"

Quicker than a blink, Tracy has Joker in a stranglehold. And Joker feels a knife edge slide across his throat that draws blood. Tracy then launches him with a kick that sets him flat against the wall, and collapses him to the ground. Joker's first instinct is to check his body for injury. He is relieved to find that the cut in his throat is no more serious than a shaving nick. He stands up and moves about. Satisfied that he is only bruised, his next reaction is to retaliate. He grabs his gun from the table and realises that it had not yet been reassembled. He appeals to the squad. "See that! See! He tried to kill me! Let's get him!"

Taigh Mór stands up from the table, leans over to Joker and slaps him hard on the mouth. Joker goes down to the floor a second time, his lip bleeding.

Taigh Mór addresses Tracy. "Good move that, Tracy. Do you have any more?"

"Lots more."

"Could you show us?"

"Sure. Right after the guns are cleaned and sighted." And so it starts. Tracy Prior trains the North Cork Flying Column 22.

Tracy's obsession is in destroying the properties of the gentry and in undermining British administration, as inspired by the Bolsheviks in the Russian Revolution. The squad's short-term objective is the RIC, but in the long term it is to dislodge all British administration and establish an independent country.

As IRA activity increases, many RIC are deserting. Some RIC barracks are no longer manned. The British administration is slipping. The Irish Provisional Government operates a shadow government and appoints republican police and judges to provide law and order. By March 1920 the North Cork Flying Column 22 is fully trained. They provide a deadly welcome to the Black & Tans, the British paramilitary police sent to bolster the RIC. Then in July 1920, on the heels of the Black & Tans, the auxiliaries come. These are the British flying columns.

The 22s disregard all protocols of conduct. Their codeword for a raid was 'payday' or 'deliver pay'. In deference to Tracy and his East London manner of speech, they change the codeword to 'pie-day' and 'delivering pie'. They are ruthless in their treatment of the enemy. Charges of misconduct and atrocities are levelled against them. They care not a whit. They scour the country from south to north, from west to east, delivering 'pie'. They become the most efficient and most feared IRA flying column in Ireland.

They permit newspapers to photograph them, and their names are freely given. All of them, that is, except Tracy Prior and the dogs. Tracy does not appear in photographs; the squad does not want it known that one member is English. Rumours and speculation arise about the unidentified eighth member, the one with German hounds in tow. This adds to the mystique.

The British post rewards for all of them. And it is not only the British administration that denounces them. The Church excommunicates each one of them. And when their home parish continues to shield them, the entire parish is placed under interdict. The squad is hated and feared by the authorities, both temporal and spiritual. Only the devil and the people are on their side.

An Irishman had joined the Black & Tan auxiliaries, and now an Englishman is in the IRA.

CHAPTER TEN

DANIEL E. KENNEDY IN IRELAND

On 25 March 1920, Second Lieutenant Edward Daniel arrives in Ireland. A total of 9,500 had been recruited into the Special Police Force. So many that uniforms were not ready. Instead, army uniforms with RIC or British police tunics, caps and belts were supplied. There was nothing 'uniform' about the issued dress except as a way to distinguish them from Regular RIC and army. Hence the RIC special force's nickname, 'Black & Tan'.

In November 1920, Daniel E. Kennedy, under the pseudonym Edward Daniel, makes a successful transition to the Auxiliary Division of the RIC (ADRIC), generally known as the auxiliaries. His display of military skill and leadership earns him a promotion. He is appointed leader of a flying column – heavily armed and highly mobile – within one of the fifteen companies mandated to operate in the south and west of Ireland where the IRA activity is greatest. Auxies are permitted to wear RIC uniforms, or their old army uniforms with police badges. Daniel E chooses to wear his old captain's uniform.

The object of the Black & Tans and auxiliaries is to break both the IRA and the newly-established Irish Government, Dáil Éireann. The 'Irish problem' is regarded as a 'police matter' by Britain. The British Army is not employed, notwithstanding their large presence in Ireland. From the British perspective this is civil war within the United Kingdom, and use of the army could lead to public condemnation. Another problem is that, due to the large number of Irish serving in the British Army, mutiny is likely. The army remains in Ireland, but avoids engaging in direct combat. Unofficially, some British serving in Ireland sympathise with the rebels, and assist them by leaking sensitive information to them. Thanks to sympathetic English civil servants in the British administration, a number of the IRA leaders avoid assassination.

Daniel's flying column is comprised of 30 men, all ex-officers and veterans of trench warfare. The men regard Daniel's accent as 'posh-Irish', common in Irish officers in the British Army. As section leader, his official rank is second lieutenant. Notwithstanding, he dresses in a captain's uniform, except for the Glengarry cap the auxiliaries are required to wear. Technically, this could be regarded as a breach of army regulations, but the protocol on army uniforms is sufficiently blurred that it is not enforced in the Auxiliary Division of the Royal Irish Constabulary. In any event, Daniel speaks like a captain, struts like a captain, and acts like a captain. The men address him as 'Captain'.

On Sunday 21 November 1920, the IRA assassinates the Cairo Gang in Dublin. The Cairo Gang were Irish undercover intelligence officers working for the British. Ten members of the gang are killed. Also killed – an RIC constable, a civilian informant and two auxiliaries. Five additional British intelligence officers are wounded.

Daniel and his flying column fly into action. The GAA (Gaelic Athletic Association) is suspected of harbouring IRA members. On that same day, at the GAA's Croke Park, Dublin and Tipperary are scheduled to play a Gaelic Football match at 3:00pm. Daniel's squad joins the British security forces/RIC under the command of Major Mills that descend on the park about 15 minutes into the game. Some RIC, including Daniel and his squad, rather than wait for orders on engagement, commence firing into the crowd, killing fourteen civilians and wounding dozens more. They later claim that they were first fired upon by IRA 'sentries'. They round up three IRA suspects and bring them to Dublin Castle. There they beat them to extract information, after which they shoot them 'trying to escape'.

Daniel's squad is attached to K Company, active in the south and west, from Cork to Mayo. What Daniel learns at the castle prompts him to go post-haste to Cork. They set out in a convoy of Crossley Tenders 25/30 hp with their .45

Webleys, firing shots into residential streets along the way.

'Captain' Daniel addresses his squad, "Pigs. And rats. That's what you're up against. Pigs you kill with one shot to the head; the rats you make suffer before you kill." 'Pigs' are republicans; 'Rats' are Republican Army.

The squad would roar into a village – Captain Daniel had a sense of where republican sympathisers might be – jump out of their lorries, firing shots and ordering all the inhabitants out of doors. Men and women, old and young, sick and infirm would be lined up against a wall with hands up to be questioned and searched. Some would be beaten with the butt end of Webleys to teach 'respect'. And then on to the next village, gathering more information and making more enemies.

It is only 21 days since the Croke Park killings, but so much is happening that it feels like much longer. The sense of urgency that is instilled in the men keeps them tense and restless, and ever ruthless. They stop in Riverstown, Tipperary, on 11 December, en route to Cork. Riverstown is Daniel's boyhood home. But under present circumstances he could not risk visiting his family at the Kennedy Stud Farm. Still, he is eager to see the place. They park their tenders away from the property in a laneway, well out of sight of the farmhouse. They approach the house by way of a wooded area so as not to be observed. When they come upon it, they see a devastated ruin of a building. Flying overhead is the flag of the Republic. The IRA had been here. The stables appear to be intact, but there is no sign of life. Daniel falls to his knees and slams his head into the ground with an agonising wail. The auxiliaries assume that he is over-stressed and is suffering from nightmare memories of the trenches. They are all veterans of the Great War; and all, without exception, endure frequent disturbing mental flashbacks.

When Daniel composes himself, he leads the men to the local village. He goes into the solitary pub there. Inside, he asks the barman about the destruction of the Riverside property. The barman recognises them as auxiliaries and is reluctant to cooperate with them. Daniel shoots at the spirit bottles behind the bar, picking them off one at a time. Liquor is spilling and splashing over the bar, and shards of glass fly around. The barman has good reason to fear for his life.

"So tell me, Pig Barman! Who burned down the Riverside Farm?"

At the first "I don't know!" Daniel shoots the barman in the knee. Then, "The 22s, the 22s! In the name of God, don't kill me!"

"And where do I find the 22s?" Daniel readies his gun for another shot.

"They travel all over the country. God knows where they are now!"

The gun levels at him…

"They are all wild and fanatical; one of them even has German dogs! He was the one that led the raid!"

An image of Tracy Prior flashes across his inner eye. He discharges the pistol an inch to the right of the barman's head, and storms out. The barman remains immobile for as long as he can hold his breath. Then fear is replaced by the pain of his shattered knee.

In Cork, the squad meets up with K Company. K Company had suffered 13 seriously wounded that same day, 11 December, at Dillon's Cross. When Daniel's flying column joins them, they commence retaliation by looting, burning and destroying a substantial part of Cork City Centre. Daniel throws himself into the work with greater zeal than before.

The next day, Daniel transfers ten of his men to other squads in K Company. The company major approves his pursuit of the 22s with his remaining 20 men. When located, the 100-strong company would rally its flying columns to engage in the extermination of the North Cork Flying Column 22.

"We're going north!" Daniel announces to his squad. This unexpected declaration takes the men by surprise.

"Hey, steady on, Captain!" they respond. And one of the men reminds him, "We were instructed not to go into 'the

North'."

"The 22s have gone north to support the nationalists in West Ulster – that's the intelligence we received. There is talk that the country might be partitioned and the 'Shinners' (Sinn Féin) want to secure a foothold in the nationalist areas there. We'll catch them as they return south. It's likely they'll rest up in Mayo. Castlebar is our next stop."

Daniel regrets not having better firepower. He intends to set up a base from which to strike, and devote some time to developing bombs. At Castlebar, he is told he could move into the RIC barracks at Ballycorry. The sergeant in charge of RIC Ballycorry is David Fox, a dedicated policeman, but not suited to anti-IRA fighting. It is a wonder the RIC barracks had not been abandoned like so many other rural stations; but the IRA is only mildly active in the region – mostly farmers who conduct a part-time campaign. The more dedicated members of the IRA are active in the cities. But Mayo is an important resting point for southern units of the IRA active in West Ulster – units such as the Flying 22s.

As Daniel E sets out, little does he know that the North Cork Flying Column 22 is in Ballycorry, just five miles from the RIC barracks. They are resting their fatigued bodies before returning to Fermanagh where they will relieve one of the other flying columns. But they are alerted by a report of the imminent arrival of Black & Tans coming to bolster the RIC contingent in the barracks.

The auxies' journey from Castlebar to Killbawn is uneventful, and only a few more miles to Ballycorry. But on the road to Ballycorry they are ambushed. The ambush is brief and deadly. It is clear to Daniel that this is no local IRA hit. This is a flying column supported by local Shinners. Daniel loses half his squad – two killed and eight wounded. He dispatches the injured back to army barracks in Castlebar, and Daniel with his depleted squad of ten finishes the journey to Ballycorry.

At the RIC barracks, Captain Daniel introduces himself to the sergeant by thrusting a squad list at him. The auxiliaries regard the RIC as too soft on the IRA. And there is no doubt that this group of auxiliaries disdains the RIC, a contempt they display at every opportunity. There are 31 names on the list, with some markings and margin notes. Daniel does not bother to introduce his men by name. Sergeant Fox, the officer in charge of the barracks, notes that there is no 'Captain' on the list, but it is clear to him that the squad has undergone serious personnel depletion, and it is likely that transfers had occurred. The auxies are weary. And ignoring all protocol and courtesy, they take over the barracks to collapse in bunks and beds and anywhere they could rest.

The following morning, Daniel still makes no effort to introduce himself or his men to the constables. The only acknowledgement is to demand food and supplies. After breakfast, Captain Daniel takes his remaining men out to the bogland behind the barracks and trains them in dodging bullets.

"You dodged bullets in the trenches! Have you forgotten how?" firing live rounds at them. "Get down! And fast! A half-inch of head above the rise is enough to get you killed!" He wounds two of his men in this 'training' – a nicked calf and a holed earlobe. Nothing serious, but he has Sergeant Fox transfer them to another RIC barracks that is undermanned. Now there are nine auxies – the eight fiercest of the bunch and a pathological captain. This brings the barracks complement to 13 – nine auxiliaries including the 'Captain', and four RIC.

The captain settles in and orders supplies for the manufacture of explosives. They arrive from Dublin inside a week.

The burning of Cork is reported in the newspapers in England. There is widespread reaction against the British handling of the Irish War. Even the King is upset. Churchill issues orders to the Black & Tans and auxiliaries to observe proper conduct. Too late. They have totally alienated the people, even those who regard themselves as 'British' Irish, including many of the Royal Irish Constabulary.

In January 1921, the RIC barracks in Ballycorry gets a phone call. It is the army in Castlebar asking for the officer in charge of the auxiliary flying column. Due to the uproar in England over reports of misconduct, orders are issued to ground all flying columns. They are to withdraw to centres from which they would be deployed by central command – in this case, the army barracks in Castlebar. Any RIC barracks that is understaffed would be supplemented by Special Forces and auxiliaries, but they must operate under the command of the RIC officer-in-charge. Ballycorry's RIC complement is for ten policemen. Second Lieutenant Edward Daniel remains there with five of his squad – the rest he sends to Castlebar Army Barracks where they will be stationed.

David Fox, the RIC sergeant, is in charge of the barracks, and Daniel is to submit to him notwithstanding Daniel's superior rank. Daniel is also ordered to provide a written report on the state of his squad and an account of his operations since arriving in Ireland. His wings are clipped but he is still afforded a lot of opportunity for independent activity. And he has time to devote to his other passion – explosives.

CHAPTER ELEVEN

TRACY PRIOR MEETS MICKEY CARR IN THE IRA IN 1920

Tracy Prior is still with the North Cork Flying Column 22 in December 1920. Their actions are concentrated in West Ulster where they operate within Donegal Command IRA. When not 'delivering pie' they are resting in Mayo. Tracy likes Mayo; so do the dogs. But his socialist activities are curtailed here for lack of opportunity. The rural IRA is nationalistic, viewing the conflict solely in the context of an Irish/British struggle, rather than as a class struggle. Tracy would like to be more active in devastating the property of Irish lords and aristocrat landlords. He is therefore on the lookout for opportunities more in line with his socialist Bolshevik principles.

The flying column is supplemented by the local IRA, varying from a half dozen to 30 volunteers. The Killbawn unit engages boys as 'runners'. They deliver messages, some verbal and some in code concealed in school homework. These runners also tip them off if they see anything suspicious or untoward. The two most frequent runners are Michael Carr, aged 13, and Ben Muldoon, also aged 13.

Mickey Carr is red-haired – small, thin and dirty. He dresses in grown-up clothes many times too large, probably his father's cast-off farm clothes – blue work shirts, blue work trousers rolled up at the ankles. He prefers rubber-soled 'quiet boots' to hobnail farm boots, or simply goes bare-footed. He is a virtual orphan. His mother died at his birth, or maybe ran away soon after – there are numerous versions of the story; his father then went to work in England and was never heard from again; his grandmother, the sole surviving family member, is in poor health. She ignores Mickey except to slap him about. So he keeps out of her way, neglected and unloved, relying on his wits and instinct to survive. They say that he is the result of a doomed marriage – a dirt-poor farmer marrying an itinerant girl. The consequence, a strange wild troublesome boy with no kith or kin to turn to. He has no friends other than Ben Muldoon, son of the local schoolmaster, John Michael Muldoon, who lives in Killbawn and who has a small farm near the school in Ballycorry. Mickey goes to school, not to learn anything, but because Master Muldoon brings him lunch, his sole meal of the day, which he eats with Ben.

Ben Muldoon is of slight build. In contrast to Mickey, he is neat and clean, his brown hair brushed at least once a day. He is usually dressed in corduroy knee-length pants, knee socks, laced shoes and a Fair Isle sleeveless pullover on a white shirt. He frequently cycles between the town of Kilbawn and Ballycorry, where he goes to school. Hence his preference for rural Ballycorry where his school pals live. His daily journeying between Kilbawn and Ballycorry provides the IRA with a reliable courier; messages are passed back and forth concealed in Ben's homework papers.

At first, Mickey only tags along with Ben. Later, the IRA realises that Mickey Carr is stealthy and cunning, and is available at all times of the day and night. He becomes so efficient that he earns the nickname 'Go-Carr'. He is keen. He learns how to handle a rifle and surprises his comrades with his skill and accuracy. Within a few months he is engaged as a sniper and supports the 22s in West Ulster. He is callous, fearless and without a conscience.

When Tracy meets Mickey Go-Carr, he recognises great potential in him, and undertakes his training. And Mickey becomes the sniper-of-choice in the unit. Go-Carr is greatly taken by the big dogs, and hence he in turn takes to Tracy Prior. Go-Carr proves to be the best student Tracy ever had – better than any of the Cork Boys. Most nights Tracy and Go-Carr would blacken their faces and disappear into the night with the dogs. The knife becomes Mickey's weapon of choice – it is silent. He could kill and move on without alerting anyone – like a ghost in the night. British collaborators and informers are found dead in their beds thanks to the Prior/Carr combination. In February 1922 Michael Go-Carr would soon get the opportunity to put his skills to the ultimate test – a multiple assassination.

On 06 December 1921 the Anglo-Irish Treaty is signed. Officially, hostilities had ceased on 11 July 1921. The Black & Tans/auxiliaries are withdrawing to major centres to be employed on an as-needed basis. In reality, many of the IRA leaders continue with their campaign against the British administration, and the auxiliaries are forced to respond.

On 12 January 1922, evacuation of all RIC barracks begins, to be completed within a year. The RIC would disband, and be replaced by 'Civic Guards'. Special Forces – the Black & Tans and the auxiliaries – are being pulled back to major centres in preparation for final withdrawal.

The reaction to the treaty is mixed. A little over 50% of the population of the country support it. Many in Ireland are unhappy with the conditions of the treaty; notwithstanding, they desire an end to the armed hostilities that are ravaging the country; they hope to pursue the realisation of a republic by peaceful means. For those who support the treaty, it is viewed as a step forward. It is expected that if most of the country achieves independence, the remaining pro-British loyalist pockets of East Ulster and South Dublin will be too small to function, and will shortly be drawn into an all-

Ireland independent country, and thence to a republic. Or so it is hoped.

But the rank and file of the IRA are overwhelmingly against the treaty. This causes a split in the IRA. Most want to continue the struggle until a republic of all Ireland is achieved. Some, a minority in the IRA, choose to accept the treaty. Both sides, anti-treaty IRA and pro-treaty IRA, scramble to claim territory. The disbanding RIC/Special Forces/auxiliaries would be a source of weaponry in the anticipated civil war.

On 12 January 1922, the auxiliary unit in Killbawn is ordered to cease all military and police engagements and withdraw from the RIC barracks as of 14 February. Whereupon, Daniel and his unit will be stationed in Castlebar, thence to Athlone and so on as British Army centres are progressively handed over to the Irish Free State. From 12 January to 13 February, the auxiliary unit is denied any meaningful activity. They are bored, disgruntled and mostly drunk as they endure their 33 days of confinement to barracks in Ballycorry. They talk about joining the Colonial Police in Palestine where there is opportunity for them under the British Mandate. Subduing troublesome Irish or troublesome Arabs – what's the difference?

Sergeant David Fox continues to police the area as best he can with three constables. Throughout the country there is confusion as to what is the legitimate or effective police force. Some towns still rely on the RIC. In strongly republican regions, the Republican Police has replaced the RIC. There are towns that have two police forces in operation, where one police force (usually the RIC) is ignored. Still other communities have no police presence at all. Fox finds himself working more and more in cooperation with the Republican Council. He succeeds, where most RIC officers have failed, in maintaining the trust and respect of the public. The locals trust Fox to look after police matters, and someone must keep the peace. More than once, Fox is required to haul drunken auxiliaries back to barracks from their unruly sojourns to town, shouting and firing their guns in the air at great risk to themselves and others. But, as Fox is warming up to the republicans, he is alienating the auxiliaries. The auxies regard him with contempt, and distrust him for his familiarity with republicans. He is still the senior officer-in-charge of the RIC barracks. But as the auxies voice their discontent ever more loudly and more vehemently, Fox is concerned that his authority over them is weakening. He wonders how long he will be able to hold them in check.

The day of the auxiliaries' withdrawal is approaching, much to the relief of both parties in the RIC barracks. Daniel E, who has been occupied in his solitary activities in the attic, has some unfinished business he wishes to conclude before departing the area – eke out revenge for the two auxiliaries killed and the eight disabled in ambush in December 1920.

On Sunday 12 February 1922, Daniel and the auxiliaries drive into Killbawn. Mickey Carr is known to frequent the market square where, even on a quiet Sunday, he sits by the river. Carr is picked up for police questioning – 'to help with police enquiries'. He is brought hooded to the Ballycorry RIC Barracks. Daniel is convinced that Carr is an IRA messenger, but he has no suspicion of his combat activities.

Daniel needs information:

- who informed the IRA about their arrival
  and location;

- who participated in the ambush;

- 'Names! Names!'

The captain permits the men to commence the interrogation and undertake the initial breaking. It should not be difficult to instill fear in, and beat the information out of, a skinny dirty boy. Daniel withdraws to the attic where he busies himself with his bombs and explosives. There will be an opportunity for revenge soon. He is contriving a plan and is making the final preparations for its execution.

The interrogation starts with humiliation – Carr is obliged to scrub the floor using his mouth to hold the brush.

"Hey Taig! You missed a spot!"

"Is it 'Shinner' or 'Shiner'?"

Carr observes the layout of the building from floor level and commits it to memory. Outside, Ben Muldoon, knowing that Carr had been picked up, is watching the barracks from a hollow in the bog, afraid to come any closer to the building.

The captain checks in on Carr, and is disappointed at the lack of progress. He has Carr hooded again and tied down in a chair. Dressed in his RIF captain's uniform, he repeatedly punches the boy with his leather-gloved fists. At this point Sergeant Fox and the three constables return from area patrol. Fox is appalled that the auxies have disobeyed orders by engaging in police activity, and he is livid at the captain in his treatment of the boy. He orders him to unhood and release Mickey. He instructs the auxiliaries to abide by the conditions of the treaty and to the requirement to duty that has been placed on them.

Daniel orders his men, "Bring him outside!" Carr, his face swollen and eyesight blurred, stumbles out, linked by two of the auxiliaries. Daniel and the other three auxiliaries follow. Fox watches them leave. He is suspicious that the interrogation is not over, that it has merely gone to a new location. He motions to the constables to prepare their Lee-Enfields. Then Fox too goes outside. At the handball alley he sees the auxiliaries kicking the downed boy. He draws his revolver and points at them ordering them to desist. They look at him and at the rifles pointing from behind the sandbags. This is a standoff between the RIC and the auxiliaries. Ben watches, and draws closer to Carr. Daniel knows that the auxiliaries could easily take down the policemen. But he also knows that they would never get away with it.

Daniel quickly snaps off his gloves to draw his pad and pencil from his breast pocket. He scribbles a quick note which he then presses into the boy's pocket. Mickey squints, unable to focus his swollen eyes. Replacing his pad and pencil, Daniel draws his men aside. Fox, who is still pointing his Webley, watches Captain Daniel straighten his fingers and insert them back into his gloves. In that quick second he observes that the little finger on the left is missing the top knuckle. Taking advantage of the tense lull, Ben Muldoon gets to Carr and leads him, running and stumbling, away from the continuing standoff. Daniel and the auxiliaries cautiously make their way to the tenders and drive away speedily from the barracks, kicking up stones and gravel as they skid onto the road, departing without further confrontation.

Fox remains transfixed pointing his Webley RIC at the now empty scene. He continues to stare in order to retain the image is his eyes – the captain in an RIF uniform, his nose bent, his finger chopped short. Satisfied that the scene is retained in his memory, he blinks to clear the image from his eyes. He blinks a second time to clear his head. He holsters his gun and strides back inside the barracks.

The auxies drive to the creamery yard where they hold a council of war. They regard Fox and the RIC detachment as

IRA sympathisers. Daniel informs his men that they would return to the barracks that night disguised as 'Shinners' and kill the constables. The auxies are all in enthusiastic agreement. The IRA would get the blame, or credit, for it.

But things do not work out as planned. After the auxiliaries drive away from the standoff, Fox is concerned that the auxiliaries might assess any information they had forced from the boy Carr, and conclude, correctly, that he, Fox, was the informant – the one responsible for tipping off the IRA prior to the attack on the auxiliaries in December 1920, and for other leaks since then. Then he considers the boy, Mickey Car, whom he has known since he was born. Dirty ragged Mickey Carr, who has endured pain and alienation all his short life. Carr would never break under auxiliary interrogation. Regardless, the strained relationship between the RIC and the auxiliaries has become unsustainable. Fox, with a sudden clarity of mind, realises that the RIC itself, not just the RIC barracks, must be abandoned.

Under the conditions of the treaty, the barracks will be handed over to the IRA, now referred to as 'the Army'. Most RIC barracks have already been vacated. Abandoning this one today in preparation for the handover is a decision the officer-in-charge is authorised to execute. He ensures that the munitions are secure in the strongroom. He checks the lock and gives the key to the constables. He instructs the constables on the protocol, and has them transport the keys, the required files and police documents to Castlebar for delivery to the new police authority. Fox takes a last look at the building that was his career for so many years, saddened that so much good has been obliterated. The RIC barracks at Ballycorry is quiet for the first time in its existence, and David Fox must now embark on a new path.

Late in the day, when the auxiliaries return to the barracks dressed as IRA insurgents, it is deserted. Daniel E relies on his set of duplicate keys to complete a check of the building. The filing cabinets are empty. The RIC personal items are gone. Daniel considers this fortuitous; it has turned out to his advantage. Now there is no need to carry out the phoney IRA attack. They are in sole charge, much to their satisfaction, freed from the interference of Sergeant Fox and his police procedures. They retrieve their kitbags from the tenders, from which they remove the whiskey that has become standard gear. The only thing that meets with their approval in this blighted place is the whiskey and the knowledge that they will soon be leaving. They secure the building, drink to their success, and rest from their day's work. There is no more work to do. In another day they will be gone from this wretched place. Soon they will be home.

There may be no more work for the auxiliaries, but not so for Daniel E. He leaves the men to their relaxation and assumes his night work alone and undisturbed in the attic. One final thing he is determined to do – exact payment of the debt from the IRA. Mickey Carr will deliver his note to Martin O'Hara, the 'Captain' of the motley North Mayo Brigade IRA. The note is an invitation the IRA cannot decline. Daniel laughs inwardly at his own cunning. The IRA will pay for the ambush of December 1920. They will pay dearly before he and the auxiliaries withdraw from Ballycorry.

CHAPTER TWELVE

FOX BECOMES MAC A'TSIONNAIGH

12 February 1922

After the RIC-auxiliary standoff, the constables report to Castlebar where they deliver the required reports, and thereupon apply for transfers – all in accordance with the terms of the treaty. The RIC are being accepted into the newly-formed RUC, into English police forces, and even into the newly-formed Irish police force. This last option is unlikely. Only those RIC who could demonstrate a pro-republican stand during the War of Independence would be accepted – a small number successfully make the transition. The three constables effectively arrange transfers to the Manchester City Police Force.

David Fox goes to visit Martin O'Hara, the 'Captain' of the North Mayo Brigade IRA.

"Hello, Mrs. O'Hara. Is Marty in?"

"Oh, hello, Sergeant. Sure I don't know…"

"Mrs. O'Hara. We both know where Marty is." (...at the IRA meeting place.) "Can you please send him word that I need to see him? It's important. And it is sensitive."

"Oh. Secret stuff like."

"Yes, Mrs. O'Hara. I'll wait inside, if you don't mind. I don't want to be seen hanging about here in uniform, you know."

Mrs. O'Hara is an active officer in Cumann na mBan, a women's paramilitary organisation, in which she is known simply as *'Bean Ní hEaghra'*, or 'Maura Rua', although she no longer has red hair. She is suspected of hiding arms, providing shelter to volunteers, helping to run Republican Courts – all activities the organisation claims to support. At 52, she is widowed. She carries herself proudly in a black 'A' line skirt with broad leather belt, low-heeled leather shoes, and a pale-brown shirt with epaulets. Her hair is tied back in a bun. She has a military bearing that impresses, despite her diminutive stature, 5'2''. A requested meeting between Fox and O'Hara is totally in character with their odd cooperative relationship. She and her son have had covert dealings with Sergeant Fox over the past two years. She casts a white shawl about her shoulders as she exits the house.

Fifteen minutes later Martin O'Hara strides in. He is small in stature like all the O'Hara clan, 5'5'', but walks and talks with authority. His attire is tan military, even wearing a bandolier, over which he wears a light-brown trench coat – most likely army-surplus. His boots are black, common among local work crews.

"Sergeant Fox?"

"Hello! Martin!"

"Is this about young Carr? Carr's in bad shape. Muldoon has him over at 'The House' and he's telling the wildest story about an RIC/auxiliary standoff."

"Yes. That part is true. But there is more. The auxiliaries have gone berserk and are out of control. I wouldn't put it past them to attempt to kill us – I mean, kill the RIC detachment in Ballycorry. I'm not sure anymore. You know how ruthless they are; it is not difficult to read them. Marty, I have abandoned the barracks and sent the constables away."

"So why are you here? Are you going too, and just want to say goodbye, Foxy? I don't think so."

"Marty, I am joining the IRA."

"An RIC sergeant joining the IRA?"

"It's not a first."

"No. You're not married; or are you planning to?"

"No ties."

"You're a bit old for jumping walls and crawling through ditches."

"I'm fit. And at 31 I'm a year younger than you."

"All right, Fox…"

"Mac a'tSionnaigh!"

"As Gaeilge?"

"'S é! Daithi Mac a'tSionnaigh."

"Right you be, Daithi. I have a lot going on at the moment. The treaty was ratified on 14 January as you know, and the Republican Council is in disarray as a result. It looks like we'll have civil war. The brigade is not sure of the chain of command anymore. They are looking to me for direction. And then there is that thing with the Carr boy beating and all. The lads are all riled up. You'll spend the night here – you cannot be seen in an RIC uniform. Tomorrow we'll handle your transition. Best you transfer to where you are not recognised.

"Ma, Daithi Mac a'tSionnaigh is spending the night here. Put him in the back room." Martin O'Hara hurries back to 'The House', the IRA meeting place.

Mrs. O'Hara is a witness to the exchange. "So it's 'Daithi' now, is it? Well, Daithi, here's your room."

Fox has just joined the IRA, but only later realises that it is the Irregular IRA. Getting in was not difficult. Getting out of the IRA would prove to be more challenging.

Back at the safe house, O'Hara informs the brigade that he has received intelligence that the RIC has abandoned the barracks, and it is now manned solely by the auxiliaries. He checks on the condition of Carr. Carr is badly bruised, but no broken bones. His face is puffed up and his eyes are half closed. He does not complain – brave lad. O'Hara removes

Carr from any planned action for now. Ben Muldoon and Tracy Prior tend to him. Normally, Carr would not let anyone touch him except Ben Muldoon or animals. Tracy, an outsider with dogs, is accepted by Carr, up to a point. They had formed a relationship in the context of assassinations and close combat. Under Tracy's training, in addition to his sniper skills, Carr is now a proficient quiet killer.

O'Hara might need a runner that evening; he asks Muldoon to remain. He sends Prior to the O'Hara farmhouse with Carr to have the bruises dressed, and to rest up.

At the RIC barracks, Captain Daniel E. Kennedy drags out two cases of Lee-Enfields, loads them onto a tender, and drives to the Blackwater. He deposits the cases under the bridge. Then he goes 50 yards back up the road and waits. He keeps the engine running and the sidelights on so that his lorry is discernible from the bridge. Chances are he has already been observed by one of the runners as he deposited the boxes. The note he sent via Carr was addressed to the IRA brigade leader:

Auxies withdrawn –
Pulling out tomorrow –
Two cases of rifles and ammo for sale £100 –
Hope you Shinners kill each other off –
Blackwater bridge 11:00pm –
leave money under black stone

O'Hara suspects a trap. But being anti-treaty, the IRA has no source of weapons. Other anti-treaty units have successfully purchased arms from withdrawing Black & Tans and auxiliaries. They desperately need guns and ammunition. O'Hara reads again the note that Carr had brought. So the auxies are pulling out. The IRA supply is almost entirely exhausted and, unless they re-arm, they will be unable to engage the Regular Army in the expected conflict.

It is a risky venture. The auxiliaries are not to be trusted. He ought to send a runner to check for the presence of auxies, and he would need one volunteer to approach the arms shipment to check it out in case of a trap. He makes the decision. A Ford Model T farm lorry, five men and a runner are selected to execute the pickup speedily. They draw straws to select duties. The runner would go ahead by bicycle, circle the area before the pickup time, and continue to watch for the presence of auxiliaries. Mrs. O'Hara, as bursar of the council, provides the funds from her 'Republican Bank', a tin box up the chimney. She is mindful that the council may not approve of this expenditure, but any agreement on anything is unlikely for the foreseeable future. O'Hara writes a note 'GO TO HELL!' – wishing that this would be the only note delivered. Do the auxiliaries seriously expect the North Mayo IRA to tender more than a year's pay for two cases of guns? Still, he needs the guns, and if he delays by bargaining, he could lose the opportunity. He must act before the munitions and arms are removed from the barracks for delivery to the National Army, and that could be any day now. He provides Loftus, the detachment leader, with ten £10 notes. They set off at 10:35pm.

The runner, Ben Muldoon, spots the auxiliary tender with one occupant. The occupant places a cigarette in the corner of his mouth. He lights his cigarette. In the flash of the igniting match his face is illuminated. There is no sign of any other occupants. Ben leaves, undetected, and goes farther back around the bend well away from the tender. He climbs a sycamore. From a limb high up, he strikes a match and tosses the still-flaring match up and away from the tree in a brief glowing arc. He counts to ten and repeats the ritual. Then he sits on the limb with his back to the trunk and waits to see the result.

Soon, Daniel hears the sound of a motor and sees the sidelights of a lorry approach the bridge from the other side. Slowly and cautiously, the lorry crosses the bridge, makes a three-point turn, and faces back the way it came. It sits idling on the bridge, its one working tail light illuminating the stone walls. Daniel flashes an acknowledgement. One volunteer waves a wad of banknotes in response, visible in the glow of the tail light, and stands next to the black stone, the distinctive stone at the end of the wall. One other volunteer makes his way below the bridge. It is almost totally dark. He calls for the lorry to adjust its position to afford him some light. He locates the gun cases underneath. He approaches them with a long stick. He prods, and then eases up the top of a box – then the other. Now he more bravely digs in and lifts out two guns. This looks like a genuine exchange. He waves, and three more lads join him. They examine a few more of the guns and, satisfied, they haul the boxes up the bank to the road. The volunteer with the banknotes fans them again so that they are seen. Then he folds them within a paper note and places them in the space under the black stone. Daniel cannot see clearly from the tender. The tender windows are fogged from his breath in the frosty air. He leans out the side window to better see in the dim glow of the tail light. He is satisfied that the money, or some amount of money, is placed in the agreed spot. Neither side trusts the other, but what other arrangement could be wrought at such short notice? The men load the gun cases on the back of the lorry and drive off. It is then that Daniel sees the runner. He knew that there had to be one watching him. A boy on a bicycle rides past him and follows the farm lorry.

Daniel had indeed set a trap. He had planted a very

small but deadly bomb inside one gun case. It has a timing device attached, triggered when the lid is lifted, set to detonate in 10 minutes.

The lorry accelerates uphill away from the bridge, rounds a bend and the tail light is lost from sight. The cyclist, having crossed the bridge, slows as he struggles up the hill. Then a fiery explosion flashes from behind the hill – and five IRA are blown to bits.

Revenge!

Back at the IRA house, Tracy Prior is leaving the IRA. He has no interest in the Irish Civil War. He no longer accompanies the North Cork Flying Column 22 in Donegal and Fermanagh. This is not his war. His war is elsewhere now. He conducts his last job with Go-Carr that same night. Carr is hurt. But the hurt increases his hatred and his resolve to act against the auxiliaries to appropriate retribution. Mrs. O'Hara dresses his bruises and gives them both some food. Then Carr and Prior and the three mastiffs depart the O'Hara farmhouse.

In scrubbing the floor of the barracks, Carr had observed a coal chute to the coal cellar – a holding pit under the kitchen door. However, the RIC do not burn coal. They stack their turf outside, beside the handball alley.

It is a little after 11:00pm. Prior and Carr and the dogs approach the barracks by way of the bog. Only the auxies are known to be there now. Carr is able to squeeze through the coal chute, but not Prior. The auxies had been drinking. They would be leaving soon for Castlebar, and probably thence to Dublin for withdrawal back to England. The stock of whiskey should not go to waste as they celebrate what might be their last night in Ballycorry RIC Barracks.

Using his night vision, Carr intrepidly makes his way through the kitchen, guided by the sounds of breathing. The breathing is noisy and heavy from intoxication. There is no lamp burning, no light in the dark interior. The auxies must have fallen asleep while it was still daylight. He encounters the first snoring auxiliary and dispatches him silently with his knife. He finds four more sleeping in the two adjoining rooms, whom he treats similarly. But he cannot find the captain, the one whose face he had never clearly seen. Then he remembers the note, the one he delivered to Captain O'Hara of the North Mayo Brigade. Mickey is unable to read, but he astutely elicited the contents of the note by observing O'Hara's mouth move silently in reading it. Mickey Carr reckons that the captain is not here; he must be out transacting the arms exchange with O'Hara. Mickey Go-Carr's work here is done for now.

Mickey Carr presses the latch in the front door. He pulls it open and looks out at the front yard. At first he cannot see Prior whose face is darkened and whose head is covered by a black balaclava. Prior moves. Now he sees him. Mickey steps outside. Prior walks towards the open front door. They both stop momentarily to eye each other in silent communication like sinister black feral creatures. The dogs lie silent and invisible at the edge of the bog. Their red dots are faintly discernible, gently bobbing as they scrutinise the vicinity with tense alertness. Prior enters the building. Carr stops, and turns to watch him disappear inside. Carr remains fixed at the spot. This is how they operate. Carr is keen to leave an assassination scene once the killing is executed. Prior takes a minute to survey the aftermath and to check the result. Carr waits for Prior.

Inside the building, Prior sweeps his hand to the left of the open door. He feels the presence of an umbrella/hat stand.

He moves his hand higher and expectantly touches the lamp inside the doorway. He removes the globe, sliding it up and off, and places it carefully on the lid of the glove box of the umbrella stand. Taking a box of matches from his pocket, Tracy shakes it to warn Mickey. Mickey shields his eyes in expectation. Tracy shuts his eyes tight, strikes a match and waits for the sound of the flare to subside. When the match is burning silently, Tracy opens one eye slightly. He is careful to avoid adjusting his eyes to the light. He touches the wick, replaces the globe and turns the wick down to a thin sliver of flame. He lifts the lamp from the hook and holds it aloft behind his head. He avoids any direct light hitting his eyes. Now he opens both eyes to observe the scene.

From outside Mickey whispers, "Leave."

Tracy whispers in response, "One hundred."

Audibly, Mickey counts, "One, two three..."

Prior walks with deliberate purpose. He sees two dead auxiliaries, and then one more. But his attention is not on the lifeless auxies. If Mickey says he killed them, then it is so. He notices the Lee-Enfields, but dismisses them. He goes to a plain flat door. He attempts to open it, but it is locked. The munitions room?

"...10, 11, 12..."

A second door beside it opens easily. It is the supply room. Hurriedly Tracy unhooks a kitbag from the wall. From the shelves he selects trousers and shirts, socks and underwear, and slides them into the bag. The kitbag is unused, in its issue state. Good. That means the pockets contain the standard-issue shaving kit and soap and sewing kit, and tin opener and metal knife, fork and spoon.

"...51, 52, 53..."

This is taking too long. He views the army-issue boots. He places his foot alongside to compare size and picks up a pair. He knots the boot thongs to the strap of the kitbag.

"...58, 59, 60..."

Next, he goes to the kitchen, and to the pantry. Tracy knocks tins of food from the shelf into the kitbag – sardines, beans and bully beef. The larder. What's in there? Big thick slices of steak, and cooked ham and roast beef. He wraps the cooked meats in a tea cloth and stuffs the lot into the kitbag. Except the raw meat. He selects three steaks and places them on top of the bag and hurries to the front door.

"...85, 86, 87..."

Tracy hangs the lamp back on the hook. On a hunch, he takes a quick peek inside the glove box of the hallstand. There he sees what he most urgently needs – Webley ammunition. It is in an opened box, about half full. Thankfully, he grabs the contents and stuffs the ammo into his pockets. He flips the lid shut and extinguishes the lamp. He steps outside.

"...98, 99, 100."

Tracy Prior and Mickey Carr stand nose-to-nose for a moment, like two cats in whisker-to-whisker silent communication. Tracy then walks to the edge of the bog and throws the raw meat to the dogs. Each dog catches a steak in the air. Mickey saunters to the roadside and rests on the stone wall. He sits facing Prior and the dogs. Tracy Prior is visible against the skyline. Mickey listens to the snorting of the dogs tackling the meat. He watches Tracy adjust the straps of the kitbag to reposition his load. Tracy waits for his eyes to readjust to the darkness. Meanwhile, the dogs finish their meal. Tracy Prior turns and takes a last look at Carr. He can make out the faint dark outline on the limestone wall. The shadow waves. Prior returns the salute. And thus Carr and Prior part company. Prior runs off into the darkness of the bog, three pairs of dancing red spots from the dogs marking his progress. Carr remains transfixed until he can no longer discern them. Mickey Carr would not see Tracy Prior again for 25 years.

Carr has a bad feeling. He is not happy about the assassination. Nor is he discontent about it either. In fact, he has no feelings at all about his kills. But the dogs. That's different. The dogs are gone. That can only mean that things have changed, and changed for the worse. He looks at the silent barracks outlined against the night sky and moans, "They're all dead! The dogs are gone!"

Mickey Carr speculates on the future. What will happen now? Something bad? Something about the note he delivered to Captain O'Hara? Has O'Hara been duped by the auxiliaries? No! Maybe not! Are they not all here, dead, except for one? And one auxie is no threat to the whole brigade. But Mickey is unable to shake off the feeling of dread. He sits at the roadside to steady his breathing for a few minutes, and then sets off at a jog to the IRA house by way of the road.

At 11:50pm O'Hara is anxious. The lorry should have been here by now. Then he hears it. No, he hears a number of vehicles. It is the Flying 22s and the rest of his brigade returning from Fermanagh where they were engaged with the Donegal Command IRA. The Corkmen are worried. They had pulled out of Fermanagh because they had run out of ammunition. They need armaments immediately. To make matters worse, they report that the Regular Army has just taken over Finner Camp from the British Army. They need to re-arm and return to North Cork. They are unsure how the disagreement between pro- and anti-treaty parties will play out in the IRA chain of command. They know for sure that North Cork is wholly anti-treaty, and that is where they need to be. The Flying 22s cannot wait – ammunition now.

"Stay calm!" Shouts O'Hara. "We are expecting guns and ammunition this very minute!"

Then a garble of questions from everyone at the same time.

"Calm down!" He sees Ben Muldoon arrive on his bicycle. "Ben! Over here! What's the news on the pickup? Are the guns on the way?"

Panting, Ben leans on his bicycle and mumbles while fighting for breath. "They are wiped out! Explosion! All dead!"

"All five? And the lorry with the guns?"

"All five; the whole thing blown sky-high!"

Those who were itching for action because of Carr's beating are further incensed at this news. All is in turmoil now. The death of five volunteers has shaken them. They are agitated and eager to retaliate. The brigade is anti-treaty, but none so much as the Corkmen. The 22s are impatient to conduct a raid at the barracks to secure the Ballycorry RIC arms and weaponry.

Fifty miles away, Captain Brendan O'Rourke is sitting in the front passenger seat of a Rolls-Royce armoured car armed with a Vickers .303 machine gun. His uniform is new and he is not yet comfortable in it. It is a British Army uniform, modified for the IRA, dark-green serge worn with a Sam Browne belt holstering a Webley revolver. He fingers the three blue cloth cuff bands. His peaked cap is resting on his lap. He turns it to view the cap diamond with the familiar insignia *Óglaıġ na hÉıreann FF*. There is no direct translation. The accepted English rendering is 'Irish Republican Army'. They are directed henceforth to refer to it simply as 'the Army' or 'the National Army of Ireland' to distinguish it from the British Army. His officer boots are brown, not as familiar to him as his once beloved hobnail farm boots. Reading the insignia aloud he says "FF. Fianna Fáil – Soldier of Destiny."

"Excuse me, sir?" his driver enquires.

"Nothing. Just thinking aloud. We are Soldiers of Destiny."

"Yes, sir. We are Soldiers of...?"

"Destiny."

The driver returns to silence, not sure how to respond.

Captain O'Rourke is leading a convoy from Athlone to Claremorris IRA Command – correction, to Claremorris ARMY Command. In the second vehicle, a Peerless armoured car fitted with two turrets armed with two Hotchkiss machine guns, is Captain Richard Stapleton, previously of the 5th Royal Irish Lancers. And behind him are ten Lancia armoured cars, built in Dublin in 1921 for the RIC, packed with Lee-Enfield rifles, Vickers machine guns and ammunition. In addition to Captains O'Rourke and Stapleton and their two drivers, are 20 soldiers, previously under the command of Captain Stapleton, 5th Royal Irish Lancers, now former British Army, new soldiers in the National Army of Ireland.

The journey from Athlone to Claremorris is 60 miles, about two hours. So why is O'Rourke in North Mayo, en route to Claremorris, a journey of 160 miles?

West Mayo IRA is leaning towards anti-treaty. Pro-treaty units are required to pull together into major centres, to hold strategic positions in the event of civil war, now considered inevitable. O'Rourke is to meet up with a 50-strong pro-treaty brigade under the command of Sergeant-Major Sean Burke, who will join the convoy. The combined force of 74 fighting men is sorely needed to bolster the position of the Claremorris Command.

The convoy reaches the agreed meeting place. O'Rourke knows all the IRA leaders in Mayo. They have been his close comrades throughout 'the Troubles'. He instantly recognises Burke. The brigade is accommodated in the Lancias, but organising the arrangements takes longer than originally estimated. Due to the lateness of the hour, O'Rourke decides against completing the journey to Claremorris until the following day. They are now less than 50 miles from the RIC barracks in Ballycorry, a spacious rural location with multiple buildings that can accommodate the entire convoy of men and vehicles. It is now close to midnight, and Captain O'Rourke's convoy of the National Army is en route to Ballycorry.

Back in Ballycorry, the North Mayo IRA Brigade wants revenge for the loss of five volunteers – and guns/ammo. The 22s just want guns/ammo. Hitting the RIC barracks would achieve both, if it succeeds.

"Captain O'Hara, do we have enough bullets for an assault on the barracks?"

"Calm down. We have enough guns and ammunition for an assault. However, if the initial assault fails, we will have exhausted our entire supplies."

O'Hara knows that he should refrain from attacking Black & Tans' or auxiliaries' positions during the ceasefire. This engagement, he feels, could end in disaster. But the energy of the men is too strong to rein them in, and the Carr beating calls for retribution. Better to direct them in an organised assault than permit them to engage in worse folly. The North Cork Flying Column 22 and the North Mayo Brigade have two pressing reasons to attack the barracks. O'Hara orders an immediate night-time assault.

En route to the barracks, O'Hara sees Carr coming toward them on the roadway. He slows the lorry. "Mickey. I thought you were back at the farmhouse."

"They're all dead, Captain!" pointing in the direction of the barracks. "They're all dead! The dogs are gone!" Mickey jumps onto the step of the lorry and it speeds up again. Mickey leans in to shout over the engine noise. "They're all dead! The dogs are gone!"

But everyone is shouting; no one is listening to Mickey. They continue to the RIC barracks, unaware that the National Army is also on the way.

CHAPTER THIRTEEN

THE IRA AT THE RIC BARRACKS

12 February 1922

Captain Daniel returns to the barracks and parks the tender inside the stable. He consults his watch and sees that it is almost midnight. He is smug that he has completed the day with a successful mission. Tomorrow he will figure out a plan of withdrawal, that is, his own withdrawal. Daniel E is still a wanted man and he needs to disappear again. Yes, tomorrow he will come up with a plan.

Walking from the stable to the barracks building he is aware that it is unusually quiet. Upon entering, he lights the oil lamp at the door, and turns up the wick. This is not right. As a rule, the lamp should be kept burning all night. He swings the lamp around above his head to wash the light about, and he quickly sees in this room, and in the next, and in the next, that his squad is wiped out. What irony – five dead for five dead. The IRA assassin team must have been here. So who is outfoxing whom in this conflict? The bodies are still warm. He must have missed the assassin team by mere minutes. The Flying 22s, he wonders? The building has not been stripped of the supplies; the dead men's guns are still there beside them. This can only mean that the IRA brigade will soon arrive to occupy and/or scavenge the building, the same brigade that has just lost five men. Yes, the same brigade that desperately needs munitions.

Daniel E needs to get out fast. But first, his bomb material. And he decides to set a few booby traps – he has explosives already prepared in a state of readiness. All they need is a trigger to set them off, a trigger like the action of a door opening. He loads up his more valuable stuff and carries it out to the tender. He makes two quick trips to the stables and goes back for one last load. High up in the attic, just beneath the slates, his precious detonators, fuses and explosive devices are carefully stored. This would be his last load. Set the trigger on the booby trap as he leaves. And then what?

He is filled with anxiety. It is folly to stay in Ireland; he cannot go to Britain where he is sure to be apprehended. Before he could consider a third option, the 22s and the brigade descend noisily on the barracks. Lorries and motorcars crunch to a halt in the gravel and men shout as they jump to take up firing positions.

Although the brigade releases a hail of bullets, there is no return fire from the barracks. Go-Carr is shouting at them. "I keep telling you they're dead! I killed them! And the dogs are gone!" The front door is ajar. He runs through it and shouts back "Come and see!"

Gingerly they approach and enter. In the lamplight they count five dead. Strange that they are out of uniform. Where are the others? O'Hara perceives that Fox's information is accurate – only the auxiliaries are here, the RIC had indeed withdrawn.

Carr tells them, yet again, of the standoff between the RIC and the auxiliaries. It is sinking in to the incredulous volunteers that there really was a falling-out between the RIC and the auxiliaries.

Captain O'Hara addresses the brigade. "It is clear what happened here. The RIC have left. The RIC, like many of their colleagues elsewhere, have abandoned the station in anticipation of the handover. The auxiliaries remained behind, and Carr here, 'Go-Get-Them-Carr', executed his most daring, most effective assassination. Now stop gawking and get to it! Get the supplies!"

There is a buzz as the phrase is repeated among the men. "Go-Carr killed the auxies, and the dogs are gone." They understand 'dogs' in this context to mean the auxiliaries.

Carr shouts to correct them. "No! Not the dogs! The Dogs!" No one notices the absence of Tracy Prior and the dogs.

The 22s and the brigade search the building for stores. They proceed to load what they can. Daniel E observes all this through the attic window. He abandons his preparations for a booby trap. There is no time now. Taking advantage of the darkness and disorder, he places the detonator fuses in his pockets and steals out through the back window, across the roof of the lean-to shed, and makes his way to the stable. From the roof of the stable he observes the flying column's two motor-cars parked on either side of the turf stack. The Corkmen are running to and fro loading supplies into the boots. None of the brigade have checked inside the stable yet. They are unaware of the tender parked inside. It is only a matter of time until the search spreads to the outer buildings. When they discover the tender and approach it, they will surely smell the hot engine. A hand placed on the hot bonnet or against the hot exhaust pipe will indicate that the tender was driven just a few minutes ago. So where is the driver?

Daniel E realises that this will undoubtedly prompt them to conduct a thorough search. He drops quietly to the ground in the darkness, and makes his way into the stable. From his supplies there, he selects two of his prepared bombs and two of his detonator triggers from his pockets. He then steals to the flying column's cars parked at the turf stack and slides under the front of each one in turn. Under each car he attaches a bomb behind the slot for the starting handle. As soon as a starting handle is inserted to crank the engine, it will trigger the bomb. He then slips into the stable and climbs up to the rafters, hoping that he would not be observed under the roof.

The Corkmen, gathering up the guns and ammunition, are shouting impatiently, "Enough! Load the stuff! Quickly! Quickly!"

The brigade and the squad are in disagreement. The brigade is in no hurry, and wants to widen the search to the outer buildings to collect every possible item of value. The flying squad is satisfied with the cache of weapons from the storeroom and is anxious to leave immediately. They are still arguing when the National Army arrives.

It is evident to Captain O'Rourke of the National Army what is happening – the IRA is raiding the RIC barracks in order to collect weapons and munitions. But is it pro-treaty or Irregulars? He hails the barracks, and orders that they acknowledge the authority of the army. O'Hara's brigade takes cover inside the building. They fire a few shots by way of answer, but neither side wants to engage. O'Hara realises that they are hopelessly outnumbered and to engage the army would be futile.

O'Rourke wants the brigade to acknowledge the army's authority and surrender. O'Rourke hails the barracks a second time and promises amnesty for any who will join the pro-treaty IRA. Lieutenant Steve Plunket, O'Hara's second-in-command and five members of the brigade, exit the barracks with hands up in surrender. They quickly jump behind the parked Lancias, where they join the pro-treaty IRA, the National Army. Their previous comrades-in-arms whistle and jeer, and release shots in their direction. They are accepted without hesitation and instantly become part of the army's force in their siege of the RIC barracks. Plunket provides

O'Rourke with information of the strength of the occupying brigade. O'Rourke decides against an assault in the dark. In the morning light, the National Army will take possession of the barracks.

Because of the unexpected arrival of the National Army, the IRA has no choice but to abandon their occupation of the barracks and relinquish the supplies they had gathered. It doesn't look good for the occupants of the barracks. They need to act quickly and attempt an escape while it is still dark. The brigade members run out the back of the building into the darkness of the bog. A few shots are fired, but no hits. The brigade members would later be absorbed into the community.

The Corkmen are in a difficult situation. Unlike the Mayo men, they would not blend in; they need to get farther away. And being anxious to save their newfound supplies, they decide to make a run for it in their cars before the army blocks them in. By ramming through to the roadway with guns blazing, they may be able to escape in the darkness. It might work. The army does not know the laneways here, and the Flying 22s can navigate them in the dark.

The army captain observes the flying squad as they make for their cars. They are running with guns pointed at the army positions, discharging shots with considerable accuracy. He considers engaging the 22s to thwart their escape. He knows that by doing so in the dark, he could lose some men in the shootout. Unexpectedly, a British Army captain darts from behind the turf stack and flops down beside him on the ground.

"Captain Stapleton…?"

Captain Daniel places his hand on his arm. "Don't engage them! Let them get to their cars!"

Captain O'Rourke looks at Daniel quizzically, but

before he could ask, Daniel continues, "The cars are rigged to explode! Keep down!"

O'Rourke orders his men "Keep down!"

Taigh Mór and three Corkmen make it to the first car; Joker Kelly and the remaining three reach the second car on the other side of the turf stack. Barry McCarthy swings the starting handle and sticks it in the grove to crank the engine to life. Instantly the car blows apart killing all four men. The second car is partially shielded by the turf stack. Joker is preparing to insert the starting handle in the second car when he is knocked to the ground by the blast. One side of his body is scorched, and he is deafened and dazed. The three remaining 22s, in confusion and fear, hurriedly abandon the second car; they grab Joker to his feet, still grasping the starting handle, and run into the dark bog. The deafened Joker's agonizing cries could be heard fading into the distance.

The soldiers approach the Corkmen's abandoned car, oblivious to the danger. Daniel E shouts, "Don't go near the car!" They watch him as he slides under the front of the car, clearly visible in the flames of the burning turf stack. He disarms and detaches the bomb in two twists of the wrist, and holds it aloft. He shouts back, "It's safe now!"

O'Rourke looks at him in the firelight and exclaims, "You're not Stapleton!"

A shout emanates from the house. "Captain! You must see this!" He directs some men to extinguish the burning turf stack and enters the house. Five dead; their blood soaked into the couches and beds. IRA dead? A search of the bodies reveals that under the outer coats are British Army uniforms. The Glengarry bonnets found on them identify them as auxiliaries. This is a dirty business – five dead auxiliaries disguised as civilians. O'Rourke orders the bodies removed to the stable, and to dispose of the blood-soaked materials.

What a report he would need to file on this one. There has not been any military hostility, so far, between the opposing IRA sides. This could trigger unwanted repercussions. He shouts, "Captain Stapleton! And Captain whoever you are! Into the office!" The three captains go into the first room that could pass for an office – telephone, typewriter, empty filing cabinet, desk etc. They need to formulate their next course of action.

In the subsequent published report, the incident is described as IRA losses suffered in an assault on an auxiliary-held RIC barracks. Ironically, in connecting it to the Blackwater Bridge incident and to the actions of Daniel E, attaching blame on the auxiliaries rendered the report more accurate than the authors believed.

Daniel E introduces himself as Captain Edward Daniel.

Stapleton approaches him, shakes his hand and says, "Great piece of work out there, Old Boy." He observes his insignia and remarks, "Ah. An old 'Fog', eh?" and introduces himself, "Richard Stapleton, former 5th Royal Irish Lancers, now being disbanded, alas!"

O'Rourke addresses him, "Yes. Nice piece of work, Daniel." and glancing at his uniform, "It's a bit improper to wear the British Army uniform without the Irish Army insignia. Are you still active in the British Army?"

"No, sir. In transition. I need to reunite with the regiment in Armagh first, before the transfer to the National Army is processed."

"Well, you'll travel with us to Claremorris. We'll arrange for you to connect with the withdrawing British Army."

Daniel E. Kennedy needs to avoid this. But if he declines the invitation and O'Rourke insists, he could be compelled to comply. He crosses his fingers and responds casually, "That's not necessary, Captain, but thanks for the offer. At present I am en route to Finner to connect up with the withdrawing British Army there."

This appears to satisfy O'Rourke. Kennedy continues, "After that, the transition is just paperwork."

"Ah, yes. Paperwork," says O'Rourke eyeing the typewriter and the stack of blank paper spilt on the floor. His attention is redirected away from Kennedy's situation.

O'Rourke is clearly the senior officer. He appoints Stapleton to fix up the place and take inventory, first thing tomorrow. For now, Stapleton appoints a sergeant to arrange a meal for the men from the barracks' ample larder, after which he orders them to rest, and to organise sentry watches.

IRA Brigade Captain O'Hara knows that the Mayo men can blend into the community. Not so the Corkmen, not so Daithi the Tipperary man, ex-RIC sergeant. February in the bog is dark at night, and very wet. The murky cloud cover obscures any possible light from the sky. Gas from decomposition surfaces noisily in a breathy gurgling sound, and emits a smell akin to foot odour or rotten eggs. One can easily get lost in the bog; and even though the bog is worked out to its bedrock, there are bog holes that can swallow a man whole without trace should one be unfortunate to stumble in. O'Hara fears that the Corkmen may die out in the bog. He goes in search of them, and has little trouble finding the Corkmen – Joker's screams lead him to them. It takes a few hours, but he succeeds in leading them through the bog and to the safe house before sunrise. The four surviving members of the Flying 22s are wounded, fatigued, wet and soiled. Joker Kelly is still moaning in pain and is not fully aware of what is happening. O'Hara goes to a neighbouring farm and commandeers an open-back lorry. He puts the Corkmen and

Daithi in the lorry, three of the 22s in the cab, Daithi and the wounded Kelly lying in the open cargo bed. Mickey Carr jumps on board and joins Daithi in the back. There is no time to dissuade him. Off they go in the direction of Cork in the gathering light of the predawn. O'Hara wonders how much petrol they have, or how much luck. He does not consider his own luck as he warily plods his way back to his house, still sporting his bandolier and IRA captain's badge.

At the RIC barracks, it is already the start of a new day. O'Rourke takes a detachment of the army to pay a visit to the Republican Council. Stapleton directs the remaining army to clean the barracks, and arranges disposal of the auxiliaries' remains. Broken windows are boarded. Other than that, the stone buildings have survived unscathed. O'Rourke has completed his report typed in triplicate, and it is ready for posting. Munitions and supplies, left behind by the Irregulars' hasty withdrawal, are tabulated and loaded on army lorries. Surprisingly, the phone line is still working.

O'Hara is dropping with exhaustion when he arrives home. He is unprepared for the detachment of Regular Army that is waiting for him. Why should he be surprised? But fatigue has dulled his mind. Of course, he is well-known to be the local IRA brigade leader. And here he is, still dressed for combat. O'Rourke, who knows O'Hara's abilities, and who fought alongside him for two years, pleads with him to join the pro-treaty IRA with the rank of captain. In response, O'Hara draws his revolver and is shot dead by O'Rourke's escort.

After mid-day lunch, Captain O'Rourke addresses his men. "Tomorrow we leave Ballycorry. It is of no strategic value. We have stripped the barracks of anything of value to the Irregulars, and we leave the buildings in good shape for the use of the 'Civic Guards' – the new Irish police force."

O'Rourke uses the phone to give a brief verbal report to HQ. The Ballycorry RIC Barracks is stripped of all weapons and items and is officially listed as vacant.

The next morning, Daniel E says goodbye to the National Army, including the auxiliary tender, his only means of transport. Captain O'Rourke wishes him luck in reaching Armagh. He cautions him against travelling by the direct route. Better to make his way to Armagh via Dublin with the main body of withdrawing British forces. But if he still chooses to go via Finner, then so be it.

14 February 1922, the National Army vacates Ballycorry RIC Barracks. The entire convoy, now with an added auxiliary tender, reaches Claremorris without further incident. However, their effective presence in Mayo is short-lived. They encounter a series of major setbacks from the four West Mayo IRA battalions. The army is forced to evacuate West Mayo. It is not until June, when Seán Mac Eoin GOC of Western Command enters Castlebar, that they are able to make strategic progress and hold ground. Mac Eoin's campaign eventually succeeds in pacifying West Mayo by November 1922, nine months after the Ballycorry Barracks incident.

Captain Daniel Edward Kennedy RIF, remains behind in Ballycorry, alone in the abandoned barracks. The 'Civic Guards' never arrive. The barracks is forgotten by them, and is avoided by the locals.

CHAPTER FOURTEEN

TRACY PRIOR LEAVES IRELAND

Sunday 12 February 1922, just before midnight. Tracy Prior is crossing the saturated bog in the darkness. His three black mastiffs are jogging ahead of him. He follows the red phosphorescent triangular dots behind their ears, the only part visible on the dogs. The snorting breathing of the dogs is matched by the sucking sounds of his jogging boots, as they pass over the malodorous bog. The bog is shallow here, and sometimes they run on the exposed igneous bedrock of schist, gneiss and quartzite, rocks formed 1800-1900 million years ago as igneous intrusions. Soon they have crossed the bog. Prior slows to a fast walk as he enters farmland – the shale-based and later limestone-based land, where grass and trees present the pleasant sweet scents of the country, even here in North Mayo's wet winter. He stops at a stream to wash the black from his face, shifts his load, and continues his journey.

Getting back to England with three big dogs is not difficult. Getting back **unnoticed** with three big dogs is a different matter. By and large, people regard Prior and his dogs as a friendly oddity. But he is cognisant of a danger from two sources. He needs to navigate his way back to England while steering clear of flying columns from both sides, auxiliary flying columns and IRA flying columns.

British Special Forces are under orders to disengage and withdraw. Officially, this means that the auxiliaries are not a threat. Unofficially, some retreating auxies still seek the opportunity to settle scores. There is a risk that three large dogs would attract attention and might draw a connection to the IRA flying columns' 'Mad Mystery Man'. Prior decides to avoid big towns and British Army garrison locations.

The North Cork Flying Column 22s would view Tracy's departure as desertion. Joker Kelly would kill him in an instant should the opportunity arise. However, with the split in the IRA, everyone is regarded as a traitor by the opposing side, about 20,000 in all. High-ranking members on both sides are at risk of assassination. In this context, Tracy Prior does not warrant any special attention. The IRA would not come after him. He just needs to keep out of harm's way.

His options – don't go east to Dublin; don't go south into anti-treaty IRA strongholds; stay away from flying columns' corridors of activity and areas of engagement. The best option is to go to Ulster.

Prior knows that cattle are shipped from Dundalk and Derry to Scotland. He considers passage by this means of transport and decides to make his way to Derry to get passage on a cattle ship. He is careful in how he refers to the city. 'Derry' is favoured by the nationalists, and 'Londonderry' by the unionists. He could get by with 'Derry City'.

From North Mayo, Tracy decides to travel by foot for the first half of the journey to avoid being noticed. He knows that some in the farming community serve in the IRA. Any one of them could recognise the 'man with the dogs' from the Flying 22s. This route is also used by the IRA flying columns that travel from Mayo and the south to the Belleek/Pettigo triangle where there is heavy engagement. There are an estimated 700 IRA from the south who are active in West Ulster. The North Cork Flying Column 22 travels this route frequently.

Tracy avoids main roads, walking across country in the off-hours mostly at night. He works his way around Ballina in the first day and reaches County Sligo. Sligo City is widespread, and it takes him a long time to skirt it, necessitating him fording the river in order to avoid populated areas.

He engages in the art of staying dry in the rain. This is something he has learned from his IRA activities. **Staying** dry is easy, notwithstanding the constant wet winter wind blowing from the ocean. **Getting** dry, when one is wet, is a different matter. The woollen clothes he wears are good water repellents, but wet wool stinks and rots. Observing the clouds and keeping possible shelter in view are constant requirements. Stone humped-back bridges, of which there are many, provide good shelter. But they are cold and draughty, and only serve as temporary resting places. Farms have alert dogs, which he needs to avoid. Outbuildings at villages provide the best resting places. Village dwellers have too many buildings, and too few watchdogs.

On day three he is heading east from Sligo, past Ben Bulben and the Dartry Mountains. The mountains are snow-covered, so he keeps below the snow line. Rabbits are plentiful here. He organises the dogs to scare the rabbits into running in his direction. A quick throw of the knife and the dogs have a meal. He rests while the dogs eat. In the distance, on the Sligo coast of Donegal Bay, he views Classiebawn Castle Estate, completed in 1847 by Lord Palmerston, Henry John Temple, 3rd Viscount Palmerston, KG, GCB, PC. The distant castle appears like a closed fist with the little finger pointing upright. Its current owner is Edwina Ashley, daughter of Wilfrid Ashley, 1st Baron Mount Temple, and one of the richest women in Britain. She is well-known for her close relationship and expected marriage to Louis, Earl of Mountbatten. And as with all rich women, there are the usual hush-hush scandals. Tracy Prior rests long enough to muse on the destiny of the country estate. How long before it would be targeted by the IRA and by the socialist elements within the nationalist movement?

Prior sets his course to Derry again. Getting to Derry would mean passing through disputed territory. Derry is one of the counties 'opting out' of the Free State and, although it is a mostly nationalist city, Derry City is situated in 'Northern Ireland'. The unionist population is strongly against joining the Free State. They are also hostile towards nationalists and republicans, who they regard as a threat. Many nationalists had been forced out of their homes. The unionist population had appealed to British forces and to the RUC to protect them against the IRA threat. Now, some unionist communities find themselves on the Free State side of the border, and some nationalist communities are on the Northern Ireland side of the border. Just as the RUC rushes to protect the unionist communities, the IRA rushes to protect the nationalist communities. As a result, some border areas in the Free State are under British control, and some border areas in Northern Ireland are in IRA control. Derry remains largely nationalist, but it is solidly under British unionist control.

Day four is delicate for Prior. He leaves Sligo, crosses the narrow four-mile coastline of Leitrim and enters Ulster. He is now faced with navigating a narrow neck of Free State territory. On one side is the Atlantic and on the other side is a current hotspot with Northern Ireland. The Free State neck of land is less than four miles wide; to pass through it, Tracy must cross the Erne River, and there is only one accessible bridge. Added to this are the high military activity and the location of the principal army camp of the northwest at Finner, recently handed over to the National Army by the British. Bundoran is where he decides to travel by train. This is a peculiar town. It is the terminus of the Great Northern Railway line. It is a summer holiday seaside town, popular with northern unionist and English visitors, and is accessible from Belfast by the 'Bundoran Express'. Many of the seafront buildings are reminiscent of English seaside towns; architecturally Bundoran is very 'English'. Against that, the town's population has a strong republican presence. Yet, the economy of the town requires that political and ideological differences are subdued. Local Irish, many with nationalistic leanings, engage in hospitality services with unionist guests in this Atlantic coastal town. In Bundoran his English accent would not attract undue attention.

The Bundoran railway station is on the Sligo side of town, and Tracy locates it easily without drawing attention. It is February, and trains are not frequent. There is no express service this time of year. Tracy studies the timetable to plan his route. It is late in the day, so he waits until the following morning.

Employees of the GNR render careful courtesy to both nationalist and unionist customers, and they secretly recognise the profitable business in accommodating traffickers of contraband. They 'see no evil' and 'tell no evil'. Prior's request to travel in a goods wagon is not out of the ordinary. He previously utilised this service to move 'stuff' to the flying column at Belleek.

Day five is Friday 17 February, the Fair Day in Ballyshannon. It is a busy morning as he travels the five miles from Bundoran to Ballyshannon, a short distance by train, but it gets him past Finner Army Camp unobserved. Four miles beyond that, the GNR line crosses into Northern Ireland, at the IRA/RUC military hotspot. Tracy decides not to travel any further on the GNR line. Taking advantage of the Fair Day activity, he disembarks from the train at the station on the outskirts of Ballyshannon. Passing the station's 'Visitors Information' stand, he selects a limp map of the town from the rack of pamphlets. The blue dog-eared brochure sporting '*Things to See – Things to Do*' will guide him through the town without the need to ask directions. He makes his way with the crowd – people, ponies, bullocks, sheep, hawkers and pedlars – to the fair green on the other side of the river by the only bridge available. No notice is taken of Prior's dogs in the crush of sheep and dogs crossing the bottleneck bridge. Once across, his options open up.

Crossing the bridge, with its plaque to the poet William Allingham, he glances downriver towards the ocean and to the island in the estuary. This must be a good omen for him. According to the guide map, the island is Inis Saimer, the site of Partholon's settlement in 2,700 BC. In the legend, Parthalon suspected his wife Dealgnait of unfaithfulness. To get even, he killed her dog, Saimer. In subsequent remorse he buried the dog on the island and relocated his community. The island was thus converted to a sanctuary in memory of the dog. Shortly thereafter, the Partholonians were wiped out by plague and the settlement was abandoned by the survivors. The dog's island sanctuary is all that remains of them. Tracy hopes that this island is an omen that the dogs will endure.

Tracy continues walking. He passes the fair green to the other side of town. Here, he is walking against the herds of cattle entering the town. In the midst of all this, his three dogs don't appear all that big. No one pays him attention. Consulting the guide map, he navigates to a second railway station in Ballyshannon. It is the terminus of the Donegal Railway Company's Ballyshannon line. It is a small narrow-gauge rail service that connects Ballyshannon to Derry via Donegal. The Donegal Railway Company runs a passenger and goods service throughout the county. Prior purchases a train ticket to Derry at the booth, and chooses to travel in the goods wagon with his dogs, sharing space with bicycles, newspapers and parcels. It is slow, very slow, and the train makes frequent stops, sometimes for ten minutes at a time. The goods wagon is accessed a few times to accept bicycles and farm produce. The presence of dogs is considered normal. The stops afford Tracy time to get water for the dogs, and to pick up on the 'talk'. He learns that in the context of the border hostilities, the two factions of the IRA are united, although there is confusion over the chain of command. The National Army is not authorised to cross over into Northern Ireland. The Irregular IRA, which does not recognise the state of Northern Ireland, has no inhibition. IRA fighters from the National Army are suspected of joining the Irregulars in cross-border incursions.

Prior arranges himself comfortably on a stack of newspapers. He relaxes. He is now travelling away from the most precarious part of his journey. There are no auxies from here to Derry, and the IRA is focused on the Belleek/Pettigo border. He is unlikely to encounter a confrontation from this point on. To be prudent, and not to tempt fate, he decides to continue riding in the privacy of a goods wagon. At Donegal, where the train stops, the guard from the guard's van enters the goods wagon. He disturbs Prior to access a bundle of newspapers which he throws onto the platform.

"Excuse me, German. It's the daily paper for town." He smiles with a know-all twinkle. "Hah. How do I know you're German, you're wondering? Well, I heard you talking to the dogs, that's how." He leaves the door half opened. A minute or so later, he returns with a mug of scalding hot tea. Balanced on top of the mug is 'toast', a thick slice of white bread toasted at the fire in the train's engine. One side of the bread is still white. The other side is blackened by fire and smoke. It is folded in half with strawberry jam dripping from the edges. "There you are, German; it's a cold morning and all. I thought you could do with something to warm you up.

And just give me a minute; I'll get some scraps from the stationhouse for the dogs too." He returns, as good as his word, with a slop bucket containing left-over stew. He slides the door shut, blows his whistle, and hops on the guard's van at the rear of the train. And they continue on their journey.

Prior is relieved at how well things are going. He is able to relax for the first time in five days. He turns over another bundle of newspapers to arrange into a seat. He pulls back the edge of the wrapping paper of the bundle to view the date. Curling back the wrapping he reads, 'IRISH INDEPENDENT'. Peeling back more he sees the date, Friday 24 February 1922. He is able to make out the headline, and is in danger of breaking the seal on the twine as he tugs a bit more to view it in full:

15 DEAD AT KILLBAWN RIC BARRACKS

In an incident late Sunday, instigated by errant auxiliaries at Ballycorry RIC Barracks in Killbawn, County Mayo, ten republican volunteers lost their lives in a confrontation that also resulted in the death of five...

That is all that Prior could see without breaking the twine or tearing the page from the paper. Sunday night? It was on Sunday night that Carr killed five auxiliaries. But ten IRA dead? Prior wonders what could have occurred at the barracks that night after he left.

The Donegal Mountains are snow-covered. There is a delay crossing at Barnesmore Gap, a pass in the Blue Stack Mountains, to remove snow and rocks that had fallen on to the tracks. It is late in the day when the train crosses the border into Northern Ireland at Strabane. The border crossing is uneventful. The Irish customs officers show no interest in people going into Northern Ireland, and just wave the train through. The Ulster customs officers are unconcerned about a man and his dogs with nothing to declare. Smuggling from the Free State into Northern Ireland is not likely. At a subsequent security checkpoint, the train is stopped and boarded by a police special unit. Some of the local Irish are questioned by a unit of 'B-Specials'. After a few insults, they are permitted to continue. Tracy Prior is sitting in the rear goods wagon with his dogs; the door is wide open. A 'B-Special' officer approaches him.

The Ulster Special Constabulary (USC), commonly called the 'B-Specials' is a quasi-military volunteer reserve police force in Northern Ireland. It was set up in October 1920, shortly before the founding of Northern Ireland. It is an armed corps, organised partially on military lines and called out in times of emergency, such as in the current insurgency. This period, the first half of 1922, is the USC's most intense period of deployment in the conditions of a low-intensity war along the border between the Irish Free State and Northern Ireland. Each special constable is armed with a Webley .38 revolver and a Lee-Enfield rifle and bayonet. Their uniforms are exactly like the RIC. Tracy wonders if they are the same as the other special force, the Black & Tans, except staffed by local Irish unionist volunteers.

"Hello, Mister!" the officer addresses Tracy. 'Mister' is rendered more like a slur than a courteous greeting. "Not a very comfortable way to travel. Is it?"

Tracy grips his Webley concealed under his coat. He has difficulty understanding the question rendered in Ulster Scots, but understands it sufficiently as the special constable gestures at the interior of the goods wagon and points at the dogs.

"It's the dogs, Constable. I travel with my dogs."

The officer picks up on Tracy's English accent, and

studies him for a moment. He adjusts his speech in deference to Tracy's English ear. "English? Where are you headed?"

"I'm going back to England. The dogs need to travel in cargo. I expect to travel by cattle ship."

"I think you should come with me." Tracy is tense and is ready to use his gun. But the special officer continues in a lower voice. "It's not decent that you should travel like this, with Shinners and Fenians. I can get you to Londond'ry in better comfort." The officer gestures invitingly. "Come on. Follow me."

Tracy is still suspicious, but less tense. He continues to finger his gun, but follows the officer, who engages him in friendly conversation. "My name is Andrew Norton, Special Constable. These men", pointing to the other five officers, "are 'B-Special' police." He pauses. "What's your name?"

"Terence Prior." Tracy is relieved now and relaxes his grip on his concealed gun. The officer did not ask for identification, which would have been proper if it were an official questioning.

Andrew shouts at his comrades, "We have a passenger. He needs a lift to Londond'ry Queens Quay to catch the cattle boat!"

One of them shouts back, "Not today. You've missed today's boat. The next boat isn't until Monday, in three days time." They are already climbing into their tenders. "Come on Prior. Hop aboard." Next, Tracy Prior and the dogs are riding with the 'B-Special' Police Force. These young men, if a bit officious on duty, appear to be pleasant.

Tracy learns that there are 65 in the platoon, and that most of them are engaged one day per week. This unit of six special constables checks for republican sympathisers and supporters along the border at Strabane. Inspecting the train from Donegal to Londonderry is a routine duty.

They drive north along the Foyle River, in the direction of Londonderry, to their police station where they will file the day's report, after which they will go about their normal lives. Andrew Norton's family runs a farm near Londonderry.

Driving to the police station, the 'B' men are relaxed, their stint of duties concluded for the week. Rounding a corner, they see that the road is blocked by a disabled donkey cart. Prior, in an instant panoramic view of the site, immediately suspects an ambush. He shouts "ambush!" The tender stops. The second tender, following behind, stops too.

"Hey, Prior! Did you say 'ambush', or do you mean 'bush'?"

"It could be an ambush," Tracy reaffirms cautiously.

"Reverse the tenders!" shouts Norton.

From behind the bend in the road they peer around. Nothing untoward. They decide to investigate the cart with the broken wheel. Two constables approach gingerly on foot. Tracy gets out of the tender with Rex, who follows them. Then Rex sniffs and snorts and lowers his front legs while looking at the cart.

"Bomb!" shouts Prior. *"Rex! Voraus!"* as he and Rex dive through the bushes into the drainage sheugh. The two constables jump in close behind them as the cart explodes in a ball of flame. Johnston, the last men into the sheugh, drops his rifle as he stumbles over the bank. His lower leg, partially exposed to the blast, suffers a scorched shin. Shots are heard coming from the field above.

All the 'B-Specials' are now crunched low, entrenched in the sheugh. They attempt to identify the source of the shooting. Tracy and his three dogs dash into action. Grabbing Johnston's fallen rifle from the ground, Tracy performs a rapid crawl along the sheugh to the shelter of the hedgerow. He quickly makes his way up the hill by way of the neighbouring field's thick hedge. There he spots ten IRA snipers behind the knowe of the hill, firing blindly without aiming so as not to expose their heads to any return fire. They had hoped that the bomb would have caused more damage and that in the ensuing panic they could deliver a lethal attack. Tracy's alertness has thwarted their strategy.

Tracy opens fire on their flank and they disperse hurriedly. Yes, he could have shot one or more, but it's not his war. He waves to the 'B' men, and shouts "All clear!" The 'B' men are in awe of Prior and ask him how he knew about the ambush and the bomb. "Well, to answer number one: the Somme in 1918 taught me a lot; as to number two: *'Rex, ein Bombendetektor Hund'*.

They leave three constables with one tender at the site, to warn traffic, and they continue to the RUC station to report the incident. The sergeant in charge takes over the situation with a unit of RUC. Johnston's leg is paining him, but there is no serious damage – just scorched surface skin. The station duty officer gives him first-aid treatment.

Andrew Norton transfers Tracy and the dogs to his Land Rover, and drives to the farm. "Prior, you are coming to the farm tonight. The dogs have earned a good meal, and a good grooming. And so have you. You look as if you slept in a field last night." And before Tracy can respond, "And don't argue. You've earned it." And continues in conversation, "What are the dogs' names? The old one is 'Rex', I gather."

"Rex, Donner und Blitz," indicating which is which.

"They are called after Santy's reindeer?"

"It's German. 'Thunder' and 'Lightning' in German."

"Ah, yes, good names." And they talk about the dogs' skills and training en route to the farm.

It was a good decision to go to the Norton farm. First, the dogs had not been fed properly in five days; neither had

Prior. Furthermore, they all needed a bath and grooming. And best of all, the farm had four large red setters that romped excitedly at their newfound companions. The trip to England could wait a few more days.

The Norton farm is a dairy farm with a herd of cows requiring milking twice a day. The house has two live-in maids and the farm has a daily workforce of ten farmhands. Milk is placed in stainless steel creamery cans which are picked up daily by the creamery, where the milk is bottled and delivered to its customers. Prior spends the first day grooming the dogs and resting. It is a very active farm. He keeps out of the way until evening when the evening's milking in concluded.

Six o'clock is 'teatime'. They gather for 'high tea'. Notwithstanding the designation 'tea', tea the beverage is not required for the meal. This is when the family meets and the day's events are discussed.

Tracy meets the family. Captain Philip Norton is the senior member. He is former Royal Inniskilling Fusiliers, and dresses in riding breeches with chapettes and hobnail boots for work. He changes into cavalry twills and ox-blood brogues for the evening. A dark-tan jacket is worn over a light apple-green shirt with a rich yellow tie and a pocket handkerchief to match. His speech and bearing are British Army officer. Tracy is put in mind of the Irish officers he knew in France, and one in particular.

Joyce Norton looks younger than 40, which is unlikely, considering that Andrew, her oldest child, must be 22. She surprises Tracy by appearing in black-and-white 'flapper' attire – straight loose dress layered in alternating black and white sections, arms bare, waistline dropping to the hips, silk stockings and black high-heeled shoes. The exposed neckline is adorned with a silver chain and locket. Her auburn hair is bobbed with a fringe. Very fashionable for Londonderry, and considered daring – a statement of independence and emancipation. After the meal, Joyce remains with the men, drinking and smoking. Tracy had not seen this in Mayo. Actually, Tracy hadn't seen this anywhere except in magazines or newspapers.

Jane Norton, daughter, works in a bank in Londonderry, and is dressed more conservatively in slate-grey skirt and white blouse and black pumps. She has all the gossip from the city.

Andrew and Simon both work on the farm. White shirts over grey flannel trousers, navy-blue blazers for both. Andrew favours brown shoes and a red tie; Simon has chosen black shoes with a blue tie. Tracy does the best he can with army surplus brown on brown on brown.

Captain Norton's nephew is staying with them. He had arrived the previous day. He is dressed in the dark-green (almost black) uniform of the disbanded RIC. Sergeant Robert Norton RIC had recently withdrawn from the Royal Irish Constabulary, where he had been the second-officer-in-charge in Clonmel. For Tracy's benefit, he relates his recent experiences in the RIC, a repeat of his account of the previous evening.

"Terence..."

"You can call me 'Tracy'."

"Tracy, you may find this hard to believe. You know who Ernie O'Malley is?"

Before Tracy can admit to knowing him – everyone in Ireland knows who Ernie O'Malley is – Robert Norton continues, "Ernie O'Malley is the leader of 800 anti-treaty IRA fighters."

"IRA hooligans!" interrupts Phillip Norton.

"Last Saturday, 18 February, his unit seized the RIC

barracks in Clonmel. Some of us managed to fight our way out. But 40 RIC were taken prisoner by them. Can you believe that? Taken prisoner by the IRA."

"By the IRA hooligans!" interrupts Phillip Norton again, as he blows cigarette smoke through his nostrils.

"They captured and obtained 11 motor-cars, 293 rifles and bayonets, 273 revolvers and pistols, three Lewis guns, 45 shotguns, 324,000 rounds of ammunition, 4,247 cartridges, and sundry small stores. I know this because I was required to complete the inventory report. The handover was intended for the Provisional Government forces, but the materials had been appropriated in the pre-empted strike."

"By O'Malley's anti-treaty IRA hooligans," Phillip Norton points out.

"Well, to continue. This is an acute embarrassment to the Government of the Irish Free State and it has raised the ire of the British Government. The question that arises is whether the Free State is able to control the IRA. Churchill is offering to send the British Army into the Free State to support the National Army, but I don't see this happening."

Sergeant Norton continues with his narrative. Since his release from the RIC, Norton has been accepted into the Colonial Police. He is in Londonderry, biding his time, waiting for confirmation of his appointment.

The conversation at the table changes focus. They are curious to know more about Terence Prior – how he had learned the skills displayed on the previous day.

The captain surmised correctly, "You served in France? In the Great War?"

"At the Somme. I was at the second Battle of the Somme for the Great Offensive, and for some time before that."

"In what capacity?"

"I was a sapper."

"Engineering. I can only deduce that you worked in mines and explosives."

"I was engaged primarily in tunnelling to the German lines to plant bombs. My preference was to plant surface explosives close to the German lines."

"Your dogs are German-trained, I see. Any connection?"

Robert interjects, "Wait a minute. I remember when serving at the Somme, there were stories about an eccentric soldier, a loner with a German dog, who inflicted damage on the Germans. I thought it was a made-up story, that we were only told this to strengthen morale. You're not him, are you?"

Prior acknowledges Robert. "I don't know what myths there were, but Rex and I went to enemy lines almost every night to plant bombs – up to the offensive, that is."

Speaking about the Great War in general terms establishes common ground for comradeship. Questioning any deeper into personal experiences would be intrusive. Andrew unpretentiously asks, "And you killed Germans? Well, good on you. They deserved to be killed."

Both Captain Philip and Sergeant Robert look at Prior. They observe Prior in pensive thought, and expect him to avoid a direct answer.

Unexpectedly, Prior answers, "No. I don't think anyone there deserved to die. The men in the trenches – the Germans, the English, the Canadians, the French. No one deserved the horrors of that war – the gas, the dirt. Not one of them deserved to die, not in that way."

Joyce Norton attempts to change the subject. It's getting too heavy. So too do the others, except for Andrew and Simon. Joyce asks, "Terence? May I call you 'Tracy'?"

"'Tracy' is fine."

"Tracy, what are your plans for the dogs now? I mean, what **do** you do?"

But Andrew and Simon are still inquisitive about Tracy's killing capability. Andrew asks, "The Fenians yesterday – you could have killed some of them. Why didn't you?"

Tracy answers Andrew. "It isn't **my** war!" And to Joyce. "I train dogs for dangerous situations – military and police work." Without excusing himself, Tracy gets up and leaves the room.

An argument now ensues at the table. Joyce lights a cigarette and admonishes her two sons for insensitivity. The captain supports her and addresses the two boys. "God. You should know better. Refrain from discussing specifics about the war. Who knows what scars Prior bears from the past."

Robert gets up from the table, and says, "I'll go to him. See if he's all right."

"Good idea, Nobbie."

Tracy is sitting in the drawing room in the dark. Robert goes to the decanter and pours a whiskey. "It's Black Bush. Would you care for some?" Tracy does not answer. Robert does not pursue it. Instead, he talks about himself. Robert is interested in dogs, specifically, to utilise dogs in the police force. He discloses his intention to set up a canine unit. Tracy utters a grunt in interest. (Good, Tracy's mind is off the war.) He asks Tracy's opinion.

Tracy responds, "The Germans and the Belgians are ahead of us in this. They use police dogs for bomb detection and crowd control."

"If what I perceive in you is true, Prior, you have a gift with dogs. Would you be interested in working with the police? With the canine unit? Assuming that I will command a unit, I will need an expert trainer and handler."

"Where? Here in Ulster?"

"No. In Kenya. I expect a letter any day now confirming my placement in Kenya with the Colonial Police."

Tracy does a quick think. He has two passions.

Dogs are his primary love; the upper class is his primary hatred. The greed of ruling classes of Europe was the underlying cause of the Great War. By doing away with the established elite, and by exercising fair and equitable distribution of wealth, war could be eliminated. But in the short term some 'removing' is called for. The Colonial Police is a perfect vehicle from which to operate. Just as he demoralised the Germans at the Somme, he could damage the imperial elite in the colonies.

Robert prods for an answer. "So, what do you think, Tracy?"

Tracy thinks aloud for Robert's benefit. "Not much to go back to in the Isle of Dogs (in London's East End)." And then directly at Robert Norton, "I'll need to choose my own dogs."

"It only makes sense that the handler chooses the dogs."

"Mastiffs are my choice for combat situations. But they have a short work-life – they get stressed out in five to seven years. For police work, Alsatians – the German dog of choice in Westphalia and Rhineland – are favoured for crowd duties. And Labradors for sniffing. And then...well, different dogs with different skills for different situations."

Robert Norton is cradling his glass of Black Bush, savouring the aroma induced by the warmth of his hands, and asks, "Well, is that a yes?"

"It's a yes."

"Yes, you are pondering or..."

"Yes. I'm in. How do I get into the Colonial Police? With you?"

"Stay here a few more days. When my confirmation comes through – it should come in the post any day now – I will report to the Foreign Office in London. I want you with me when I report in. I have been asked to recruit suitable candidates from the RIC, but your qualifications put you at a premium. I'll give you an application form tomorrow which I will approve upon completion."

Three weeks later, on Friday 17 March 1922, Sergeant Robert Norton and ex-Sapper Terence Prior enter the Foreign Office in London for their final meeting. Three hours later Superintendent Robert Norton and Constable (Constable-in-training) Terence Prior exit the building. The British Army had confirmed Prior's honourable service record. There was no record of his association with the IRA. Norton and Prior have orders to depart for Nairobi in one month. And so starts a working relationship that will last 25 years.

CHAPTER FIFTEEN

CORK

Monday 13 February 1922

The farm-lorry is in poor shape. It is bumpy and slow and noisy. At every bump, Joker screams in the back.

The Corkmen question Daithi. "Who the hell are 'ou? And where is Tracy and the dags?"

Mickey Carr doesn't look up. His head is down between his up-drawn knees. His bruising is hurting much worse now. "Tracy's gone; the dogs are gone," he says quietly. "This is Daithi."

The Cork lads ask, "And can Daithi handle a gun – can he now?"

"He can handle a gun…!" and Carr falls asleep despite the discomfort.

They stop briefly to siphon petrol with their engine running, and continue on. "Get out of Mayo, get out of Mayo," chanting like a mantra. At Tuam, in Galway, they stop. A fierce ragged-looking bunch, looking for all the world like Irregulars on the run – which is exactly what they are.

Carr, when he is awake, continues to bemoan the absence of the dogs. Joker cannot sleep and could not be calmed. He is still deaf, and he would not stop screaming and moaning. They pull into the hospital. Their ragged and desperate appearance is in stark contrast to the white-walled building with flowers out front – the snowdrops are almost finished, the crocuses give a cheery appearance, and the daffodils buds are opening.

Here they receive treatment. The medics are worried at

the state of the men and implore them to remain. Looking at Joker, the doctor on duty says that he might die without hospitalisation care.

"If we delay, we will all surely die!" the Corkmen reply.

The hospital staff is well aware of the situation here. They have encountered it before – IRA on the run. They dress Mickey Carr's and Joker Kelly's wounds. Joker is given a painkiller injection. They give Joker's painkiller pills to Daithi, the only sane-looking member of the wild bunch, with instructions on dosage. The staff members pull a mattress off a hospital bed and put it in the back of the lorry, complete with clean sheets and blankets. They could do a lot more, but the Corkmen are anxious to leave.

The hospital staff look at the lorry driving away, belching oily smoke. "I wonder if they'll make it."

The North Cork Flying Column 22, what's left of it, travels through County Galway. They cross the Shannon at Portumna rather than proceeding directly south via Limerick. The situation in Limerick is unknown and is best avoided. Crossing at Portumna they enter Tipperary, and thence travel to Cork, each mile bringing them deeper and deeper into the safety of undisputed anti-treaty territory. Late in the day, they stop at the house of a known trusted sympathiser, who feeds them and gives them fresh clothes. After a night's rest, they continue to North Cork.

They survive the journey and join up with the North Cork Brigade. The brigade is shocked to see their poor state of health and their diminished numbers. At the safe house they are given a staff-room. The brigade is undecided what to do with them. Joker Kelly is unfit for combat. The other three members of the squad have the look of defeat – not a good thing to see. The Tipperary-man is too old and does not look the part. The beaten-up boy appears too young and puny.

What has happened to the feared North Cork Flying Column 22 that was the scourge of Ireland just a few weeks ago?

The members of the group, the remnant of the 22s, take to bickering among themselves and are excluded from most activities. They call Mickey stupid 'amadan'. Mickey has difficulty with a lot of things and avoids people. He amuses himself by taking things apart and reassembling them. The brigade notices Carr's dexterity with machinery. He is assigned to equipment maintenance duties, fixing up the guns and the lorries mostly. He avoids human contact and spends most of his days sitting under the trees staring at the dark waters of the Blackwater – a different Blackwater to the one he knows in Mayo, but just as dark.

A few weeks later, there is heightened excitement in the brigade. They receive intelligence that a senior minister of the Provisional Government is coming to Cork, and would be passing through Tipperary. The details of the route are leaked to the IRA, and the North Cork Brigade is planning an assassination. To be successful, the brigade would need a superior marksman, one who could hit a target squarely on the first shot. Secondly, they would be up against stiff resistance from the Regular Army escort detail, and would require plenty of firepower.

The brigade assembles their available volunteers to prepare them for the event. Details are not revealed, except to advise that a major raid is being planned. They ask for sniper volunteers for a 'delicate job' and Daithi steps forward. He volunteers himself and Mickey Carr. They test them both and find them superior to anyone else in the brigade. Surprisingly, they discover that Mickey is uncannily talented. Even at a distance, he can always hit the target, in any kind of weather, in any breeze. He also amazes them in his ability to hit a moving target from a moving vehicle, something none of the others are able to do. There is something odd and unnatural in the manner in which Carr controls a gun. He does not appear to take aim. He can send a bullet to its target with the same ease as putting a forkful of stew in his mouth. Everyone is in awe of his skill, but fearful of his strangeness nevertheless. The brigade captain is in no doubt. Carr is the undeniable choice. The ability to hit a moving target is a prime requirement in the planned assassination.

Their intelligence proves correct. On the scheduled day, the brigade is positioned in a copse on a low hill overlooking the planned route in Tipperary, just across the county boundary. There is a slow curve in the road, sufficient to block the view of the target car from some of the army escort detail. On the lower side of the hill, on the other side of the road, a farmer, like most farmers in the area, is preparing the ground for spring planting. It is unusual but not suspicious to see a tractor chugging through the field. Small farmers still favour the horse for ploughing, but progressive farmers in Tipperary have recently taken to the Fordson tractor. Poor small farms in North Mayo don't have machines like this, but South Tipperary is in Ireland's Golden Vale, the richest farmland in the country. On this tractor, however, tiny puny Mickey Carr is standing on the drawbar and leaning concealed against the mud-guard. This is Mickey's first encounter with a Fordson.

The farmer is singing loudly

" 'Twas early, early in the spring..."

The motorcade snakes down the road as expected. The government minister sees the flock of gulls over the field, a sure sign that ploughing is in progress. Upon glimpsing the Fordson tractor, he orders the driver to stop. He rolls down his window to admire the tractor.

"...The birds did whistle and did sweetly sing..."

"Now this is what will make Ireland great," he declares to his escort. "Since the end of the Great War, these tractors are produced in only two places in the world – the USA, and Cork. After the USA and Canada, the richest market is Britain. This is a lucrative export for the New Ireland."

"...Changing their note from tree to tree..."

He leans out the window, the better to hear the farmer singing over the roar of the tractor. Ah, the future of Ireland.

Carr is judging the rise and fall of the tractor as it lurches over the wet ground, and at the correct moment, releases a single shot, fearlessly and without emotion.

"...And the song they sang was Old Ireland free..."

A portion of the minister's head disappears in a splatter of blood and grey brain matter. Little puny amadan Carr successfully executes a mortal blow from a moving tractor at a distance. The escort rushes away with the dying minister, leaving two tenders to engage the IRA ambush. One tender drives in the direction of the tractor and sniper. It sinks into the soft earth, its spinning wheels lodging it deeper into the ground. The six occupants are at the mercy of the brigade – or rather, at the lack of mercy. They dash on foot, attempting to reach the safety of the remaining tender. They are annihilated, mowed down in a hail of deadly bullets. The occupants of the remaining tender fire a few volleys and then make their escape. Provisional Government losses, seven; Irregular IRA, nil.

Carr is now the brigade's number-one sniper. They move Carr from vehicle repairs to elite squad. The North Cork Flying Column 22 is revived and is being built up again.

Carr also amazes them with his skill in dismantling and reassembling a rifle blindfolded faster than anyone else could with both eyes. Mickey shows them how to keep their guns in good condition and how to clean, repair and maintain their equipment in the dark.

The brigade captain asks Mickey how he can be so calm about killing.

"I kill. That's what I do best. Some things are meant to be killed. I kill what is meant to be killed. At the right time I too am meant to be killed."

Mickey is a celebrity, but still an outsider. He spends much time alone, withdrawn from the group. He retreats to his private spot among the trees by the river, sitting for hours at a time on a log, staring at the black water.

Daithi, who was a participant in the ambush, is sickened by the callous disregard for life. He sees no glory and no positive outcome in the anti-treaty IRA campaign. There is no doubt about his anti-treaty sentiments, but he does not approve of the anti-treaty IRA methods of resistance, such as the assassination of the government minister. The country must return to a law-abiding state, and fighting should be conducted nonviolently at the negotiation table by the representatives of the people.

On 02 April 1922, the RIC ceases to exist and is replaced by a new force – the Civic Guards in the Free State and Royal Ulster Constabulary in Northern Ireland; the Black & Tans and auxiliaries had left the country. The British Army would hold on to some facilities for another year to ensure handover to the proper authorities. Daithi is a policeman at heart and, three months after joining the IRA Irregulars, he decides to join the newly-formed Civic Guards.

On 01 June, Daithi makes a trip to the post office. For some time he had been sending post and receiving post from the Phoenix Park – from the government Department of Justice. Daithi Mac a'tSionnaigh picks up his post. It is his acceptance letter for the interview for entry into the Civic Guards. The postmaster tips off the North Cork Brigade.

Daithi, previously David Fox, goes to the brigade captain to inform him that he would be leaving. That's when he learns that one does not leave the IRA. The captain is fully informed of Daithi's postal exchanges. Daithi-David is tied up and detained in a room pending a 'trial'.

That night, the brigade captain calls a meeting of his senior officers. The prisoner is brought in, tied at the ankles and wrists, and placed in a chair – the 'dock'. Although they all have come to like Daithi, they cannot risk his going to work for the government – the pro-treaty Free State government. Daithi knows too much, and in the guards he could be pressured to work against the Irregular IRA. He cannot be permitted to leave – not alive. After some heated debate they agree to execute the prisoner.

This kind of execution is distasteful to the men – Daithi has always been loyal, and there is no suggestion of betrayal. However, any leak, even innocently slipped, could have disastrous consequences for members of the brigade. The execution, though unpleasant, is deemed necessary. An executioner is required, one who can act unhesitantly without emotion. They decide on Mickey Carr. Disregarding the lateness of the hour, Carr is summoned. He is given a command to carry out the execution.

Without so much as a blink, Mickey stands and says "Untie his feet." He takes out his newly-acquired Webley & Scott Mk VI Caliber .455. He motions to Daithi to walk outside. The captain tells him not to leave the body where it might be seen. Mickey prods Daithi in the small of the back with the pistol. Some of the men follow them out into the darkness.

"Where are you going?" they ask.

"To the river. No body left lying around, you said."

They stumble along at a fast pace. Mickey, thanks to his training with Tracy and his innate feral skills, is able to adjust his night vision faster than the others and is far ahead of the men as he walks to his familiar private spot at the riverbank. Behind him, in the distance, he can hear the men stumble, and they go back to the house for a lamp. Mickey stops at his log seat at the riverbank. He draws his knife and cuts through the Daithi's remaining ropes.

"Daithi, when I shoot, fall down by the edge of the water." He shoots into the ground and pushes his favourite log into the water with a splash. "Go back to being David Fox." The others are just catching up to him as they hear the splash. "Daithi Mac a'tSionnaigh is no more!" he tells them.

They peer into the darkness at the black water, swinging the lamp high in a futile attempt to penetrate the blackness of the river. Some are satisfied that they see a body floating out in the current. Mickey turns, his blank face displaying apparent disinterest, and calmly walks back to the house.

Fox waits. He hears the men re-enter the house. He waits a while longer. Then crawls; then walks; then runs – putting distance between himself and the IRA. He checks his pockets. His things are still there – the acceptance letter, some coins.

The following day he passes through a number of villages before he has the courage to go to a post office. He pulls his post office savings book from his back pocket and withdraws enough money for the bus fare to Dublin – and to the Phoenix Park.

Two years later, on 24 May 1924, Mickey Carr leaves the IRA at the end of the civil war. He returns home after five years of killing. He is 18 years old. His grandmother has died in his absence – no sorrow, no loss. He now owns a small unproductive farm on barren land bordering the bogland in Ballycorry in the Irish Free State – *Saorstát Éireann* – a dominion within the British Empire. He avoids friendships, and embarks on raising pigs and collecting junk. And continues to dismantle and reassemble things.

CHAPTER SIXTEEN

MURF AT THE SPORTS EVENT

Sunday 10 August 1947

As promised, Murf arrives at the Fox residence on Sunday after Mass. "Been to Mass, Murf?" Mary asks by way of greeting.

"Yes. Sorry I'm a bit late. Counting the collection, you know."

"Would it have been to confession you were, Murf? I hear you're big on confession."

They are interrupted by two children, running in ahead of Foxy. "Yeah! Murf's here!"

Murf could just reply to Mary, "No. But why mention 'confession'?"

Mary replies teasingly, "I believe you have a 'confession', Detective Inspector John Patrick Murphy. At dinner tonight."

Foxy is herding in his grandchildren. "Children! Children! Let me finish my cup of tea…"

"…and goldgrain biscuit," interjects Murf.

"…before we leave."

The three adults stand in the kitchen waiting for Foxy to finish his tea. Mary is dressed in a yellow sundress patterned with big green oak leaves, short sleeves and sandals. The sundress is tight at the waist and billows out when she twirls. In her hands, she is holding her floral-patterned broad-brimmed sunhat which she bought in Casey's for 7/11 (without the discount). Fox is dressed 'for the country' in a dark-green tweed suit, cream shirt with a burgundy wool tie. His shoes are high-laced brown walking shoes which he wears with moss-green socks, and on his head is an autumnal-speckled tweed hat – one that the 'King of the Fairies' would wear. Murf pictures Fox sporting a clay pipe, and suppresses a smile.

Murf is smartly dressed – well, smart attire for Murf. Plain laced black shoes, dark-blue (matching) socks, light-grey flannel trousers (with a crease) and navy-blue double-breasted blazer with gold shiny buttons with anchors on them, sky-blue shirt and red tie. Murf unbuttons his blazer to perch on a barstool and reveals a little can-can girl on the tip of his tie.

"Murf," exclaims Mary. "Were you at Mass wearing that tie?"

"I made sure to tuck it into my shirt during the collection," demonstrating how he can tuck it in.

"I hope you did. And how did you come by such a swanky tie?"

"I got it in Casey's on Friday; Suey McBride picked it out for me…"

"Suey McBride from 'Accounts'? She's the moody attractive one they keep away from the customers. Right? What was she doing in 'Drapery'?"

Fox interrupts to explain. "That's Murf's 'contact' in Casey's…"

Mary, to herself, but audible to all, "What kind of 'contact' I wonder."

Fox continues without pause, "…who keeps him informed on who is buying what, and who is selling what…"

Murf, red-faced and uncomfortable, is eager to change the subject. "So, how's Foxy treating you, Mary?" he asks, while looking at Foxy.

Mary segues into the fresh subject without pausing. "Foxy has my heart broken. Do you know what he did?" And without waiting for a response, "Well, I'll tell you what he did – what he DIDN'T do. Now, every year it falls to the husband of the ICA president to judge the bakery competition."

"Ah," thinks Murf, "that would be the husband of President Mary Fox." And aloud he asks, "There's a bakery competition at a sports meet?" knowing quite well that there is, at least in Killbawn.

"Well, of course there is, Murf. You know that! It's the most important part of the event. And Foxy here..." looking at Fox with hostility "...declined. The Superintendent of the Garda Síochána declined to judge the ICA baked goods. How's that for a 'how-do-ye-do'?"

Fox jumps in with a remark. "Murf, judging ICA baked goods is the most dangerous assignment ever to befall a guard. Never do it."

Murf asks Mary, "So what is going to happen with the judging? Can you not..."

But Mary is not finished speaking, just taking a swallow, "Fortunately, at the last minute..." She pauses momentarily to shoot a critical look at her husband, and resumes, "...fortunately, I was able to get Dean Pilkington from the Church of Ireland. He is such a lovely man." And glaring at her husband, "And unlike this cowardly lump here, Dean Pilkington has..."

"...de Valera on a horse!" shouts Foxy.

"Foxy, what on earth has got into you?" and continues speaking to Murf, "...he has such a discerning palate."

To conceal his smile, Murf declares, "Then let's go to the sports and see the cake stand," and in the direction of the children, "Come on!"

"Yeah! Murf's taking us to the sports!"

Connor and Macushla are excited to go to the sports meet. They go by way of the riverside pedestrian walkway. The children skip along, sometimes running, sometimes stopping to examine a twig or pluck a buttercup. Blonde Connor is seven-and-a-half. He is wearing running shoes, because he will be running today, fawn ankle socks, brown shorts and tan short-sleeved shirt. Macushla is four-and-three-quarter-years old, and also blonde; she wears a broad yellow bow atop her head, her hair falling to her shoulders in a ponytail. She is dressed in a light-blue dress, surrounded by a buttermilk-coloured pinafore – to 'keep it clean', primrose ankle socks and shiny red pumps with strap-and-buckle fasteners.

They enter the park and look for a place to sit down. It is

a parish and community holiday for families and children – no major qualifying events for the county sports meet. The ICA, the Irish Countrywomen's Association, is much in evidence, its officers supervising many of the award categories – crocheted items, lamps made out of whiskey bottles, but most of all the baked goods section. Foxy and Mary are there, of course – Garda Superintendent David Fox and Mrs. Mary Fox, President of the ICA, in her 7/11 summer hat. So are all the elders of the community – the priest, the canon, the local doctor, Casey, and all the big farmers. The wives are all dressed up, a virtual small-town rural Irish version of Ascot.

Grandad Fox takes the children in search of ice cream and dillisk, while Murf spreads the Buchannan tartan rug on the grass for Mary. Mary twirls, and sits down on the rug in the perfect circle formed by the spread of her sundress, looking like the pistil of a flower within the corolla of its petals. They both remain silent, taking in the sounds and smells of the event. Most of the sounds are from children at play, mixed in with the voices of pedlars and hucksters selling wares. The grass smells fresh, complemented by the rich sweet smell of hay. The grass had been cut a week earlier to be short enough for the event, but to permit sufficient growth to soften the stubble. The 'people smell' is exhilarating – almost all smell of cigarettes or tobacco, some emit the sweet-sour smell of porter, although drinking at the event is not in evidence. Some who pass by smell of toffee, one of the most popular items sold at the stalls. There are the smells and odours from the baked goods stands, the salty sea smell of the dulse (or 'dillisk', in Mayo), and the sweet syrupy smell of melting ice cream. As the wind drifts gently from across the river, there is the occasional wafting hint of cattle manure – ah, the fresh smell of the country.

Their reverie is disturbed by five girls, twentyish, who come stumbling along, their high heels sinking into the soft earth. Their arms are linked so as to assist each other in remaining balanced, but from their giggling and staggering, it is clear that they are of very little assistance to each other.

Mary recognises them from Casey's General Store. As they draw alongside, one of them falls over, to be rescued by Murf. There is a momentary glimpse of sparkly garter, to Mary's disapproval. Upon assisting the 'distressed damsel', they tease Murf about entering in the athletic event.

"Guard Murf, will you be running in the half-mile?"

"Or the high jump? They say that you are always getting up to things."

"Are you up to the high jump, Guard Murf?" And off they go, still giggling, still stumbling.

Mary remarks, "More of your 'contacts' Murf?"

Murf pretends not to hear. He looks in the direction of the park entrance. The name of the park is 'Home of Fitzpatrick-McHugh' written on the sign at the entrance along with rules on behaviour and anti-littering.

Murf says, "They never could get the spelling right. It should be 'Holm, H-O-L-M, of Fitzpatrick-McHugh'; it's homophonic, but has a different meaning and connotation."

Mary is leaning back propped up by her outstretched arms to angle her face to the sun. Her eyes closed. "It should be called 'Murf's Turf'; after all, you are responsible for it."

Just then Foxy returns with the children – and with dillisk and ice cream. Passing an ice cream cone and serviette to Mary he asks, "So what is Murf responsible for now?"

"The homophonic 'holm'."

"Ah, yes. I never tire of that story. It was the greatest piece of peacekeeping I ever experienced." Connor and Macushla pick up on the word 'story'.

"What story?" they ask.

"The story of how Murf got us this park," says Mary with a hint of pride in Murf's achievement.

"Tell us, Murf! Tell us!"

"All right," says Murf. "Just don't drop any ice cream on grandma's Buchanan rug."

"We won't! We won't!"

"This park, this whole big flat area, was once in the river..."

"No, it couldn't. The river is way over there." says

Connor, pointing to An Abhainn Mór – the Blackwater – at the farthest extremity of the park.

"Don't interrupt. Murf is telling the story."

"…and as the waters receded – got smaller – a large flat island appeared. That's what a 'holm' is – dry land that was once a riverbed."

Connor asks, "And that's where we are now?"

Macushla exclaims, "Don't interrupt!" punching Connor in the arm and causing him to drip ice cream on the Buchanan rug.

Murf continues, "Where you see the river now, that was once only a small branch of the river; the main stream was over there by the entrance, and all this flat area was an island in between. Thirty years ago…"

"Was that before you were born?" Another dig, another drop of ice cream.

"… there were two big farms bordering the river here – McHugh's, and Fitzpatrick's; Fitzpatrick's was over ten times larger than McHugh's, but McHugh owned the holm – the island…"

Connor exclaims, "Oh. Fitz and McHugh are both here today. I just saw them. …and don't dunt my arm, 'Cushla; you're getting ice cream on Grandma's bugle-allen rug."

As Macushla mouths, "Don't interrupt."

"…the bend in the river was the safest place for cattle to drink. Anywhere else, the bank was too steep and might collapse, or the river edge was flat and boggy. Cattle might tumble into the river and drown, or sink to their oxters and get trapped. So the bend in the river – up there near the entrance – was where Fitz watered his cattle.

"Thirty years ago there was an old mill upriver – it had not been used in a long time. The dam was still intact but in poor condition. And then there came a monster flood that was too heavy for the dam wall. It collapsed, sending a torrent of water downstream to this very place. When the water receded, …"

"Got smaller." piped Macushla.

"…well, to everyone's astonishment, the flood had

deposited a large quantity of mud all along this stretch of river. The holm was no longer an island, and the branch river was now the main river – the only river.

"Up to then Fitz and McHugh had an agreement that the bend in the river, where the cattle drank, was owned equally, 50/50, by them. Fitz expected the agreement to apply to the new route of the river too – which would give him half of the holm; but McHugh said 'No', the holm was entirely his. This was the dispute. The land title deeds were consulted. They clearly stated that Fitz's property should end at the river, but the measurements on the supporting map showed that it ended short of the holm."

Mary sits listening to the story as if for the first time. Foxy coaches Murf not to forget relevant details.

"Grandad, don't interrupt. Murf is telling the story."

"Fitz would drive his cattle down to the river; and McHugh, if he were about, would come waving his stick to drive them away. The cattle actually got enough to drink; most of the stick-waving was between Fitz's cattle drover and McHugh. Then ten years ago the present McHugh – Big Jim – took over the management of the farm. He erected a fence which prevented access to the holm and to the river.

"When I came here to Killbawn, it was the priority of the guards to keep these two feuding families apart. Fitz would cut the fence, and McHugh would call us to have him arrested. Fitz, on the other hand, demanded that we arrest McHugh for illegally fencing off access to the river. The fence-cutting escalated into hay-burnings and cattle-maiming…"

And from Macushla, "What's 'escalating'?"

To which Connor replies, "When it's bad, and then worse, and then it gets worser!"

And from Fox, "There was mayhem that might end in murder if we didn't step…"

And from Mary, jokingly, "Grandad, don't interrupt. Murf is telling the story."

Macushla jumps in, "There was no 'mayhem'. Murf said nothing about 'mayhem', so there was NO 'mayhem'. Only hay-burning and cattle-naming. Isn't that right, Murf?"

Murf continuing, "That's right, there was hay-burning and cattle-naming – and they called them some nasty names, but the cattle did not understand all the names.

"At that time there was a lot of discontent and civil unrest, and there was resentment against the big landowners. Some had left, and many farms were run-down and dilapidated. Those who remained were trying to recover social acceptance by donating land to the people. And here in Killbawn the G.A.A (Gaelic Athletic Association) was looking for a site for football and athletic games – a nice big level park. I convinced Fitz to donate five acres of land and McHugh (who did not want to be outdone by Fitz) to donate another five, to a total of seven acres..."

Connor, who could add, interjects, "Murf, that's not right! That should be ten acres!"

"Ah, you see! Fitz donated five acres which included his half of the disputed holm; and McHugh donated five acres that included the entire holm – a total of seven acres."

And from Foxy, "The next bit is genius, pure genius."

"The property was deeded to the people; legally it is now owned by the state which represents the people; but it must be administered by the parish. Which means that the state cannot alter the use of the land without the agreement of the parish. It is the parish, not an ecclesiastical diocese, which administers the park through the parish's parks council. The council is elected yearly. Fitz and McHugh are on it; so are Foxy and myself, and eight others."

Connor is trying to visualise the concept of a council. "How can Fitz AND McHugh both be on the Parish Parks Council? Isn't one a Protestant and one a Catholic? And we are Church of Ireland."

"Because the Parish Parks Council is non-denominational."

"Non-abomin-what?"

"The parish is not just the Catholic parish or Church of Ireland parish, it is the same parish regardless of which church you attend, or if you attend no church at all. Fitz is one of the people. Anyone resident within the parish boundary, Catholic or Protestant, or whatever, can sit on the council."

And from Macushla, "Where are the cows? Why aren't the cows down at the river having a drink?"

"Because one month after the agreement, a pumping station was installed that pumps water to both farms, all the water they need."

"Genius. Sheer genius, Murf. You're a shoe-in for a politician."

"No," Mary corrects him, "an angel," nudging Foxy to look over at the hoop-la stand. Murf and the children are already on the way over for the sack race and the egg-and-spoon race. Foxy observes young Ron Fitzpatrick and pretty Molly McHugh tossing rings, but it's clearly not hoop-la that they are playing. At the next stand, Mrs. McHugh and Mrs. Fitzpatrick are viewing the cakes and are exchanging recipes, but the approving nods reveal that more than cakes are being considered favourably.

Macushla is holding Murf's hand while Conner tackles the sack race. "Murf?"

"Yes, Macushla?"

"You're a guard, right? You don't look like a guard. What's a guard anyway, if you don't dress like one?"

Mary, shading her eyes with her 7/11 sunhat, reads Macushla's lips, even at this distance. She is unable to hear Murf's reply, but knows anyway. "Well, it's actually 'garda' which means 'guardian'."

"So, you're a guardian, like a guardian angel?"

And Mary whispers, "A guardian angel."

Foxy, who is finishing the dillisk, asks, "You think Murf is a guardian angel? You're not falling for a younger man, are you?"

"Of course not, Foxy. Everyone loves Murf. Don't you?"

"Yes, actually. I'd go to hell and back for him." And to himself, "but I hope I never have to."

CHAPTER SEVENTEEN

CASEY'S GENERAL STORE

Patrick Joseph Casey is simply known as 'Casey'. He operates a retail/wholesale business in Killbawn. It is a shop, and a warehouse, and a supply depot for farm implements; it is also an import business of sorts. 'Emporium' does not adequately describe his operation, so Casey settles on 'General Store' as the most appropriate designation. Peter Meehan is Casey's delivery service, and is Murf's most valuable source of local information.

Every day Peter travels his rounds with his donkey and cart. Peter is well-known. He is a bachelor by conviction. There isn't a door in the townlands where he is not welcome. Peter updates everyone on the local news in exchange for a cup of tea, a slice of bread or a light for his pipe. He is obliging; he delivers personal items for his customers while on his rounds, which gives him more opportunity for news – who is delivering what to whom and for what reason. Peter is dwarfish, not even five feet tall, but with long arms and large hands. At school he was clever, and still is. He can read and write, and 'do sums' in his head. He is always clean-shaven, and dresses in black, from his black bowler hat to his black well-polished boots. His pipe is black brier; his three-piece suit is black, over a black shirt and black socks. He wears a bright scarlet ascot cravat with matching handkerchiefs flopping out of every pocket. His donkey, Maeve, also wears a bowler hat with holes for her ears, and Peter dresses it with sprigs from hedge and field – hawthorn, holly at Christmas, shamrocks for St Patrick's Day. Maeve knows the delivery route and can execute the daily routine unaided. The donkey cart is painted shiny black, except for the shafts that are stark white. The shafts are fitted with white and red reflectors like a car, so that the cart, despite being black, can be easily seen at night. The front of the cart is fitted with a seat and footplate, like a handsome cab, so Peter can conduct his deliveries with a degree of decorum. His apparel includes two waterproof capes, one for himself and one for Maeve. No one can rightly remember when Peter Meehan first started to work for Casey's General Store.

Every customer of Casey's General Store possesses a red 'ration book'. Peter Meehan turns up at the agreed location – the back door, the barn, the stile at the crossroads, or wherever – and reads the list in the page dated for that day. He notes, in pencil, the price in the appropriate column. At the end of the day he delivers the requested goods, and records the amounts in indelible ink. Sometimes, if Peter is unfamiliar with the item, the price might change – but most items are familiar to Peter and to the purchasers. Corrections are seldom necessary. At the end of each week, the current column is totted up and a balance due is reckoned. Depending on the agreement with Mrs. Casey, payment is due on the following Monday, or at month end or at an agreed future date.

Many of Casey's customers also have a blue book. This is the ledger to record the goods that farmers sell to Casey, who in turn makes them available for general sale as a part of his merchandise. If you are fortunate, your blue book balance exceeds your red book balance, and you receive money from Casey. This arrangement works very well and greatly aids the local economy.

Casey is a very astute businessman. If a requested item is not in stock, he can always obtain it. Even prohibited goods are transacted, as in the case of dynamite for removing tree stumps. How Casey does it, no one is sure. Maybe he runs an under-the-counter blue book with the county quarry manager who can slip him some supplies now and again.

He does not permit politics to interfere with business either. He had supplied the RIC, the Black & Tans, the Irregulars, and the Free State garrison in turn. He even purchased supplies from the Black & Tans when they withdrew from Castlebar, before they departed the country – which he then sold to the Irregulars whose stock of ammunition needed replenishing. The ladies of the county receive fashion magazines from London via Casey's, and if any item takes their fancy, he obtains it for them from the high fashion houses.

Peter Meehan does not worry about how Casey gets the stuff; he just delivers, and tallies up the red and blue books. Mrs. Casey 'does the books', and keeps a record in the store of all the red and blue books held by customers. She enforces payment policies with an iron fist. Her bookkeeper is Suey McBride, who keeps the books updated and neat for 'herself's' inspection. It was due to Garda Murphy that Suey McBride got the job in Casey's. Suey is very pretty and very moody – two good reasons to keep her away from customers; but she is excellent at working in accounting with Mrs. Casey (who could not care less about how moody or pretty she is). Casey himself considers it dignified for Mrs. Casey to have an assistant. Murf considers it an advantage to have a set of eyes inside Mrs. Casey's inner sanctum; and Suey McBride is a first-rate (and willing) espionage agent.

The guards know that some of Casey's transactions are not quite legitimate. They keep an eye on things, assisted unwittingly by Peter Meehan and intentionally by Suey McBride – watching for the sale of half-dried barley which is favoured by the poteen distillers, and any other suspicious transactions. And to give Casey his due, he is careful about providing dangerous and prohibited products. He supplies some farmers with bullets for their guns to shoot rats, but only to those he considers responsible and experienced. If any order does not add up to good sense, Casey tips off the guards. Casey's General Store is highly regarded by all in the region of Killbawn. And he gives 5% off to members of the Garda Síochána.

The old RIC barracks is Casey's strangest customer. But it was always a profitable client, and Casey was content to let it develop. He frequently scanned the orders in an attempt to obtain some understanding of the mysterious client; but no, he could not get a handle on him. Casey had instructed Peter Meehan, his delivery man and local daily reporter, to glean whatever information he could – to which Peter had willingly agreed. And it registered in Meehan's head that whenever Garda Murphy ('Murf') greets him he frequently slips in an enquiry about the occupant of the old RIC barracks.

Back in the old days, before the Great War – the 'War to End All Wars' – a custom was established with the constabulary. They didn't want newsy-nosy Peter Meehan picking up tidbits of information to spread around the countryside, so he was instructed to drive his cart into the stables – there were no horses there anymore – and refer to the 'ration book' on the book rack there. The items purchased were the usual – mostly tea and sugar. Except for milk. Peter actually delivered milk to the barracks daily, the only customer he delivered milk to. All the other customers had a cow or a neighbour who supplied milk. But the RIC barracks was remote from the farmland and did not have any close neighbours. Peter Meehan called in twice daily and exchanged a wave of the hand with the duty officer as he passed the front.

Peter did not know, or care, how the RIC paid for the goods. He knew that they did. Periodically Mrs. Casey would give him a figure to enter in the ration book with the remark – 'Payment received with thanks' – and he would bring forward the revised balance. It appeared that Casey and His Majesty had a payment arrangement.

In 1920, the Black & Tans arrived to supplement the constabulary. The barracks was sandbagged and coils of barbed wire were strung all over the place. The stables were still accessible, and the delivery routine did not change. But the list of requested goods changed – now a lot of whiskey and cigarettes. Payment was received in cash paid upon each delivery. They paid in large bills, and never asked for change. A credit accumulated in the ration book, but they never asked for repayment.

On 12 February 1922, the British auxiliaries and the RIC abandoned the barracks. It was immediately claimed by both factions of the IRA. The local IRA, which was anti-treaty, stepped in first and held the barracks for less than a day. The better-armed pro-treaty IRA wrested the barracks away from the local Irregulars, and then they promptly abandoned the barracks on 14 February for reasons that it had no strategic importance. Both factions stripped the barracks of items of a military nature, but left the buildings in good condition. It was a bleak place with no shelter nearby. Throughout the IRA fighting, a temporary ceasefire was observed for the safe passage of Peter Meehan and his cart, who continued to bring supplies daily – paid from the Black & Tan credit.

On 15 February 1922, Peter Meehan has no reason to approach the barracks. It is empty. The British had withdrawn. The RIC were in the process of being disbanded, so they would not return either. And the IRA had vacated it. The donkey turns to enter the gateway. Peter steers her back to the roadway, and they pass on by.

The next day, the donkey enters the barracks' yard and stops in the stable before Peter remembers that it is no longer a scheduled customer stop. Ah, well! He needs to retrieve the ration book for Mrs. Casey. He takes it off the rack and flicks it open to the current page, curious to see what credit balance remains from the 'Tans – extra profit for Casey he thinks. Peter nearly drops the book. There under the previous day's entry is an order for staples – bread, flour, salt, tea, and sugar and more. Actually, it is quite a long list, one that a housewife might make to stock up on an entire month's supply of groceries. Surely there is no one living in the barracks; it looks unoccupied. Still, he is too nervous to put his suspicions to the test by entering the building – he had never been inside the building, and ten years of conditioning is difficult to shake. He pencils in the value of the requested items, and notes that it exceeds the credit residue. He writes "£1-03-11 owing. How will you pay?" and replaces the ration book.

That evening, Peter returns with the delivery. Surely he was mistaken. He must have opened the book at an old date instead of the current day's date. He would be relieved if indeed he were mistaken, no one would learn of it. He checks the book and as he fans the pages to the current date, a £10 note flutters out. Could the Black & Tans be back? No! There are no requests for cigarettes or whiskey. Peter Meehan continues to supply the barracks. Payments are always made. But he never sees or hears a human being.

On 16 March, Peter Meehan is running late. People are ordering in extra stuff for St Patrick's Day, just like every year, and they delay him with festive drams. It is after dark when he enters the stable at the old barracks. The bleak place gives him the creeps. It is dark, too dark to make entries in the ration book, so he just leaves the supplies on the bench as usual. As he makes his way back around the house to the front yard, he glances at the front door. He is unable to discern if the door is open or closed – it is a black door and the house is completely in darkness. He feels someone watching. He halts the donkey to listen better. He peers into the doorway – yes, the door is fully open. He can make out a vague figure in army uniform inside waving a pistol.

A voice from inside shouts out to him. "Pigs! Pigs! Come on you pigs! Daniel E will make sausages out of you German pigs!" It sounds like an English accent. And then, *"Fág a' Bealach!"* Why did he switch to Irish? *'Clear the way!'* Peter understands this to mean that he is blocking the laneway and should move on. It is unnerving, so he hastens out of the gateway and continues on, to complete his rounds.

The next business day is 18 March. Peter goes to Casey with his news update. He tells Casey, but not anyone else, at least not until he can make sense of it. "His name is 'Donnelly'!"

"Who is 'Donnelly'?" Casey asks.

"The resident of the old RIC barracks."

"So, how did you get that information?"

"He shouted out to me two nights ago."

"Is that a fact? And what did he shout?"

"Well, he has a funny accent; he could be English. But he said that he was 'Donnelly' – at least I think he said 'Donnelly' in a funny sort of way."

"And? Is that all he said?"

"He said that he wanted to make sausages and needed German pigs."

"Why must the pigs be German? Can he not use Irish pigs?"

"Well, how do I know? He told me to leave right after that."

"Hold on, Peter."

"Yes, Mr. Casey?"

Casey sees potential for business here. "We could do with good sausages. Maybe you should convince him to consider local pigs. If you can't get to talk to him, do your usual note writing. Tell him that we have good local pigs, and that we can supply him with the spices and ingredients for sausages. And bring a blue book to him to record the entries."

"Right you be, Mr. Casey."

It takes a few weeks and some puzzling written communications before Donnelly accepts the idea of using Irish pigs for sausages. Once started, it progresses quickly. Since Casey does not handle livestock, it takes a little time to establish a system. Local farmers, introduced via Peter Meehan, would deliver pigs to a holding pen at one of the side buildings. On the following day, the acceptable pigs would have disappeared, and the rejected ones left behind in the pen. At first, Peter Meehan shows the farmers how to record the transactions in a ledger in the stable, but they very soon get the hang of it. Donnelly would only accept good pigs. And they quickly learn to fatten up the pigs and have them healthy for Donnelly to consider.

Donnelly supplies sausages to Casey, and quickly builds up a credit in the account. Casey acts as the clearing bank to settle Donnelly's payment to the farmers, for a modest service fee of 5%.

As time goes by, Donnelly becomes more demanding in what he requires from Casey; and Casey is more than happy to oblige. Donnelly orders equipment to handle the increasing volume of work, and converts one of the buildings into a slaughterhouse, installing winches, hooks and pulleys. Casey is now receiving so many sausages and puddings from Donnelly that he is able to wholesale them to butcher shops in the neighbouring towns. They are labelled 'Donnelly's' and are in great demand. And throughout all this, no one ever meets or speaks to Donnelly.

There is local speculation about the mysterious Donnelly. Some swear that he could be seen at night inside his front doorway but, since he always stands or sits in darkness, his features are never seen. It is rumoured that he is black, and that is why he could not be seen in the dark.

Peter Meehan is busier than ever with Donnelly. Donnelly orders and obtains books and magazines of a military nature, clock and watch parts and timing devices, and pharmaceutical products. Meehan remembers that on the one time he glimpsed Donnelly, he had been wearing an army uniform – so he is ex-military. Therefore it is not surprising that he would have an interest in reading military books and papers. By the time St Patrick's Day 1923 arrives, a year later, Donnelly's (as the old RIC barracks is now referred to) is a thriving business. Since everyone benefits from Donnelly, they are prepared to overlook his strangeness. But they are apprehensive of him and keep their distance.

On 16 March 1923, Peter Meehan is running late, just like the previous year and for every year he could remember. This time, as he passes by Donnelly's darkened front door, he shivers with unease. But being of a newsy-nosy nature, he hesitates and peers through the darkness of the doorway. Again he sees the figure of an army officer, waving a pistol and talking. "Is this a sapper, or a rat? A rat slithers into the filth!" He is pointing his pistol and making popping sounds with his tongue. Meehan takes off before he is ordered to, like last time.

On 18 March he reports this to Casey. "Mr. Casey. That Black Donnelly fellow was talking to rats two nights ago; he was pointing a gun and going 'pop-pop-pop'."

"He was shooting them?"

"No. He was just making sounds with his mouth."

Casey figures that a slaughterhouse must have rats. There are hooks to suspend the pig carcasses and meat out of reach of the rats, but nevertheless, there must be a lot of stuff around for them to feed on. If word gets out that Donnelly's is overrun by rats, it would be the end of the sausage business. So Donnelly has a gun it would appear, but no ammunition.

"Peter. Find out from Donnelly if he requires bullets for his gun." Donnelly shooting rats is no worse than a farmer shooting rats.

"Right you are, sir!"

Meehan ascertains from Donnelly that indeed he does require ammunition. The calibre of bullets is the same as those used by the Black & Tans in their handguns – the stuff Casey purchased in Castlebar when they withdrew on 02 March 1922. He still has some in stock.

At first he supplies Donnelly with 10 bullets at a time, but later gives him boxes by the gross. And Donnelly shoots the rats, and the reputation of the business remains intact.

One thing that worries Casey is the pharmaceutical products that Donnelly obtains. What are they for? He mentions it to the sergeant of the guards at a social event.

"Unusual, but not dangerous – unless they are mixed with certain other ingredients – like some weed-killers and some of those new artificial fertilizers that are on the market." Casey swallows. The sergeant continues, "But that's unlikely around here. One would need military training in explosives to know how to handle the mix. Not even we, in the Garda Síochána, would know how to do it; well, to do it safely, at any rate."

Casey considers the military books and papers that Donnelly obtains, and swallows again.

"You're not supplying this stuff to farmers. Are you, Casey?"

"Oh, no, Sergeant. I saw it listed in a trade catalogue and was wondering if I should stock it."

"No. That's for a chemist to stock."

"Ah, right. Now I know. It's so hard to keep up with all the stuff they are putting out these days."

Casey conducts a mental argument with himself. "Think, Casey. There must be a good reason for Donnelly to make explosives." He lists in his mind all the possible things Donnelly would need in the sausage-making business. "Let's see... He would need to kill the pigs. That's usually done using a bolt to the head. An explosive charge is required to drive in the bolt with force. That's it! Donnelly needs explosives to kill the pigs." And Casey puts the matter out of his head.

CHAPTER EIGHTEEN

MURF AND MEEHAN

Sergeant John Patrick Murphy (Murf) came to Killbawn in 1935, two years before District Officer Superintendent Fox. In 1938, with a strong endorsement from Fox, he was promoted to the rank of garda inspector. In many respects Murf's arrival in Killbawn is a homecoming. He had grown up, and had gone to primary school, in nearby rural Ballycorry prior to 'the Troubles'. He is quickly accepted by the locals, re-establishes social contacts, and quickly gets to know everyone. Murf treats it as a priority to know the community intimately. Policing is much more effective when a vigilant officer can spot something out of place before an offence is committed. Several factors must come together for a crime to occur – the desire/motivation, the skills/tools needed, and opportunity. A vigilant officer can detect if any of these factors are present before they combine together. Murphy's motto is to prioritise crime prevention over crime punishment.

On top of his list is Peter Meehan – the reputed eyes, ears and nose of the community. Close second is Mrs. Bertha Fitzpatrick, sister of Baron Lord Kilmacneil, member of the House of Lords. Peter knows all the earthy stuff; Mrs. Fitz knows all the snobby stuff; they both know an equal amount of dirt.

Murf's knowledge of Donnelly is lacking. This bothers Murf. He could always size up people in seconds. But he has never met, seen or heard Donnelly. Over time Murf gets the story from Meehan. But it doesn't ring true. Clearly, Meehan is missing something. What the eye or ear observes may be different from how the brain distinguishes it. If only he could get Meehan to enact what he observed, without paraphrasing, embellishing or interpreting, then maybe he could get some accurate insight into Donnelly.

Coming up to Christmas 1946, Mrs. Fitz arranges for a theatre company to present a new play. The theatre company agrees. They were looking for a venue in which to perform prior to the official opening night in Dublin in January. The Killbawn performance in St Bridget's Hall would expose any flaws, and give them a chance to iron out the wrinkles. Why Killbawn? Baron Lord Kilmacneil is a patron of the theatre, and pressed by his sister, Bertha Fitzpatrick, he convinces the theatre company to perform in Kilbawn. It is a new Irish play – '*Oak Leaves and Lavender*' by Sean O'Casey.

Well, EVERYONE had to be there for the play – the Garda Síochána district officer, the parish priest, the canon, the dean, Fitzpatrick and McHugh, Casey, the ICA. Peter Meehan is there too, not because he has any interest in theatre, or desires to be seen. Peter Meehan just likes to know what is going on. And he is there too because Casey is providing the refreshments – soft drinks, wine, cocktail sausages on sticks and cakes.

Suey McBride is helping out – black-haired black-eyed Suey in black waitress dress and white apron. It appears that a theatrical crowd can handle a pretty and moody girl handing out sausages and wine. Meehan is the 'delivery service', and has to wait for the end of the show to clean up and remove the chairs. Lord Kilmacneil introduced the cast at the beginning of the evening, and concludes with gracious thanks to the theatre company and to all who attended – and Casey gets his plug. Surprisingly Meehan actually enjoyed the play. He claps as loud as anyone.

Murf glances around, noting his most valuable local 'contacts', and makes a point of spending some time with each. He makes sure to compliment Suey McBride. Two years earlier, Murf saved her from her own folly when he prevented her from taking her own life. Some people cruelly refer to her as 'Suicide McBride'. Murf has taken to looking out for her. Even hard-nosed money-grubbing Casey revealed a paternal trait in creating a position for her in the general store – a quality Casey would never openly admit to. Murf is thankful for his cooperation.

Lastly, Murf helps Meehan stack the chairs on dollies, and he wheels them out to the cart. Humorously, Murf shouts to those gathered at the doorway to clear a path. *"Fág an bealach!"*

Meehan remarks, "You know, Murf, it's the funniest thing."

"What, Peter?"

"That's the second thing tonight that put me in mind of Donnelly."

"What! *'Fág an bealach'*?"

"Except that Donnelly said it more like *'Fág a' Bealach!'*"

"Is that right, Peter? I thought you said he spoke with an English accent. You didn't tell me that he spoke Irish."

"Well, he DID speak with an English accent, even when he spoke in Irish. But it was not the same English the Black & Tans spoke. And that's the other thing. He spoke just like Lord Kilmacneil. Well, isn't that the divil-and-all? Twice in one night I was put in mind of Donnelly."

Murf is alert to this new information and his brain kicks into top gear, but he keeps up a casual conversation with Meehan. "Peter, you did his voice very well there. Can you do it again?"

"I can show you how he said 'Donnelly' in that English voice of his – 'Danelee' – there!"

It is apparent to Murf that Meehan regards the British Army officer accent as 'English', even an Irish British Army officer's. And it is unlikely that 'Donnelly' would be rendered as 'Danelee' in that accent. So he clarifies with Meehan. "Could it have been 'Daniel E'?" Murf asks in imitation of Lord Kilmacneil's voice.

"That's it, Murf. You have it perfect."

"Thanks, Peter." and in his head he repeats it with emphasis. "Thank you, thank you, Peter."

"What are you thanking ME for, Murf? This is MY clearing up your doing. I should be thanking YOU."

But Murf is already out the door. Murf is now convinced that 'Donnelly' is actually 'Daniel E', an Irish British Army officer who located in the RIC barracks just when it was abandoned in February 1922. 'Donnelly' was previously an Irish British Army officer, yes. But from which group: RIC, Black & Tans, IRA or National Army?

CHAPTER NINETEEN

MICKEY AND TRACY IN AUGUST 1947

The first Tuesday in August 1947, the 5th of the month, Mickey Motor (Michael Carr) had bought 10 banbhs from his boyhood friend, his only friend, Ben Muldoon. Mickey relies on Ben for all his market transactions. He distrusts the farmers at the market, suspecting them of putting one over on him. So he engages Ben to do the dealing for him. But today the deal is just with Ben. They are both sitting having a drink of porter at the pub in the market square of Killbawn. Neither is talking to the other, which is quite normal for them. Ben makes a comment, Mickey grunts in acknowledgement, and they fall silent again. At eight o'clock, as the clock strikes the hour, Mickey stands up, drains his glass and says goodbye to Ben. Ben is sleepy. He too should be leaving. He has a young gossoon out in the cart that should be in bed before dark – just as soon as he finishes his drink. The porter relaxes Ben, and he is in no hurry.

Mickey drives back to his farm, the 10 banbhs in the back seat – not actually the back seat – they are situated where a back seat would be, if the car had a back seat. Mickey had converted it into a saloon to transport pigs, hogs, sows, banbhs and swill. At 8:40 Mickey turns off the boreen and into the laneway of his farm. No one could miss Mickey Motor's farm – that is, if they ever had reason to travel this quiet boreen out near the bog. The farm is littered with bits of tractors and cars, and things that had been there so long that no one could possibly know what they are. Inside the house it is worse. The place is littered with things that Mickey takes apart and reassembles just for the fun of it.

As he approaches the house, he sees a black couch or rug lying at his front door. Probably some neighbour thought he could do with even more stuff. Except that the rug suddenly sits up. "Rex!" he shouts. No, it can't be Rex. Rex was one of the black-brindled mastiffs that Tracy Prior had with him from 1919 to 1922 when he and Carr both served with the IRA North Cork Flying Column 22. Rex couldn't be here. Twenty-five years have passed.

"Hello, Mickey."

He hadn't seen the man sitting on a tractor wheel amidst all the machine parts. The man stands up, the better to be seen.

"Tracy? Tracy Prior? Is it Tracy Prior and Rex?"

"Yes. It's Tracy and Rex. Not the same Rex. This is 'Rex Secundus', 'Rex 2' if you like, but he answers to 'Rex'."

"How did you get here? I don't see your car."

"A Land Rover, parked two miles back by the river. I have two fishing rods in the back seat so that any unlikely passerby would take it for a fisherman's car."

"Always secretive. Eh, Tracy?" Mickey releases the banbhs from the back seat and into a pen at the side of the house. "So what have you been up to in…what is it...25 years now?"

"…and six months," says Tracy, who continues, "mostly Kenya with the police…"

"You're with the police?"

"In charge of the Ulster K-9 division. Well, I will be as of the 01 September…"

"So that's why your getup is like a commando's."

Prior is dressed in military-style dark-green tunic over combat trousers and combat boots, a green beret on his now-greying head. "…taking two weeks off for fishing first. I thought I'd look up my old comrade."

"Well, come inside. I don't get visitors. I have no tea, and even if I had, I've no cups. Can I offer you a porter?"

Tracy follows him in and looks around. "I see you smoke and drink now, Mickey."

"Ah. Yes. Now where can you sit? I can't find a chair. Ah, here's one."

"I'm okay on this stool by the workbench." Tracy leans on the workbench and fingers what looks like a clock's works on the worktop. "I see Mickey that you still tinker around with things, but no guns to reassemble?"

Mickey sits down on a stack of car wheels. "Naw, I haven't handled a gun since leaving the flying squad. But I fiddle around with things all the time. Like that strange thing you have in your hand, Tracy. I have had it since the day you left, and I have no idea what it is. I keep taking it apart and putting it back together, even with my eyes shut, for 25 years, and I still don't know what the heck it's for!"

"Since the night of our last 'operation' at the RIC barracks?"

"That's right! I picked this thing up from beside the turf stack after the explosions."

"There were no explosions that night."

"Of course there were, Tracy! At the bridge, and another at the turf stack beside the stables. Don't you remember?"

"After you killed the six auxiliaries…"

"Five, Tracy. There were only five."

"After you killed the five auxiliaries, and you confirmed that all were dead, I left with the dogs. I didn't hear any explosions. I ran over the bog to make uninterrupted progress."

"Well, there you are. You had left before the explosions. A lorry-load of IRA was blew up near the Blackwater bridge, killing five of them. And then the IRA came and took over the barracks. And then the Regular Army arrived and one of the 22's cars was blew up, killing Taigh and three others. Joker was badly wounded and never recovered. Fourteen dead and one wounded in one day, all within a few hours. The army took over, and then they all left."

"Gee, Mickey. I'd read of an encounter in which 14 died. But nothing as you describe. I never knew."

"Ah, it was the divil of a time, so it was."

"And what of the RIC barracks now? I passed it a few minutes ago. It looks deserted except for some tracks of activity around the outside. Sheep dipping or something?"

"Oh, there's a strange hermit chap living there now. But that's not so rare – there are people all over the country now living like that. He's just one more. We don't know how he came to be there. It appears that the army left him behind, an officer authorised to hand over the RIC barracks to the guards or something. But the guards never came."

"The army left him behind?"

"Naw. That's stupid. Peter Meehan, who delivers for Casey's General Store, he says that. He also says that he's English." Mickey hesitates to gather his thoughts. "You know, Tracy, the night the army arrived, the same night that you left, there were a lot of British Army men at the RIC barracks – soldiers from the British Army taken into the Irish Army. After they pulled out, two days later, this strange fellow was left behind."

Tracy is still fingering the piece of 'clock', a mechanism with which he is intimately familiar. He has not fingered one of these since 1918 at the Somme. He murmurs to himself aloud, "...explosions...five auxiliaries killed, not six..." Then he suddenly stands up. "Mickey!"

“What?”

“I believe we have an ‘operation’ to complete.”

CHAPTER TWENTY

MURF AT DINNER WITH THE FOXES

Sunday Evening, 10 August 1947

The grandchildren are tired. They offer no resistance when Brian and Jane pick them up to bring them home. "There's a lot to do tomorrow, so early to bed."

"Aw," they protest weakly, but they are content to go.

At dinner Mary brings up the subject. "Confessions."

Foxy, Mary and Murf are sitting at the dining-room table in the Fox's house. The maid is clearing the dinner plates, and they are relaxing over cups of white coffee. Murf considers the cups too small, but in tune with Mary's sense of decorum. Mary offers to refill Murf's cup, the small white cup with delicate pale-blue scrolls. She reaches for the silver pots, the bulky one containing hot black coffee, and the slender tall pot containing hot creamy jersey milk. Murf gestures in agreement to a replenishment, a mixture of both. White coffee is popular with the county people and people with 'airs', including the executive of the Irish Countrywomen's Association. It is also a means of displaying fine silver – two silver pots and a silver sugar bowl with silver tongs. Murf calculates. Mary would not normally present the silver coffee service, unless it was an occasion; and she would offer to withdraw to the drawing room at this point of the meal. And it is clear that Foxy would be more comfortable in his easy chair.

The purpose? As Mary is pouring the coffee-milk combination, Murf asks, with an unconvincing innocent expression, "Confession?" And engages in attending to choosing the appropriate number of sugar lumps.

"Yes," says Foxy. "As in this!" plopping a copy of the Manchester Guardian, Friday edition, on the table.

The Guardian had arrived in Saturday's evening post

and Mary had the foresight to conceal it from Foxy until this evening. The newspaper is folded to display page five. There is a picture of the top brass of the British police forces meeting in Manchester on Thursday night; with Dr. Trevor Harrington, Chief Police Psychiatrist for the London Metropolitan Police, in the front middle of the group; and beside him is the newly-appointed chief constable for Northern Ireland, Sir Robert Norton. The topic of the police convention, according to the accompanying article, is 'Confessions: Psychological and Forensic Aspects'. And there, at the end of the back row – as Foxy and Mary point with their eyes – is Murf. Well, it looks like Murf, except for the spiffy formal civilian dress. Under the photograph it identifies the personalities pictured, and listed is 'John Patrick Murphy'. In the accompanying article it describes the work of Dr. Harrington who was 'greatly assisted by the input of John Patrick Murphy, a member of the Éire Police.'

Fox says, "I don't know what to ask first…"

Murf is almost blasé. "Oh that. I have been in correspondence with Trev – Dr. Harrington – for over a year now to develop a more accurate means of confession, one that is fairer to the accused and yet more accurate for the courts in delivering a verdict…"

But Murf, you HATE the brass; you HATE the courts…"

"No. I Don't HATE them. They just get it wrong most of the time; and forward-looking innovators like Trev, Dr. Harrington, will change that…"

And Mary interjecting "… and innovators like John Patrick Murphy, 'Éire Police'?"

"I was assisting him in his presentation on Friday, the part entitled 'Practical Application of Interview Techniques'. The group met for dinner and introductions on the previous evening. That is where the picture was taken by the 'Guardian'. I have been employing these interview techniques here in Mayo for some time, and Trev is pleased with the results. He needs a wider sampling to have the techniques officially adopted. He hopes to get a larger police force to adopt..."

Fox interjects, "Murf, on Thursday, the day of the police convention in Manchester," tapping the newspaper loudly with his forefinger, "...you were here, smearing muck all over my Irish Independent..."

"Thursday MORNING, Foxy."

"...and you told me that you were investigating the incident in Ballycorry. I thought you were in Ballycorry all day Friday."

"That's perfectly true. I was indeed investigating the Ballycorry homicide, but my investigation took me to Manchester."

"And how could you be in Killbawn and in Manchester on the same day?"

"Flying. There are four flights a day from Shannon to Ringway Manchester, Foxy. I got there in good time for dinner and to meet..."

"You went to see Dr. Harrington of the Met. In your investigations?"

"Don't be silly, Foxy. Harrington is not the only reason I went. Robert Norton is the other reason, the one pertinent to the case. I asked Trev to introduce me to Nobbie – that's Sir Robert Norton – whose help I need in tying up loose ends in the case. And if the dots connect, as I expect, it will provide him with grounds to make an arrest."

"And what did you talk about? Your white dots?"

Murf said one word, as if it explained everything. "Dogs."

"Gods?" Foxy asks, falling into dyslexia in his confusion. "I mean 'dogs'? You went to Manchester to talk to Sir Nobbie Norton, the chief constable for Northern Ireland – to talk about DOGS?"

"Yes."

"To help tie up loose ends in Killbawn?"

"Yes."

"And help him make an arrest?"

"Yes, but not yet – a possible future arrest. I'm still working on it. It may have a connection to the

Donnelly/Kennedy case."

"And you didn't clear it with your district officer? Or with Dublin?"

"That's right."

"And I am to approve the expense?"

"The London Met paid for my flight and hotel."

"Murf…" but couldn't think of what to say. "I need a drink. No, Mary, not more tea…"

"It's COFFEE, Foxy." She kicks him under the table.

Foxy continues talking as he gets up from the table and walks through the open double doors to the drawing room, straight to the Waterford whiskey decanters, "…a glass of Jameson. Jameson Crested Ten."

"Well, I think it's great, Foxy!" shouts Mary. "Murf, hob-knobbing with the English brass. No, 'hob-nobbying'," and starts to giggle. Mary and Murf follow Foxy into the drawing room. Speechless, Foxy drains his glass, and refills it.

Later, Fox seems resigned, whatever the outcome, thanks to the settling euphoria of a few more Jamesons. "I'm intrigued – impressed, that Dr. Harlington – or Harrington – consulted with you. Maybe this 'white dot' thing has more merit than an idiosyncrasy of yours."

"Come on, Murf," says Mary. "I'm dying to know what impressed Dr. Harrington."

"Well," says Murf. "It starts with 'mental reservation'. One can present the truth in a manner to mislead or even deceive; and conversely, one can lie to arrive at the truth."

"An example," demands Mary before he can continue.

"Lord Haw-Haw."

Lord Haw-Haw was William Joyce, an American by birth but raised in Ireland. During the Anglo-Irish war, 1919-1921, he was an informant to the British forces about the IRA rebels. He was also a senior member of the British Union of Fascists and fled England on 26 August 1939. In February 1940, as Lord Haw-Haw, Joyce was the main German broadcaster in English for most of the war.

"Okaaay. And…"

"In 1 Kings 3:16-28, Solomon instructs that a baby be split between two women to settle a dispute as to which one is the mother. The true mother of the child, in order to save the baby from death, cries out, 'Do not kill him. Give him to her; she is his mother', thus revealing that only she herself could be the true mother.

"Even today, the expressions 'splitting the baby' or 'cutting the baby in half' are sometimes used in the legal profession for a form of simple, if unsatisfactory, compromise. That's not exactly 'mental reservation', but it illustrates…"

"Okay, okay! I understand!"

"Now, one step more – to the presentation of evidence – confession. The 'black dots' I refer to are the data one is given under the aforementioned circumstances. It is unreliable. The real truth – the 'white dots' – is revealed through secondary data, the seemingly unimportant peripheral data, which is not foremost and not infected by evaluation and editing."

"Example."

"In the Book of Susanna, otherwise referred to as Chapter 13 of Daniel, a false accusation from two judges would result in the death sentence of Susanna. Daniel, upon questioning the accusers, uncovered their deceit by discussing the flora of the garden, the 'crime scene'. Whereas the two accusing witnesses could agree on the details of the crime ('black dots'), they were unable to agree upon the identity of a tree at the site where the alleged incident occurred. This inconsistency uncovered their contrived machination and their evidence was rejected. Susanna was freed, and her accusers were executed."

"Hold on, Murf. I thought this was new stuff – with Dr. Harrington et al. But this is thousands of years old."

"The truth is the truth, and anything less than the FULL truth is falsehood."

"Who said that, Murf?"

"I just did."

"Oh, Murf. Go on," laughs Mary with a dismissive

wave.

Fox pauses from sipping his whiskey. "You know, Murf, you may be on to something."

But Murf is on a roll. "Now in criminal law, confession evidence is a prosecutor's most potent weapon. However, the integrity of the confession must be protected by applying rules of confession evidence and procedure. You know, even voluntary confessions are unreliable. You remember the 200-odd voluntary confessions that were received in the U.S. in 1932 regarding the Lindbergh baby kidnapping? These were voluntary self-incriminating statements."

"Is that a fact?" asked Fox, who was now only half listening.

"My communications with Trev Harrington are for the improvement of police interrogation methods. Physical intimidation and 'baetin' it outta them' is no longer considered reliable. He, in consultation with other police forces, is working on a nine-step procedure to interrogate a suspect. One aspect, the area in which he consulted me, is to differentiate unreliable information from reliable information. I do this by the inclusion of 'innocent data'. 'Innocent data', I call 'white dots'. They are not part of the evidence, but they ARE part of the picture. They are unbiased, because they are perceived as irrelevant. For the interrogator they serve as an essential tool to measure the accuracy of the confession evidence – to see if the 'black dots' connect correctly. It is by connecting the 'white dots' that you establish the integrity of the 'black dots'."

But Foxy had dozed off.

Mary says quietly, "I do believe you put Foxy to sleep."

"Ah. So I did. Well, have a good time at the Riverstown Horse Show next Sunday," says Murf as he gets up and promptly leaves. Mary is not disturbed at Murf's lack of manners in departing abruptly; it is typical of Murf to act without preamble or forewarning, and she accepts it as an endearing part of his eccentricity. He is gone before Mary could ask what he means.

Riverstown Horse Show, in County Tipperary, is a

swanky affair for the 'County' people. No doubt Mrs. Fitz would be there. As Mary pictures herself in a stylish new sundress and sunhat, she debates inwardly, "Why shouldn't Superintendent Fox and Mrs. Superintendent Fox not attend? What a great suggestion, Murf. And Foxy's family is not far from there either."

CHAPTER TWENTY-ONE

CAPTAIN DANIEL EDWARD KENNEDY
IN 1947

Captain Daniel Edward Kennedy, Royal Irish Fusiliers, as daylight fades into twilight, sits looking out over no-man's-land from the officers' bunker in the trenches. He knows it is make-believe. He is really in an old RIC barracks in North Mayo dressed in his captain's uniform and waving his Webley Mk VI revolver, and that it is Tuesday 05 August 1947. He knows well that his life is empty. He cannot contact his family or his regiment. He cannot reveal himself to anyone. The loneliness would surely drive him mad if he did not escape nightly to experience the Second Battle of the Somme relived in make-believe. For the men who served in the trenches in 1918, the Somme was a nightmare. How he wishes for the sanity of that nightmare in preference to the reality he is now living. His only contact with living creatures is with rats and pigs. Rats and pigs are his only companions. Rats and pigs both he hates. Alas, rats and pigs are his life now, and killing rats and pigs is his life's sole purpose.

He is attentive to hygiene and neatness. Notwithstanding the building's gloomy exterior appearance, Kennedy is attentive to maintaining an efficient clean operation. The laundry and scullery are converted to an efficient butchering operation, and the old holding cells are converted into cold storage rooms. The floors and counters are scrubbed clean. The tools are sterilised and sorted. His clothes are neatly laundered and pressed, and his shoes are highly-polished. A picture of George V still hangs on the wall from the time of the RIC. In all the neatness and order there is nothing of the identity of the occupant himself.

He still makes timing devices and small bombs. The timing devices he makes from clock and watch parts. He checks their precision by inserting them into clocks and adjusting them for accuracy. Some, he lets run for a week and is pleased that they lose less than one second in that time. The house is full of timing devises being tested for accuracy. They tick just like clocks, and they chime rather than explode. He tests their lethal accuracy by strapping miniature bombs to the heads of the pigs. By synchronising the timers, all pigs are killed simultaneously. Last week he killed 12 pigs, and the blasts were so closely synchronised that he heard just one single detonation. But the pigs are 'Germans in the trenches' in his fantasy.

He receives supplies from the 'quartermaster'; in return he delivers dead bodies, all meticulously recorded in the officer's log – even though he knows that it is Casey's General Store that delivers his supplies and picks up sausages and puddings from him which he records in the blue ledger. This is just more fantasy to keep him sane.

There are rats outside – 'German snipers crawling through no-man's-land'. There are no rats in the house. He has the house well-secured against them. The rats are attracted to his disposal pit which is cleared out weekly, but the rats find bone and skin and hooves to feast on. Each evening, after sunset, he throws a pig's heart onto the front yard. The rats come to devour the heart. Daniel E waits until three or four congregate. Then he commences firing with his Webley. Even in the twilight of the early night, he can kill a rat with every shot. He shouts threats at the pigs, and he shouts at the rats as he kills them, just as he shouted to the Germans 29 years earlier.

The one shot he never took, the one missed shot he

regrets, was the one meant for Tracy Prior. Oh, to meet Tracy Prior, the rat, one more time. That would be one sweet encounter.

He settles into the routine, the same as every night for 25 years.

CHAPTER TWENTY-TWO

CARR AND PRIOR AT
THE RIC BARRACKS IN 1947

Mickey asks, "Where are we going?"

Tracy replies, "To the RIC barracks. We can run there comfortably in under 40 minutes."

"It's five miles, Tracy. Why do we hafta run there?"

"It's less than three miles by cutting across the bog. And it's a covert operation. We can't be seen."

"Tracy, I don't think I can run three miles."

Tracy looks at Mickey. "You're out of shape, Mickey. Park your car behind the creamery – it will be well-hidden there – and meet me at the bend where the road meets the bog. You can run the final mile with me." Tracy pulls out a flat tin from his jacket. "Here. Blacken your face and head. We can't have you shining like the moon." Mickey understands. He had done this with Tracy many times.

Tracy moves to the door. The dog stands up and approaches his side. He pulls a balaclava over his head and says, "Don't make me wait for you."

"Aren't you coming in the motor-car with me?"

"And risk being seen with you by someone on the road?" Tracy and the dog depart, jogging over the back field/junkyard, onto the bog, and they disappear behind a ridge.

Mickey gives his car a push and it rolls down the laneway. He hops in and jump-starts it by clutch-gear-release. It is the fastest way to get it going. As he drives to the creamery he feels like a limp wet rag that is slowly drying to a hard crisp. The old assassin feeling is returning. He takes his packet of Woodbines and flings them out the window – his craving for a smoke gone. He feels young again. Maybe he should have run the three miles with Tracy and the dog.

The creamery is deserted. It is really a milk-collection station. The co-op collects milk in the morning from local farmers, and transports it to the main creamery in milk containers by noon. The yard behind is large and tree-lined. He parks the car out of sight, careful to park on a slope. He jogs to the bend where the road meets the bog. Tracy arrives at the same time. It is past 10:00pm and the sun is setting.

They run the final mile to the RIC barracks. They do not run on the road. They jog along the edge of the bog, keeping to the hollow of the sheugh – the drainage ditch that separates the roadway from the bogland. It is quiet underfoot, and they would not show against the skyline. The dog, being lower and his paws silent, runs along beside them on the road surface. The dog is familiar with the pace set by Tracy and adheres to it. Mickey, being out of shape, is starting to flag. He is wheezing as he struggles to maintain the pace. Despite his efforts, he is slowing. Tracy falls back to coax him with hand gestures. Now they are running strung out in single file.

They see a cart on the road ahead. Mickey recognises it as Ben Muldoon's. "Oh," he moans to himself. "Ben Muldoon and that northern gossoon-nephew of his are returning from the market. Why are they so late?"

The mastiff is well ahead of them now. The dog is trained to disarm an attacker. He is also trained to identify explosives. One of the many ingredients he is trained to sense is carbide. And although they are not lit, the cart is equipped with carbide lamps on the tailgate. Another part of his training is to pursue suspects attempting to escape. As luck would have it – bad luck in this case – the jennet gets spooked and gallops. The dog gives chase. He leaps up twice to investigate each of the lamps in turn. He sniffs and snorts to indicate a find, but is unable to assume the required stance. He redirects his attention back to the original quarry, the house. The cart nosily rounds the bend and, judging by the sound, is speedily departing from the place.

Tracy is troubled. He is too far away in the twilight to communicate to the dog by hand gestures, and he needs to remain concealed. He considers the import of the incident with the cart. So the boy saw a dog. So what? A dog running along a country road is not unusual. And there is no way to associate the dog with Mickey or himself.

The spooked jennet had drawn the dog too far ahead. This is not exactly as planned. Prior hears gunfire from the house, and increases his speed. The black-brindled dog is not visible in the twilight, but Prior can make out the red dots of the dog, and is satisfied that Rex is not the target. All the same, the dog is exposed to danger.

Tracy catches up with the mastiff at the open doorway of the bleak house. He sees Rex crouched inside just past the threshold. He had hoped to observe the house first, and assess the situation before proceeding. He needs to be sure of the identity of the recluse in the house. If it turns out to be who he suspects, imprudent action could be dangerous. Because of the dog's forward action, things had already moved to an advanced stage. Tracy has to see it through now – and hopes that it is not a mistake.

Captain Kennedy, sitting inside his doorway, looking out onto his front yard, hears the clatter of a fast moving cart – ahh...the sound of artillery being moved behind the lines. He shouts at the rats and shoots a few. Then a black shape fills the doorway and lands at his feet, poised to pounce with fangs bared. It is Prior's abomination of a mastiff.

For a moment Daniel E is confused. Has he lost his

ability to distinguish fantasy from reality? He moves his gun hand, just a shiver, and instantly his hand and wrist are clamped in the grip of the mastiff's massive jaw. He holds his breath, fearing to move. He exhales, and the dog's grip tightens. How long could he hold his breath? One more exhale and he feels the fangs pierce his skin; now his hand is numb. His eyes are closed in pain and terror.

Prior is panting from exertion. He stops to catch his breath and then warily steps on the threshold. He peers inside, looking past Rex, and discerns Daniel E. Kennedy. He correctly deduces that Rex had seen a man in the darkened doorway of the house waving a pistol and, true to his training, the dog removed the perceived threat by gripping the man's gun hand in his mouth. The dog has the situation well in hand.

Captain Kennedy hears a footstep on the threshold and a soft voice *"Aus."* The grip on his hand is released, and his revolver clatters to the floor. *"Platz, Rex. Braver Hund."* The dog lies down, with its alert eyes fixed on him. Feeling returns to his hand, offset by a loss of feeling all over. He hears Prior (it MUST be Prior) breathing in the darkness of the doorway, only his outline visible in the dim twilight of the doorway.

Prior is satisfied at how things are progressing. Good. He stands silently in the semi-darkness watching Daniel E, and waits for Mickey.

Daniel E can hear the snorting breathing of the short-nosed mastiff.

He hears the ticking of his timepieces.

He hears his own heart beat.

Why are they waiting? Waiting...

CHAPTER TWENTY-THREE

THE LAST ASSASSINATION IN 1947

For Mickey Carr, the assassination of the auxiliaries is being replayed 25 years later. It is time to complete the job. He makes his way to the coal chute. His breathing is steadying, the ache in his side subduing, his mind is working again, focused on the job at hand. The chute is sealed shut, no longer functional.

Mickey's mind is now up to speed, working with its old killer cunning. The hatch in the old laundry, now used to haul pig carcasses, gives him access to the laundry, which gives him access to the scullery, which in turn gives him access to the kitchen. The interior of the building is in complete contrast to Mickey's junk-filled abode. It is as neat and clean as a military hospital. All doors are securely shut, but unlocked. The latches and hinges are well-maintained, oiled and aligned. There is no rattling or squeaking. He remembers the way. It is still clearly etched in his mind from the day he was captive here. He navigates successfully in the near-darkness. He approaches the front room as silently as a shadow. A knife. It has to be a knife. Mickey is not fully prepared for an assassination; he has neglected to bring his killing knife. But, not to worry. The kitchen walls are lined with knives hanging neatly by size and shape. Mickey chooses what he regards as a fit knife for a killing, and steals into the front room.

He casts a quick eye around and sees the dark outline of Tracy in the dim light of the doorway. There is a chair in the room, pulled up close to the doorway and facing outwards. Someone is sitting in the chair, and Rex is glaring threateningly at the occupant. Mickey needs a moment to consider the circumstances. Is not this Donnelly, sitting in the dark doorway at night as is his habit? Surely Donnelly is not the intended victim of this assassination engagement. But who else could be here in the house? Surely, other than Donnelly, it is unoccupied. What is Tracy's target objective?

Tracy Prior, however, is in no doubt as to the identity of the man in the chair. He recognises the broken nose he inflicted on him years ago. Prior moves into the centre of the doorway so that he can communicate to Mickey. Mickey, still as stealthy as a shadow, reads Prior's body language. This is how they silently communicated years ago when they were the IRA's most efficient assassination unit. Mickey interprets the silent message from Prior and considers the significance of the RIF uniform. Why is Donnelly dressed up as the auxiliary captain? With a sudden flash of clarity, Mickey realises the reason for Tracy's decision in coming here tonight. This is the captain, the one responsible for his beating, the one he missed in the assassination 25 years ago.

Donnelly is Daniel E.

Donnelly is the captain.

Donnelly is the sixth and final auxiliary.

Now to finish the job 25 years after it started.

Mickey prepares to inflict a fatal cut to Daniel E's throat. Tracy inclines his head slightly. Mickey hesitates and follows the gesture to look beyond the doorway. Lying in the yard outside is a pig's heart. Ah, he understands.

Daniel E is focused on the threatening dog and on the silent Prior in the doorway. He is unaware of Mickey Carr so ominously close behind him. He has no pre-warning; Mickey plunges the knife into the heart. Daniel E exhales a long 'ah' sound as his lungs collapse and he slumps forward. Mickey pulls him by the hair to an upright position to look at his face, now staring lifelessly at the ceiling.

"Mickey, meet Captain Daniel Edward Kennedy, Royal Irish Fusiliers. However, you did meet him before, didn't you? When he was captain of the auxiliaries?"

Mickey looks hard at the lifeless face before him. In his mind's eye he sees the faces of the auxiliaries he had killed. Six, all six, all six accounted for. "We're done here."

"No, Mickey. Three things. First, tear his heart out, if he has one; get something to open the knife wound."

Mickey goes back to the kitchen and selects two sharp meat hooks. He returns to the limp body. Donnelly-Kennedy is lying with head back, staring at the ceiling with lifeless eyes. Mickey gets to work. He pulls at the wound. He draws out the knife, and tears open the wound to extract the heart.

"Throw the heart out to the rats, Mickey."

Mickey throws the warm bleeding heart onto the front yard. It lands beside the pig's heart.

"Second. This Daniel E was an expert bombmaker. This place may be booby-trapped. Disable anything that ticks, but gently. You don't want to detonate an explosion." Mickey remembers the exploding car that killed the Corkmen.

Mickey is skilled at this. He quickly and easily silences every clock and ticking device in the house. The row of now-silent clocks all display 10:20.

"Third and final. You need to contaminate the evidence."

"What do you mean, Tracy? Dirty the evidence?"

"I'm a policeman, Mickey. I know that the police will come. And they will find evidence to put you at the scene. Now this is what you do – it's what I do in these circumstances. Come back to the crime scene and muck about leaving your prints all over the place. The police will not be able to determine if your prints, or any other evidence left by you, were deposited before or after the crime. Are you taking this in, Mickey?"

"Oh, I am, all right."

"But not now, Mickey. You need to be seen by someone when you go back in."

"I hafta come back?"

"Mickey. Does anyone come here, other than you with your pigs?"

"Peter Meehan from Casey's comes here every morning at about 9:00 to take orders for supplies."

"Good. Be here at 9:00. No. Come early, in case Meehan changes his schedule, or if someone else arrives. Then, when he arrives, make up some reason to enter the house. Go into the house to find 'Donnelly'."

"Ah, yes. I get it now. I just go about inside the house, to the same places in the same order as tonight, touching the same things and muck with the evidence."

"Exactly. But don't let anyone else come in until you are satisfied that you have contaminated the evidence completely."

Mickey thinks it is a brilliant plan. "And this works?" he asks.

"It works for me. Job well done, Mickey!"

In all of this, Prior never entered the room past the doorway. He did not touch anything, not even with his gloved hands. He salutes Carr, spins around, and leaves with his dog. And like the previous time, 25 years before, man and dog run to the bog and disappear into the night.

CHAPTER TWENTY-FOUR

MURF EXPLAINS TO FOX

Monday 11 August 1947

District Officer Fox is looking out his window. No rain yet today. There was no rain on Sunday. He looks at the sky and observes dark clouds drifting in from the Atlantic. There may be rain later, he hopes. When he is feeling gloomy he appreciates sympathetic rain. He is unsure of the progress on the case. What is Murf doing? He goes here and goes there – from Ballycorry to Manchester. Where next? It's not like Murf to go in circles or on a wild-goose chase.

Fox addresses his reflection in the window, altering his focus from the distant sky to the faint image in the glass. "Murf has always been spot-on as a detective and a police officer. He reconciled the feuding farmers, Fitzpatrick and McHugh. Why, last month he solved the disappearance of Tee McDaid, when no one else believed a crime had even been committed – and he was on suspension at the time. And now he believes he has a solution to the Ballycorry murder case. If only I could share his optimism."

Murf comes to Fox's office and interrupts his soliloquy. Murf is carrying two cups of fresh tea balanced on a writing pad with a pencil stuck into the spine. He places his load on Fox's desk and sits down. Fox turns from the window and takes his customary seat. He stretches for his teacup and glances at Murf's writing pad. Fox sees that the pad contains a series of big circles with diminutive annotations jotted in each of them. Some of the circles are joined by connecting lines.

"Here's how it is, Foxy."

"How is it?"

Murf indicates to his pad. "Quite simple. Forensics confirms that Donnelly/Kennedy was killed by a sharp object, probably a knife..."

"Yes. Probably a knife..." Fox echoes.

"...his heart was cut out..."

"...his heart cut out... his heart cut out?" Fox is trying to place relevance on this fact.

"... the rats get to him and gnaw at the exposed flesh..."

"Rats? What rats?"

"It's a slaughterhouse, Foxy. Of course there are rats."

"Yes. Of course there are rats there." Fox has an image of the sausages he ate for breakfast, and feels like throwing up.

Impatiently, Murf elaborates. "Rats cannot get to the carcasses and sausages hanging from the hooks in the secure cold room. But they can get to anything lying around outside."

Fox is still feeling sick. "No. Of course not...the cold room...only stuff lying around...like dead Donnelly, er, Kennedy."

"Foxy, focus on the dots." Murf is tapping his pad.

Fox takes a swallow of tea. It settles his stomach. He feels better now. "Murf. Who could have done it? Who could have a motive? There was no..."

"Let's talk 'motive', Foxy."

Fox opens his right-hand drawer to access his biscuits. He is feeling a bit more settled, but anxious to get a credible solution in the case.

Murf is on a roll now. "'Donnelly' first appears on the scene just after the raid on the RIC barracks. That was 12 February 1922. There has to be a connection to that incident, and that is where we look to find motive and, ultimately, identify the perpetrators. I listed all known participants in that event – 31 Irregular IRA, and an unknown number of Regular Army, may have been as many as 100, and the assassination team.

"First, I dismissed the army – it is unlikely that any of them would have sufficient motive to kill 'Donnelly/Kennedy'. Ditto with most of the North Mayo Brigade members; they are old and settled now, and have put 'the Troubles' behind them. I have stricken them off the list, and that includes Maura Rua O'Hara and Daithi Mac a' tSionnaigh."

Fox is in the process of extricating a nice big round biscuit to dunk in his tea, when the mention of 'Daithi Mac a' tSionnaigh' jolts his attention. He snags the entire pack of biscuits knocking them to the floor. The biscuits shatter into crumbs on the exposed dark oak floor-board surround; the few that survive roll onto the oatmeal-coloured carpet. "I'm on the list of suspects?"

Murf is put off stride, "No, Foxy. You WERE on the list. I took you off."

Fox is now standing up, the itch suddenly bothering him.

Murf picks up the train of his development, checking off dots and circles on his pad. "The strongest motive would be with the survivors of the North Cork Flying Column 22. Four of them were killed in the explosion on the night of the raid, and one other was maimed for life. I checked with the Gardaí in Cork on the four survivors. Charles Kelly, unmarried, is manager of a Builders Providers Yard; the Larkin brothers are both married and are retired from farming; so too is O'Toole. Kelly was playing 'Twenty-five' the night of the Donnelly/Kennedy murder incident, and the three farmers were at home that night. The guards can attest to it. The Corkmen may have had motive, but motive also requires opportunity in order to execute the deed on Donnelly, or Daniel E. Kennedy, as I have reason to believe him to be. None of them were in, or near, the vicinity of the RIC barracks on the night of the Donnelly/Kennedy homicide." Murf makes a few more check marks.

Fox returns to the window. It has started to drizzle. Looking out the window at the drizzle of a dull North Mayo late-August day, he is fighting the urge to scratch. "So who DID have motive and proximity?"

"Ah. Proximity. Who was there at both occasions – the Donnelly/Kennedy murder scene, and also at the barracks the night of the IRA raid?"

"Ben Muldoon and Mickey Carr?"

"Yes. And no. 'No' to Ben Muldoon; his nephew, a valuable witness, can account for Ben at the time of the murder. But Mickey Carr? That is worthy of serious consideration." Murf is making notes and writing symbols in his circles.

Fox is of a mind to dismiss Mickey Carr as a suspect too. "Michael Carr's prints were all over the place – you don't need forensics to see that – but that was from the following morning when he and Ben Muldoon discovered the body."

"Not so, Foxy. Ben Muldoon did not discover the body; Ben Muldoon did not go into the house; Ben Muldoon did not see the body or the scene of the crime."

"True."

"Mickey Carr went to the crime scene. Mickey Carr, I contend, deliberately contaminated the crime scene."

"How 'contaminate'?"

"Foxy, are ALL of Carr's prints – handprints, footprints

and any other evidence of his presence – from the following morning? Or could they, some at least, be from the previous night, from the time of the crime?" Murf lets this sink in. "Now, Foxy, remember: way back on 12 February 1922, at the RIC barracks in Ballycorry, an IRA volunteer known as Go-Carr killed five auxiliaries with a knife. But he could not find the captain. But there was no 'Captain' on the list of auxiliaries. Was there, Sergeant Fox, RIC?"

Fox searches his memory for a second and says, "The leader of the auxiliaries was Second Lieutenant Edward Daniel, listed by surname first as 'Daniel, Edward'. And known as 'Daniel E' But he… There was…" Fox is connecting dots in his mind "…Daniel Edward. Murf, you believe he is Kennedy?"

"Yes. Captain Daniel Edward Kennedy, Royal Irish Fusiliers. Known as 'Captain Daniel E'."

"The Daniel Edward Kennedy wanted by the English police?"

"And concealing his identity in the auxiliaries."

"How do you come up with all this information?"

Murf does not answer this question immediately. He waits another second. "Think now, Foxy. Another dot to the picture. Go-Carr's accomplice in his assassination exploits, the man with the dogs, where was he that night? And, Foxy, the ace assassin Go-Carr, what was his real name?"

"Michael Carr, of course."

"The same Michael Carr as 'Mickey Motor'?"

"The same. And the man with the dogs was Tracy Prior. And not just dogs. He had English mastiffs. Big-brindled mastiffs that understood German."

"And for a while the Carr/Prior combination was the most efficient assassination team in the IRA."

The picture is crystallizing in the mind of D.O. Fox. He

thinks aloud, "Carr and Prior...and Mickey kept saying 'The dogs are gone...' Prior left that same night..." His mind comes back to the present. "One thing about this puzzles me, Murf."

"What's that?"

"Carr had been going to Donnelly's slaughterhouse with pigs for 25 years. If he had motive, why did he not act before? What made him act now?"

"Motive, means/proximity, knowledge, and opportunity. Most crimes are crimes of opportunity. Something happened to alter the relationship of these four factors, to put them into accord with each other, something that was hitherto missing. These are the dots that I still need to connect. But I believe I will have the solution imminently."

"Murf, you know. Don't you?"

"Foxy, I have the picture, but not the proof. Come with me. I'll show you."

Foxy walks to the carpeted area of the floor and retrieves two unbroken biscuits, the only survivors of the fall. He carefully steps over the crumbs of the shattered goldgrain and follows Murf to his office.

One wall of Murf's office is festooned with pages torn from his blotter, adhered to the wall by cellotape. The pages contain abbreviated notes in Murf's shorthand. Fox observes that the pages had been repositioned a number of times as evidenced by the tape marks on the wall and the missing paint. The pages are arranged around one central page entitled 'Donnelly/Kennedy Murder'. Running from the outer pages in the direction of the centre page are coloured cotton threads.

"Foxy, here you see the possibility and probability of each suspect's connection to the crime. The different coloured threads indicate the nature of the connection, and the length indicates the degree of certainty."

"So what does this mean, on the sheet titled 'Stoat Manchester'?"

"You see that the 'motive thread' is about 50% of the way, but the other threads are very short."

"Short on means and opportunity?"

"Exactly. Not a serious contender, but a significant contributor to the full picture nevertheless."

"But Murf, how do you come to have 'Stoat Manchester' on the wall at all?"

"Read the notes, Foxy."

Fox puts his finger on the page and, line by line, follows the sequence of information thereon:

Capt Daniel E – per Peter Meehan (Dec) –

Capt Daniel Edward Kennedy – Br Army search of Irish Capts confirms one name match (10 Jan) –

RIF confirms file of Capt, file access log records family enquiry and one by Manchester P (20 Jan)

Man P confirms Daniel Edward Kennedy is wanted for the murder of five members of the Stoat Gang in 1919

Man P drops case, 25-yr statute of limitations. Man P sends info from file. (22 Feb)

"Jaypers, Murf. You had this information on Kennedy back in February?"

"I was building a profile on him. I had been for some time."

"And that is how you got the old 'wanted poster'." Fox looks at all the pages stuck to the wall. There is a page on

'DF'; he notices that the threads are short. Like 'Stoat Manchester', 'DF' must contain some pertinent information. He sees the notation *RIC 12 Feb 22 – IRA.*

Fox recognises the names on other sheets, mostly IRA participants.

There is a sheet on Terence (Tracy) Prior. This one looks interesting –

Name appears on court-martial in Kennedy RIF file. Striking an officer – not guilty (20 Jan).

Intro to IRA by Connolly Dublin from Connolly London – per Old IRA Cork (7 Aug)

Confirmed – contact in London – Active communist member in 1919 (8 Aug)

IRA Assassin in 20-22 – German-trained military dogs – coincidence? German-trained police dogs in RUC. Checked up with Nobbie Norton – Man meeting (8 Aug)

Must confirm ASAP

Fox notices that the Prior sheet is not fully connected to the centre crime sheet, only about 50%. Fox continues to the bottom of the wall. There is a page entitled *'Murty Muldoon Witness'*. It is connected laterally to a sheet entitled *'Black Pig'*, which in turn is connected solidly to the centre crime page.

"Murf. Your strongest suspect is the Black Pig? Are you nuts? I thought that your strongest suspect was Mickey Carr? Look. You have connected Carr to the centre – well almost. Is there some doubt there? Is the Black Pig, the ghost pig that you said does not exist, is this your chief suspect?"

"Foxy, this is why I brought you here. There is something missing in the Carr connection. Something that does not fit the picture, unless..." Here Murf strikes out the word 'Pig' and inserts 'Dog'. "...unless you consider a black-brindled short-nosed mastiff with short legs."

"Like one of Prior's dogs?"

"Now watch." Murf removes the 'Black Dog' page from the wall and re-attaches it to the 'Prior' page, thus connecting Prior solidly to the crime page at the centre. Murf continues, "And what changed for Carr? The arrival of Prior. Carr/Prior, the most efficient assassination team in the IRA, is reconnected."

Thereupon, Murf removes the 'Carr' page and reattaches it to the 'Prior' page. Carr & Prior are jointly solidly connected to the centre crime page. "There, Foxy. The only possible fit for the picture."

"Good God, Murf. But can you prove it?"

"Just a few more steps – evidence, confession, confirmation – standard police work. Let's go back to your office."

Back in Fox's office, seated with their lukewarm tea and broken biscuits, Murf holds up a sheet of paper. "Foxy, something I need to confirm."

"Yes."

"Look at the old 'wanted poster' again." Murf holds it up for him. "Did the 'Captain' have a broken nose like this?"

"Yes. But the poster is very faded. It looks like him, but I can't swear to it."

"Now look at the picture from the scene of the crime." Murf slides a photograph from inside his pad, one of the crime scene photographs, and holds it aloft for Fox. It shows the dead 'Donnelly' in his chair, his head back, staring at the ceiling with lifeless eyes, his hands hanging limp by his side. He is dressed in his old army captain's overcoat. In alarm Fox stands up and grabs the picture, dropping his two remaining biscuits to the floor. He steps back, crushing the biscuits under his feet. He looks keenly at the picture and notes the RIF captain's overcoat, the broken nose and the mutilated finger. His mind flashes to a scene from the past, one that he had long forgotten, but that is now superimposed on the picture he holds trembling in his hands. In the scene from his memory he is pointing his Webley RIC revolver at the standoff with the auxiliaries, at the captain in an RIF uniform, the one with the bent nose, his little finger chopped short on his left hand. Foxy is looking at the captain of the auxiliaries of 12 February 1922.

Murf is still talking. Fox hears him say, "...you don't have to."

Fox realises that he had not been listening and asks, "I don't have to what?"

"You don't have to swear to the identity of the deceased. But we need independent confirmation of his true identity in order to confirm the connection. This is just ONE link that requires securing."

"But Murf, when did you figure it out?"

"Oh, Foxy, I have had an understanding of the crime from the first day. It was easy. But I did not know the identity of the perpetrators, other than a list of 20 suspects. My priority now is to narrow down the list of suspects by connecting the remaining dots, and to collect adequate evidence to build a sufficiently strong case to apprehend the killers. Time is of the essence. Daniel E is not going anywhere, but..."

"But YOU are?"

"And so are you, Foxy!"

CHAPTER TWENTY-FIVE

MICKEY CARR SULLIES
THE EVIDENCE

Tracy Prior and Rex run off into the darkness of the bog. Mickey Carr is alone with the dead 'Donnelly'. Mickey looks about in the dark. Even if he wanted to, it is now too dark in the old RIC barracks, 'Donnelly's Place', too dark to do any thorough cleaning or mucking, or tampering with the evidence. He retrieves the killing knife and the two meat hooks. He considers cleaning them and replacing them on their hooks. He decides to take them with him – he would be able to explain his fingerprints on doors and wall, but not on the instruments of mutilation. He shuts the front door. He locks it from the inside with the big key that is stuck in the lock. He exits the way he came in – through to the kitchen, to the scullery, to the laundry room and out through the loading hatch. At each doorway he makes sure to leave each door ajar. Daniel E could have installed devices in the locks that rendered them self-locking when triggered by shutting the doors, or placed the locks on a timer. Thus he is certain that he will have uninhibited access on the following morning.

Yes. Mickey can get in easily, but he fails to consider that so too can the rats.

He walks back to his car at the creamery, and returns to his farm. He is badly in need of a smoke, but he had disposed of his cigarettes. He does not retire to bed. As is his usual practice, he prefers to sleep wherever he happens to be sitting at the time. Only tonight, sleep eludes him.

At first light he loads the two fat pigs in the car. He needs a legitimate reason to be at Donnelly's. He drives slowly searching for the pack of Woodbines he had discarded the previous night. He finds them on the roadside, damp with dew. No matter, he manages to light one, and draws heavily on it.

At the old RIC barracks he pulls in to the roadside, rather than into the yard, so that the car's presence wouldn't be missed by anyone passing. He notices that the two hearts had disappeared from the front yard, probably devoured by the rats. He pauses and looks again. Where are the dead rats? Didn't Donnelly shoot and kill four rats? Mickey considers this. Do rats eat other rats? He shivers at the thought. Or do rats remove the bodies of dead rats in a kind of rat funeral? He shivers again. The absence of rat carcasses unsettles him. He looks around. Is there someone, or something, here other than himself? He shakes himself to restore his confidence and resumes his walk across the front yard. He waits by the front door for the arrival of Peter Meehan, or whoever would first pass on the road. From here he is able to view the road in both directions – along the mile-long stretch, and at right angles where the road swings sharp right.

It is after 9:00am, and Peter Meehan has not arrived. He hears the sound of voices approaching and two cyclists come into view. Oh no! Not Ben Muldoon. Why couldn't it be someone other than Ben? And that gossoon 'cub' is with him. Ever since that northern boy arrived, Ben spends less time with Mickey. Here goes the charade.

Unaware of the pretence, Ben innocently complies. He waits outside the house for Mickey to gain entry through the back. Mickey goes through the same route as the previous night – touching the walls, the doors, the tables, benches and everything he could possibly have touched before. Hardened as Mickey is, he is shocked at the sight of the dead British army captain in the chair. Rats dart away from the corpse. He feels sick. But he needs to complete his work of contaminating the evidence. That means handling the body. The rats disperse at his approach and disappear. He catches Daniel by the hair as before, then he pushes and prods around the gaping wound where had previously hacked with the meat hooks. A rat jumps out of the wound and scurries off. The surprise of this causes him to jump back; he slips on the bloodied floor and falls against a wall table knocking it over. He holds his mouth to stifle the urge to vomit. "Concentrate, Mickey!" he wills himself. What else needs to be touched? He cannot recollect, so he places bloody handprints all over the walls. When he can no longer endure it, he turns the key, opens the door and stumbles out. He vomits. He restrains Ben from entering. He needs to think. "Did I cover all the possible evidence?" he asks himself, and pictures in his mind the sequence of actions of the previous night.

When satisfied that he had completed his task, he grabs a cigarette out of the pack. He is unable to light it. Twenty-five years ago he would have been rock-steady and calm. Now he has the shakes.

Leaving Ben at the house, Mickey goes to notify the guards. He drives in the rain with his head out the window because his wipers are broken, a wet limp cigarette hanging from his mouth. He is vaguely aware that Ben's nephew from the North is in the car with him. At the boy's prompting, he drops him off at his grandmother's house, and proceeds to the guards to report a 'mysterious death'.

Later, back home, Mickey Carr experiences a sense of self-worthlessness bordering on despair. He considers the futility of his existence. Yesterday's assassination, the killing of Kennedy, now seems pointless. During 'the Troubles' it was different. There was a reason for it then, when Mickey Go-Carr was a valuable asset held in high esteem by the flying columns of the IRA.

But now? 'The Troubles' are long over, and things are different. Kennedy has been gone for 25 years – gone with 'the Troubles'. Donnelly is not the same as Kennedy. Donnelly IS? No, Donnelly WAS. Donnelly is gone too, and Mickey has no buyer for his pigs. Tinkering with bits of machines is also pointless. Nobody gives him things to actually fix; they just dump useless stuff on his front yard. No one has use for him anymore. He sits smoking Woodbines and drinking porter until the darkness of the night envelopes him in sympathy with the darkness of his spirit.

What will Mickey Motor Carr do now?

CHAPTER TWENTY-SIX

MICKEY CARR SHEDS A TEAR

"Hello, Mickey."

"Murf. Three times since…"

"…since the incident."

"Always at sunset."

"A preferred meeting time. Wouldn't you say, Mickey?"

Inspector Murphy is standing at the open doorway of Mickey's abode. He makes his way inside, uninvited. Mickey's cluttered house contains two rooms – this front room that opens to the outside, and another intended as a bedroom. Who knows what Mickey uses the bedroom for; he clearly sleeps in the front room, which also serves as kitchen, living room and workroom. Murf sits on a high stool by the workbench.

Mickey is sitting on a couch. It is impossible to say what exactly he is sitting on. There are items of clothing and machine parts on it, and more stuff under it and against it. Mickey is wedged in the midst of it all. He stares across the darkening room through the open door at the fading daylight outside. It is already dark inside the dim room.

Mickey has a smouldering cigarette in his mouth, and the floor at his feet is littered with empty cigarette packets. He does not respond to Murf's question. Both men sit there in silence, listening to the other's rhythmic breathing. After a few minutes Mickey's cigarette burns down. He pulls it out of his mouth and stubs it out on the wooden floor. He reaches for the pack of Woodbines beside him, draws out another cigarette, and places it between his lips. He strikes a match using his thumbnail. The flaring match illuminates his face, and the action brings him to life. He addresses Murf. "Are you gonna arrest me?"

Murf remains silent, making no response.

Mickey continues to smoke. The light continues to fade. The tobacco is loose and the cigarette smoulders quickly. In ten minutes or so, Mickey is ready for another Woodbine. He draws another cigarette from the pack. This time he taps the cigarette to settle the tobacco, and drops the now empty pack at his feet. He repeats his lighting routine. Then he focuses on Murf.

"Murf," he says, and his eyes drift back to the light in the doorway. "I know how you do it…" a pause for a drag, and he continues, "…the thing with the dots. You gather information like dots, and you put them together to make a picture. It's the same with me; that's what I do; I make a picture in my head. That's how I see in the dark – inside my head I see the picture. I can draw the picture in my head with one blink of the eye, and then I see it inside even with my eyes shut." He pauses for a drag. "I can do the same thing by touch. I can touch something in the dark, and I can see it inside like a picture. That's how I could take a gun apart and put it back together again, even in the dark. I am looking at the picture in my head. I can see the picture by feeling the gun in the dark." Mickey takes the cigarette out of his mouth, holds it between his thumb and index finger, and leans forward. "Do you ever get it backwards, Murf? Like, the black dots and the white dots mixed up?"

Murf responds, "All the time. Sometimes it is black dots on white, and sometimes it is white dots on black – like a negative. But it doesn't matter; the picture is just as clear either way."

"A negative? Is that what it is? My pictures are negatives too, and it doesn't bother me neither."

"In what way are your pictures 'negatives', Mickey?"

"Well, when I take something apart – say, a gun – and I put it back together from the picture in my head, it's always pointing the other way." Mickey has finished his cigarette. "I'm out of fags."

Murf lobs a pack of 20 Woodbines to him. "I brought some for you."

"Just the 20?"

Murf lobs over another pack, and another – five packs in all. Mickey pulls out a cigarette from a fresh pack, and lights it.

Mickey, still perched at the edge of his seat, looks at Murf and says, "You have a picture from the other night! The night...." and draws a circle with the glowing cigarette. "Right?" He does not wait for a response. "I have a picture too. It's the same picture. Isn't it, Murf?" They sit in silence for a while. Then Mickey says, "I could kill you here and now, Murf."

Murf is unfazed. It is an observation, not a threat. Murf realises that Mickey, notwithstanding his dependence on cigarettes and porter, is still an efficient killer. It is a skill that was once admired and gave him status. But now it is unemployed and unrecognised. Mickey has no other admirable skill. His ability to take things apart and reassemble is viewed as an oddity. He is unable to fix a broken item unless it is first introduced to him in its working state; only then can he reassemble it to the template in his mind.

Mickey sits back against the back of the couch and lowers his head. The cigarette smoke drifts from his mouth up to the top of his head, and disappears into the darkness. There is silence until his cigarette burns down. He removes it from his mouth and, leaning forward, he stubs it out. "Well, aren't you gonna arrest me?" It was not a question.

Silent pause, then Murf says, "Well, Mickey, aren't you going to kill me?" And neither was that a question.

Mickey leans back again. With no cigarette glow to light his face, Murf cannot read him. "You know, Murf, they all think I'm an amadan."

"I don't."

"No, you don't, Murf. That's because you see pictures in your head – you and me both."

"Ben Muldoon? Does he think you're an amadan? And HE doesn't see any pictures."

Mickey is agitated at that. "No, Ben's my friend."

Murf pauses. After a moment, he asks, "What about Foxy?" Some minutes pass. Murf can tell from Mickey's breathing that he is wide awake.

Then Mickey says, "Sergeant Fox of the RIC would play handball with me at the back of the barracks. He protected me from the bigger boys that threw stones at me and called me names. He would let me sit there, hanging around the stables, when I had nowhere to go. Once or twice, when I did not go home, he let me sleep in the 'black hole'; he left the door open so that I could go when I please."

"What else did Sergeant Fox do?"

He pauses for a minute, then says, "He saved me." Mickey flips out another cigarette and asks, "What did he save me for?"

Murf isn't sure if Mickey is referring to Fox's motivation in saving him, or if he is lamenting his current situation. On reflection, probably both.

This time when Mickey strikes the match, Murf sees that his cheeks are wet. Mickey reaches forward and picks up an empty cigarette pack from the floor. He carefully restores its shape. Then he takes a fresh cigarette, rolls it on his cheeks, drying them, and places the tear-stained cigarette in the restored pack as in a sacred ritual. Then he carefully places this pack, with its sole cigarette, in his inside jacket pocket. "My last cigarette," he says.

Murf corrects him. "You still have 100 cigarettes, Mickey."

Mickey, in turn, corrects Murf. "I have 97. But this one…" patting his pocket gently, "…is my last one." Some minutes pass. Then Mickey says, "I will smoke my last cigarette with Sergeant Fox."

"Shall I tell him so?"

"No. First I'll smoke the other 96. Then I'll see him."

"When?"

"How long it takes me to smoke 96 fags." Mickey's cigarette burns down. The smouldering cigarette generates a small sphere of light around his face. He stubs it out. It is now totally dark. Some more minutes pass. Then Mickey says, "Tell Ben he can have the banbhs back; …and the two fat pigs.'' Mickey's breathing changes to a relaxed rhythm.

Murf says, "I'll do that, Mickey." He waits for a response. There is none. Murf gets up to leave. "Is there anything else I can do for you, Mickey?"

"I need a pencil. Do you have a pencil, Murf?"

Murf plucks the pencil from the notepad in his breast pocket, and passes it in the darkness to the sound of Mickey's breathing. Mickey takes it from him unerringly. Murf hears Mickey shift position on the couch, and then the sound of relaxed breathing. Mickey is asleep.

Murf navigates his exit from the dismal house by the sound of his feet. The hollow sound of bare uncluttered boards from the couch to the door guides his feet along the narrow dark pathway through the clutter. Outside, the low cloud bank screens any light from the sky. No moonlight, no starlight. Only the crunch of gravel underfoot directs his progress to the bottom of Mickey's lane. There, he collides gently with his black Ford Prefect 10hp car. The roar of the starting engine and the lights of the departing car are an irreverent intrusion on the silent sombre night.

CHAPTER TWENTY-SEVEN

MURF VISITS THE RUC

Sunday 17 August 1947

Murf is at Lough Erne in County Fermanagh. Sir Robert Norton is the newly-appointed chief constable for Northern Ireland. In Northern Ireland it is termed 'inspector general'. Sir Robert has just concluded a three-day conference with his district inspectors and higher-ranking officers at a secluded private estate at the lough.

In Northern Ireland nothing is scheduled for a Sunday. Except for essential services, it is a day reserved for worship and for rest. Most of the D.I.s have returned to their districts. Several are taking in a few hours fishing at the lough. Norton never takes time off. Even on a 'day off' Norton is as busy as ever. Recognising this need, the RUC Station in Enniskillen has provided a room and staff at his disposal while away from RUC Headquarters in Belfast.

Robert 'Nobbie' Norton had served in the Great War and, at its conclusion, with the RIC in Clonmel until 1922. He then transferred to the British Colonial Police, serving in Kenya. He rose quickly in the ranks and successfully promoted the use of canine units in his overseas operations. Terence (Tracy) Prior, who was recruited by Norton into the Colonial Police, followed him to every posting, acting as his chief dog handler. In Ulster, Norton has appointed Prior in charge of forming a K-9 unit – not a division in itself, but a unit to serve the entire policing region. To date, there has been no public announcement on the formation of the new K-9 unit, and no mention of Terence Prior's appointment.

Nevertheless, the rank and file will learn of it tomorrow. The formation of the K-9 unit was one of the key subjects of the conference. Terence Prior holds the rank of lieutenant-colonel equating to the police rank of district inspector in the RUC. He will assume his position officially on 01 September 1947. Prior made a brief appearance at the conference on Friday.

K-9 units in the U.K. are still underutilised, chiefly because of poor understanding of a dog's ability, and hence inappropriate training. Prior explained, with practical examples, how properly-trained dogs and properly-trained handlers can detect bombs, disarm an assailant and be used for crowd control. Norton hopes that a successful K-9 unit in Ulster will demonstrate to U.K. police forces how a K-9 unit could be employed to great advantage in a variety of policing situations.

"Excuse me, sir."

"Yes, McSorley. What is it?"

"An Inspector John Patrick Murphy, requesting to see you, sir. He says he is expected. He didn't show me his identification, just a verbal message – 'Practical Application of Interview Techniques' – if that makes any sense to you, sir."

Norton, who seemed irritated by the interruption, immediately brightens up. Drawing out his watch, he snaps it open, saying to himself, "Is it that time already?"

Sergeant McSorley coughs. "Sir?"

"Show him in, McSorley. Show him in. By George, if it isn't Murf himself."

McSorley raises an eyebrow at the unfamiliar term 'Murf himself', but Norton says it loud enough to be heard in the outer office in the hope that Murf would hear his name rendered in West of Ireland idiom. McSorley attempts formal correctness of admittance and introduction, but Murf blusters past him, placing his briefcase at the door, and is met halfway by Norton, both of whom engage in handshaking and backslapping.

McSorley commences, "Inspector Murphy, you may..." It seems redundant to say "enter". He continues, "Inspector-General..." but this is rendered redundant also. So McSorley completes the introduction, inaudibly, to thin air as he exits, "...Inspector Murf himself."

The inspector general's temporary office, utilised by him for the duration of the conference, is a small carpeted office with a desk, a phone, a typewriter and a window. But no view of Lough Erne from here. Tomorrow he would be at his spacious and impressive office at RUC Headquarters in Waring Street, Belfast. For now, this small quiet office in Enniskillen affords him an opportunity to put his conference notes in order without distraction.

Norton had aged well. He is fit at 55, one year younger than David Fox, and has the tanned features of one who served in the sun. He is dressed in a two-piece blue lounge suit with a red-and-blue paisley ascot cravat and ox-blood brogues – it is his day off. Murf is modestly dressed in navy-blue jacket over grey slacks and black shoes. Murf detects the faint aroma of Dutch pipe tobacco in the room. Dutch tobacco, Murf reflects. Now that's an exotic choice in a time of austere rationing. It's also a departure from Norbert's usual strict no-smoking policy. Even inspector generals, it seems, loosen up the rules when away from the city.

"Murf. Nice to see you again! It's only been a week since Manchester."

"That it is, Nobbie."

"So, Murf. What is so important that you couldn't do it over the phone?"

"It's a homicide…"

"You didn't come up here for my help with a homicide…"

Murf raises his palm to denote 'silence', and continues, "…with possible links to multiple 'situations of interest'. I have arranged the dots, and formed a picture – no proof yet, mind you – a picture with a piece missing."

Norton returns to his desk. "So who/what is the missing piece, Murf? Someone I know?"

Murf goes back to the doorway to retrieve the briefcase. Norton gestures in invitation to the guest chair. Murf is speaking as he approaches the chair. "A man and a dog – actually a brindled mastiff."

"That's… are we talking about Prior here, the head of Ulster's new K-9 unit?"

"Good," thinks Murf, "you just confirmed that Prior is here in Ireland." Aloud he continues, as he opens his briefcase and draws out a manila folder. "Nobbie. There is something you should see."

Norbert is clearly unhappy with the portentous tone. "Murf, I'm not too sure where this is going. Tread carefully."

Rather than speak, Murf slides one piece of paper after another from the folder onto the desk. Norbert speed-reads. It documents the history of Prior's activities during the Irish War of Independence, 'the Troubles'. It starts with Prior's introduction to the IRA by the Connolly Club in London, and concludes with the North Cork Flying Column 22.

"This is accurate? True?"

"All confirmed, Nobbie. But there is more."

Norbert slumps in the chair. "How much more?"

"Prior was introduced to the IRA from the Communist Party in London. He, with a member of the North Cork Flying Column 22, was an active assassin against the Crown and against the pro-British landed gentry from 1919 to 1922.

He left the IRA after an engagement at Ballycorry RIC Barracks involving the RIC, the auxiliaries, the anti-treaty IRA and the National Army, all on the 12 February 1922. He disappeared after that, and..."

"St Patrick's Day."

"No, Nobbie. 12 February is not St Patrick's Day."

"On St Patrick's Day, 17 March 1922, Terence Prior was accepted into the Colonial Police..."

"...and he hasn't been heard of again until..."

"...until he turns up in Northern Ireland..."

"...until he turns up in North Mayo."

"North Mayo? No. That couldn't be right, Murf."

"At Ballycorry RIC Barracks, to be exact."

"And you are sure of this?"

"No, Nobbie. I am not sure yet, but there are strong pointers to him. But bear with me. I am still putting my dots in order to form a rational picture consistent with facts."

"To form a picture? Or maybe fail to form a picture."

"Exactly. Just assist me in filling in the missing dots. It will take a few minutes. And if the picture does not fit, well..."

"Very well."

"Consider this. Prior was an active communist during 'the Troubles'. He wrought havoc on perceived capitalists, destroying property and engaging in assassinations."

"Just like other members of an IRA flying column."

"But an ENGLISH member of the IRA, Nobbie. Irish nationalism couldn't have been his cause. Now, here's part of the missing picture. Did he suddenly change his stripes on St Patrick's Day 1922?"

Norton stiffens in his chair. His eyes display rapid computations at work in his head. His silence is an indication to Murf to remain quiet and still. Norton taps his desktop with a pencil, a slow beat alternating from the dull eraser tip to the sharp pencil point over and over. A minute passes, two minutes – tap-tap, tap-tap. He stops. His eyes come back from pensive inward gaze to a sharp presence. "Sergeant! Sergeant McSorley!"

McSorley enters at the first syllable, probably waiting at his master's door ready to do his bidding. "Sir."

"McSorley, get me an outside line." He taps the black phone with his pencil to indicate the phone he intends to use. "I'll be making a trunk call."

"Sir, if you give me the number, I would be happy to place the call..."

"Sergeant, do you understand my request?"

McSorley stiffens to attention. "Yes, sir."

"Then execute it."

"Yes, sir." McSorley leaves the room red-faced. He glowers at Murf as he shuts the door. Norton's change in temper could only have been initiated by the Free State policeman, 'Murf himself'. McSorley wonders what has set Norton off.

Norton extracts a writing pad from the top drawer, and commences his pencil-tapping again. His phone rings. He lifts the receiver. "Thank you, Sergeant."

Murf has not moved or spoken since the first pencil tap. Norton spins the handle at the back of the phone to alert the operator. Murf listens to Norton's side of the communication, hoping that he can construe the other side from the context.

"Operator? Priority Red Five.

"Yes, this is the RUC! Priority Red Five. Trunk call to England – Hounslow two-double-two.

(Pause) "No. I will NOT wait! Do you understand 'Priority Red Five'?"

Tap-tap, tap-tap. Murf hears the buzz-buzz of the phone

connecting, and the click when Hounslow 222 picks up. No voice, no 'hello'. Just a click, then silence.

Norton speaks. "Who killed Cock Robin?"

Now the sound of a further connection, buzz-buzz, click, silence.

Norton: "Who killed Cock Robin?"

A voice, too faint to distinguish.

Norton: "Mother Hubbard here. I wish to speak to the Piper's Son."

Another voice this time.

Norton: "Bow-wow"

Murf suppresses a smile. The Brits are to be admired. They know how to communicate in code – unless Norton has connected to a children's nursery school.

"Piper's Son, I need you to cast your mind back – and it's completely off the record, you understand. You remember the Humberland case?

(Pause) "Lord Humberland, yes. You felt at the time that we executed the wrong man.

(Pause) "Desmond Nzeki. Why were you so sure that Nzeki wasn't our man?"

(Pause) Norton repeats back the information to confirm. "The evidence was assembled too quickly. Nzeki's alibi was suppressed – regarded as unreliable?

(Pause) "Piper's Son, your gut instinct. What do you think?

(Pause) "Evidence may have been planted?

(Pause) "And there is the other case? What case?

(Pause) "But that case was dropped. 'Accidental death' – the high commissioner's driver stepped on a nail and died from blood poisoning.

(Pause) "Are you suggesting that a contaminated nail was deliberately placed in the driver's shoe, but in error? That it was intended for the high commissioner?

(Pause) "Okay, so the valet gave both sets of shoes to the scullery maids for polishing. Cut to the chase – what do the two cases tell you? You are suggesting that they have some connection.

(Pause) "And you think it may have been within the police? Who do you suspect?

(Pause) "There is no proof, I understand...exhaustive analysis of the evidence...come up clean...just a bad feeling.

(Pause) "I don't care about that; give me the names of the officers.

(Pause) "Only three names in common to both cases.

(Pause) "In alphabetical order, okay. Give them to me."

Murf strains to watch Norbert write.

Campbell
Pratt

An audible sigh of relief from Norton, and "Confirm 'Pratt'.

(Pause) "P-R-A-T-T – At first I thought I heard you say 'Prior'."

The point of the pencil snaps off. "That's the third name? Confirm!

(Pause) "P-R-I-O-R? And first name?

(Pause) "Thank you, Piper's Son. That's all for now. Mother Hubbard out."

He hangs up the receiver.

Murf opens his mouth to speak. Norton raises a finger to silence him. Tap-tap, tap-tap...

At length Norton speaks, primarily to himself, but quite audibly for Murf's benefit. "There were more. All those years, there must have been more. And no evidence to nail

Prior."

The finger of silence again, and a resumption of the tap-tapping. Murf waits expectantly for some disclosure. Clearly Norton's policeman's mind is sifting through information. Norton stops tapping. "We need to detain Prior while we investigate. As it is, we have no substance, just conjecture and speculation. No grounds for an arrest. Unless, unless..."

Norton spins his chair to reach for his conference notes, his supporting data on the advantages of employing an effective K-9 unit. He flips through the papers, extracts a section held together by a bulldog paper grip. "The timeline. Now let me see...

"Look at this, Murf. Prior favours German-trained dogs. In January 1938, he contracted for, and expensed, a black-brindled English mastiff. I, myself, authorised the payment. See, a copy of the contract, with the address and location of the kennel."

Murf, peering at the paper, exhales a whistle and exclaims "Germany."

Norton turns to the accompanying page. "See, Murf, Prior went to Gibraltar to pick up the dog in Spain in December 1939."

"A neutral go-between due to the state of war between Britain and Germany..."

"But the principals to the contract, notwithstanding the location of the transaction, were German..."

"..and during wartime."

"Trading with the Enemy, an offence as per the Trading with the Enemy Act passed on 05 September 1939." Norton slaps the file loudly on the desk in an expression of accomplishment. "McSorley!"

McSorley enters immediately. Norton addresses him. "McSorley, get me a pot of tea and some biscuits. Bring three cups. I want you in on this meeting."

McSorley coughs, and remains standing. "Sir."

"Yes, Sergeant?"

"There is no tea left. And no sugar. And no biscuits. The station has exhausted all the available coupons."

"Hold on," interjects Murf. He fishes into his briefcase and extracts two sachets of folded paper. "Tea and sugar from my rations."

McSorley goes off to communicate Norton's request for a pot of tea. Both Norton and McSorley know full well that Murf, from the Free State, has no ration book.

Norton smiles at Murf and jokes, "Lucky for you I'm not a 'water-rat'. I would arrest you for tendering contraband."

Murf is not finished fishing in his briefcase. From amongst his pens he extricates two small slender bottles of Power's 'Three Swallows'. Three flying swallows, displayed on the neckband of each bottle, are a subtle indication of the liquid capacity of each slender bottle.

McSorley returns just then, in time for Norton's added request, "...and two glasses."

McSorley, observing the whiskey, raises an eyebrow at the request for 'two glasses', which is noticed by Norton.

"Sergeant, Inspector Murphy and I are off duty today. You, on the other hand, are on duty. Two glasses."

A few minutes later the three police officers – Sir Robert Norton, Inspector-General of the Northern Ireland Royal Ulster Constabulary; his junior assistant and 'wheelman', Sergeant Alex McSorley; and Garda Inspector John Patrick Murphy – are seated around Norton's desk. They are refreshed and fortified for a meeting session by a pot of tea (with extra sugar) and Powers whiskey. The desk is crowded now. In addition to the usual telephone and typewriter, there is the tea tray with teapot, sugar and milk, cups and glasses, two briefcases, and a number of pages fanned in orderly array.

Norton extracts a page of his official letterhead from his briefcase. He selects two paper onionskins and two carbon sheets from the desk, places them in the typewriter, and spins the roller to align the paper to his satisfaction. He types rapidly while speaking to McSorley. "McSorley, I have an assignment for you. A delicate assignment, to be conducted in strictest secrecy. You will not tell anyone, not even your closest colleagues. No hint of where you are going, or why you are going. Nothing."

"I understand, sir." McSorley is not surprised at this request. When working for the inspector general, undertakings of this nature are not unusual.

Norton whips the paper out of the typewriter, signs the bottom of the page, replaces the carbon paper in the top drawer and places the onionskins in his briefcase. He takes an envelope and addresses it by hand, inserts the newly-typed letter, seals the envelope and hands it to McSorley. "McSorley, you'll take my car, drive to Aldergrove. From the time you step from this office, until you complete the assignment, you will speak to no one; you will go directly to Aldergrove – no stopping for a clean shirt or for a cup of tea. Deliver this letter to the senior officer-in-charge of the RAF. You'll wait for his answer. His answer – he will provide you with a letter authorising your passage to, and return from, your location of investigation. Passage will be provided to you, either by army transport from Aldergrove, or by RAF, whichever is the first available."

Norton waits for this to sink in. "Now, McSorley, here is an address." While Norton is talking, he is copying an address from a document in his file, writing it on a sheet of notepaper.

McSorley reads the address. "That's Germany, sir. And isn't that a dog kennel?"

"Yes, it is. It is a facility that trains dogs for military and police work. And it's not just in Germany, Sergeant. That's the British Zone of Allied Occupied Germany, currently under martial law. You will be cooperating with the British military police jointly with the German Hannover police. You understand that you have no jurisdiction there. But you will find excellent cooperation from the German police."

"What's the nature of the case, sir?" His question infers the obvious. What investigation in Allied Occupied Germany requires the cooperation of the RUC, British military, German police, and unavoidably the Foreign Office?

"Trading with the Enemy." Norton continues, "Don't worry about the protocols. Just do your police work. I'll arrange all authorisations so that you will be escorted upon your arrival in Germany until you are boarded on your return flight."

"Begging your pardon, sir. Are you sure this address still exists in Germany? It may have been destroyed in the war."

Norton glances at correspondence papers held together by the bulldog grip, in particular, the paper from which he copied the address. It is the response to an inquiry into obtaining trained police dogs, dated March 1947. The letter expresses regret that English mastiffs are no longer available, and to consider Alsatian/German shepherd (*Deustcher Schaferhund*) or Doberman Pinscher. "It is a business address, a business that has been in operation for thirty years and is currently thriving. I trust that their German efficiency extends to quality record-keeping."

McSorley glances around expecting to see a file marked

'Secret', or at least a brown envelope with instructions. There is none.

Norton continues, "You will not write your report until you return to Belfast. However, you will communicate to me as soon as you have information of substance. You will contact me by telephone with the message 'I have located the dog's collar'."

McSorley repeats the code. "I have located the dog's collar."

"I have not told you the name of the person under investigation. Have I, Sergeant?"

"No, sir."

"You should find his name numerous times going back to 1919. He has had legitimate dealings with this kennel since then. Your investigation is to ascertain what, if any, dealings were conducted in wartime."

McSorley is uneasy, apprehensive at where this is leading. He heard something about German-trained dogs at the conference on Friday, the section on the history and development of dogs serving in the military and police. He mouths a name simultaneously with Norton's pronouncement "Terence Prior."

"Terence Prior, also known as Tracy Prior, currently lieutenant-colonel in the RUC. Watch for the spelling. It is 'Terence' in his records, but it sometimes appears with two 'R's – T-E-R-R-E-N-C-E"

"Yes, sir. I am to check the records at the kennel for possible 'Trading with the Enemy' by Terence Prior under this or other name, or any persons engaged by/with Terence Prior, in contravention of the 'Trading with the Enemy Act of 1939'." And then asks, "Oh, sir? How will you get to Belfast? I will have your car."

"Sergeant, as of now, concern yourself solely with the

assignment. That's all. I expect a communication on your progress within 24 hours. Good luck."

There is silence for a moment after McSorley leaves. Then Murf and Norbert speak simultaneously.

"Sorry, Nobbie. You go first."

"No, Murf. You go first. After all, you came here to request something, did you not?"

"Nobbie, I need to collect evidence to nail Prior. I don't have anything solid yet."

"Both you and I, Murf."

"Could I have your cooperation to examine Prior's flat, his car, his clothing, personal belongings?"

"Yes, of course. Actually, Murf, I was about to ask you for help in our case too." Norton lifts the whiskey glass and drains the last few drops. "Murf, the case against Prior is weak. A charge of Trading with the Enemy may buy us time, but not much else. I know Prior. If he gets wind that we are investigating him for past crimes... Well, best to keep him locked up while we assemble sufficient evidence. I am not optimistic about this, Murf, so could I have your cooperation in interviewing Prior? I could use those highly-touted procedures that were presented at the recent police conference in Manchester – 'Practical Application of Interview Techniques'?"

"Nobbie, you have a deal." And they shake hands.

Murf is packing his notes into his briefcase. "Nobbie, one last thing, if you don't mind. I see that you have pictures of K-9 units with your conference presentation notes. Do you have a picture of an English mastiff?"

"Actually, I have a few. Would you like one? Here's one of Prior's current favourite dog, 'Rex Secundus'. You can take it." Murf places the picture of the dog in his briefcase. "You're on your way back to Mayo now, I suppose. Good luck!”

"To Donegal, actually. But thanks.”

Norton walks him to the door, and Murf departs. Norton returns to his desk. He appears to have aged in the past hour. He vainly attempts to extract another drop of whiskey from the empty glass.

CHAPTER TWENTY-EIGHT

AT BELL TRA BEACH

It is Monday 18 August 1947 – thirteen days since the incident with Black Donnelly. This is how I, Murty Muldoon, recall the meeting with Inspector Murphy at Bell Tra Beach.

There are rocks below the cliffs at Bell Tra Beach. My father had taken me to the beach to collect dulse. He has no love for the beach, or the sea. He remains at the inn overlooking the strand; I can see him watching me through the window in the lounge. The tide is coming in, almost halfway now. I watch the progress so as not to get cut off on the rocks.

"Murty Muldoon?" A question rendered in a Mayo accent.

I knew a man would come. Subconsciously, I was awaiting his arrival. I saw him make his way from the inn parking lot, across the strand, and down to the rocks. He is not dressed for the beach – wearing laced shoes. "Yes? You're a guard."

"How did you figure that?"

"Sooner or later you would be coming." A brief silence and, "Why do you guards hold your mouth tight just before you speak? Do you need to think first? And why are you wearing shoes on the rocks? You'll slide on the wrack (brown coarse seaweed) and fall and break your skull."

"You can call me 'Murf'. Everyone does."

Silence, as Murf removes his shoes. "No school today?"

"One more week of holidays. And there would not be any school today anyway, because of the weather."

"Why? The weather is perfect."

"That's why – because the weather is perfect. This may be the last chance to win and save the hay – the farms need the children to help."

"But you're not working on a farm, are you?"

"I don't work at a farm anymore. I'm gathering dillisk."

"I thought you called it 'dulse' in Donegal?"

"I call it 'dillisk'. My Dad calls it 'dillisk'. He's from Mayo, like you are. Do you know him?"

"No. We are not the same age. I met him for the first time back there in the inn. Look, there he comes now walking across the strand to join us. But I know your grandfather, 'Master Muldoon'. He taught at Ballycorry National School. Your uncle John teaches there now."

"Yes, I know. Ballycorry is where..." I cannot say 'Black Donnelly's' so Murf finishes my sentence.

"...where the old RIC barracks is."

Murf slings his shoes around his neck by the laces. "I'd like to show you some things in my folder. Would you mind walking back to the inn with me?"

"Sure. There is no dillisk here anyway. It's farther out, and the tide has covered it."

"...and you don't have a basket," Murf adds.

As the three of us walk back across the beach, Murf remarks that there are donkey droppings in the sand. "I see you had a donkey here yesterday," he says, pronouncing it 'dângkee'.

"No, it wasn't a donkey." (Pronounced 'dungkee' – to rhyme with 'monkey'.)

Murf smiles and rhymes. "You say 'dungkee' and I say 'dângkee'; You say 'mungkee' and I say 'mângkee'".

I correct him. "It was a shaggy-haired Shetland pony. They bring it here on Sundays – 6d a ride." Murf is easy to talk to. "Do you know something funny, Murf? Maggie Molloy."

"Maggie Molloy is funny?"

"She's the maid who cleans house for us. She swears that it is a big dog with hooves."

"What? The Shetland pony is a big dog with hooves? And why would she think that? Do you know why?"

"Well, how could she know? Sure she had never seen a

Shetland pony before. But she has seen lots of dogs."

We reach the inn. Murf checks that his feet are dry and puts his shoes back on. His Ford Prefect is parked near the entrance. He fetches a folder out of the boot, and we enter the inn. The lounge is quiet, unlike the previous day. Murf places the folder on a small table by the window, and we sit around it. There are no customers in the lounge. Other than the three of us, the only other person here is the barman, and he is busy clearing empties and rearranging his spirit bottles after the weekend activity.

Opening the folder, Murf says, "Donnelly – 'Daniel E' actually – full name is Daniel Edward Kennedy. Sadly, he was murdered. We have two suspects. You may hear it on the news. I wanted to give you some advance warning. I believe you have the right to know. Here is a folder with some notes of explanation for you. And, if you like, I will keep you informed."

I agree to that. Murf pulls out a photograph from the folder. It is a picture of a military dog handler and his dog. The dog is huge. Its coat is black with shading. The nose is not long and pointed as a dog's nose ought to be. It is crushed in like a snout and there are two lighter spots over his dark eyes.

"This is an English mastiff, the largest dog in the world by body mass. One hundred years ago, every big house in the country had one as a guard dog. Then these big mastiffs declined in popularity. Today, there are very few. Take a look at its nose, Murty. See how short it is. Well, because of its short nose, it breathes in a snorting manner when exerted."

"Like a pig."

"Yes. Very much like a pig. Look at its legs. They are short for a dog of this size. Compare it to another big dog, say, an Irish wolfhound. An Irish wolfhound, with long legs, is much taller than a mastiff, but it has less body mass. See also the girth of the mastiff; well you could easily mistake it..."

"...for a pig."

"But it does not possess hooves or crubeens. This one here is trained to sniff out bombs and mines. For example, carbide cart lamps might excite him to investigate."

"What I saw was a PIG!"

"I believe what you say. But I can only convey to you what is supported by evidence. Remember Maggie Molloy. You told me she knows dogs. Yet she sees a Shetland pony as canine, rather than equine."

I study the picture more closely and attempt to superimpose the image in the picture over the image in my memory. "Is that the murderer? The soldier with the dog?"

"One of them. He's a British colonial policeman, actually. You may keep the picture. It's for you."

"Do you think I saw a dog like this?"

"No, Murty. Not a dog LIKE this. This IS the dog you saw. There is not another one in all Ireland like this."

"Why did this happen, Murf? The awful thing to Donnelly. Why do things like this happen?"

"Murty, there is a troubled history behind..."

"Did you say 'Troubles'? I should have known. Donnelly was in 'the Troubles'. That's why it happened."

"Well, you could say that."

"That's why no one speaks about 'the Troubles'. There were killings back then, and talking about it brings back the past. It might bring killing back again."

"Ah, yes. It's best not to dig up the troubles of the past."

"Will I have to go to court – as a witness or anything?"

"No."

"Murf, I'd like to know what happens. I mean, how it all

comes together – how it all ends.”

“Murty, for you It HAS ended. The phantom is exorcised. It’s gone – it was never really there. Everything is okay now.”

“But promise to tell me everything.”

“I promise. But later, when it is all over.”

My father, sitting next to us, speaks with Murf for a while. Then Murf rises, fastens his shoes which were still undone, and says, “I’ll keep in touch.” And he is gone.

My father leans over, takes the folder, and says, “Let’s go home.”

For the first time in two weeks I feel light again, like a weight has been lifted off my back. I can stand erect again without feeling a knot in my stomach. “Murf is right. It’s over. Let’s go home.”

“Can I have a lemonade first?”

CHAPTER TWENTY-NINE

MARY FOX REPORTS ON RIVERSTOWN

18 August 1947

"Oh, Murf, you won't believe it. It was wonderful." Mary Fox is talking to Murf by telephone. "I have to tell you all about it. Why don't you come over? Foxy won't mind if you take time off – actually, he says that he doesn't know where you are half the time. Come right over. I'm making sandwiches."

Murf is not in his office at the garda station. He had just arrived in Killbawn, having driven two-and-a-half hours from Donegal, and is considering some pub grub. He needs to check some things with Mary before reporting to District Officer Fox back at the station. He foregoes the pub grub in the hope that Mary's sandwiches will be more satisfying.

A short time later, Murf enters the Fox house. He is still dressed in his 'visit the RUC' clothes – light-grey trousers, white shirt with burgundy tie and blue jacket, over black laced shoes – a step up from the mismatch he usually wears. He is feeling peckish, and is pleased to see that Mary has laid out afternoon tea, complete with miniature sandwiches cut diagonally into triangles with the crusts removed.

He notices that Mary is dressed in the 'New Look' – a slate-blue fitted short-sleeved jacket with a peplum and full skirt to mid-calf; rounded shoulders replacing the still-popular padded shoulders; the neckline modestly low – just enough to warrant a string of pearls; white medium-heeled shoes with a small hole at the toe. And clearly part of the ensemble, a pair of white gloves and matching handbag on display on the chair next to her. Christian Dior must have been at Riverstown too.

"Hello, Mary. I see that Riverstown has rubbed off on you."

"Nonsense, Murf. This is nothing, really. I have a new Royal Doulton gold-blue-and-white tea set and I want to see how it shows off. There is one just like it in Riverstown."

"So you went to afternoon tea at Riverstown?"

"Well, let me tell you…" pouring tea, "…we went with the Fitzpatricks – but you know that – and we met Lord Kilmacneil, who is Bertha's brother – but you know that too."

Murf thinks to himself, "Last week it was 'Mrs. Fitz; today it is 'Bertha'."

"Well, Lord Kilmacneil knows EVERYONE and he got us in to EVERYWHERE. Did you know that Riverstown Stud is restored? It is now part of the Carrickmore Syndicate; they have breeding operations in Tipperary, in Kentucky and in Australia. The Kennedys – that's Donal and his nephew James – are shareholders. The Kennedys manage the Riverstown stud. And do you know that they are training not one but TWO stallions for the King? No, that's not quite right – it's for Queen Elizabeth; she's the one who's REALLY into horses."

"So how is the Kennedy family coping with all the work?"

"Oh, there are a number of stud farms and training stables in Cork and Tipperary, and in County Down too; and they are all working in this together – oh, I don't know – whatever horsey people do to cooperate. But you know, Murf," pausing to bite elegantly on a cucumber sandwich, "there is one sad note."

"What's that, Mary?" biting a sandwich as daintily as he could rather than popping it whole into his mouth.

"Well..." a sip of tea and a long sigh, "Captain Daniel Edward Kennedy was to take over the farm in 1919, but he never returned from the Great War. It's the strangest thing. They have pictures of him on the mantelpiece. The most recent one was a photograph taken on Armistice Day, 11 November 1918, in France, just before he was to return home. He had been through the whole war uninjured – except for a broken nose, which you can see in his picture. And then… he just disappears. He was expected to report to RIF HQ – that's Royal Irish Fusiliers Headquarters, Murf – in Armagh, but he failed to show. Not a word of him ever since."

"What does Foxy think of all this…?"

"Oh, Foxy has no interest in the Riverstown County people. He enjoyed the horses, and then went to visit his family. And Fitz went off to view the prize livestock. Only Bertha and I went to Riverstown for afternoon tea."

"Didn't you tell Foxy any of this – Captain Kennedy and all that?"

"Well, yes, all of it. However, he didn't say a thing. He was quiet throughout. As I say, it did not appear to interest him. Foxy doesn't even know about the new tea set."

Prudently, Murf takes Mary's cup and saucer from her, and moves the delicate plate away from her elbow, and places a picture flat on the table. Mary looks at it and, had she been holding her cup and saucer, she most certainly would have dropped them.

"Lord have mercy!" she exclaims. "Murf, that's the exact picture the Kennedys have on the mantelpiece, the one of Captain Daniel – the one of him with his broken nose. Why on earth do you have it?"

"Mary, and this is a sad state of affairs, I have reason to believe that this is the man who was found dead in Ballycorry last week."

"In the old RIC barracks? But isn't he... wasn't he 'Black Donnelly'?"

"I believe it was 'Daniel E' – not 'Donnelly' – 'Daniel E. Kennedy'." Murf slides a second picture to Mary. "This is a picture of the deceased, taken by the medical officer – just the face."

Mary notes the unmistakable broken nose.

"We also found a flat leather satchel which contained meritorious awards from the First World War. They have been sent to RIF Armagh for verification. Once confirmed, Foxy will be getting in touch with the Kennedy family to identify and claim the body."

"And Foxy knows all this?"

"Yes, Mary. Nevertheless, not with certainty. That's why he did not tell you. Foxy and I discussed the probability. I suggested that he should go to Riverstown, and to take you too, to gather information and to take you too."

"Murf, you used me to gather information?"

"Mary, it would be distressful to inform the family that a long-lost member was found – found murdered – and then discover that we are mistaken. We needed to be sure, to avoid unnecessary distress to the family. What you tell me confirms my premise. Thus, to the true identity of 'Donnelly', I had reached that conclusion weeks ago, even before the tragic incident of last week. I just needed to be certain."

"Before the tragedy? Could you have done anything – anything to have made a difference? I mean, could you have saved him from that terrible awful death?"

"I don't know. He was deeply troubled – a victim of the war. And there was no reason to expect his demise – not now, and not in a violent manner." Murf could have said that an incident was possible, but unlikely due to the lapse of time. There were no indications of imminent menace to

Donnelly/Kennedy. Sadly, saying this might be upsetting to Mary Fox.

She sighs. "There are hundreds of victims of the war, living forlorn lives, existing in limbo between life and death…" Her voice fades and she loses interest in the dainty sandwiches, and in the Riverstown-like tea set. After a moment's silence, she comes to herself, and brushes imaginary crumbs off the tablecloth. "Foxy is due home soon."

"I know, Mary! I'll wait for him!"

CHAPTER THIRTY

THE CASE PROGRESSES

Monday 18 August 1947

District Officer Fox is standing in his office, looking out the window at the rain. He peers at the wet street below; he studies the drops sliding down the windowpane, and observes his own faint reflection in the glass. This must be the rainiest summer ever in Mayo. O'Reilly knocks and enters with his tea and the Irish Independent. It is 08:00 hours. The file is on the desk, 'Donnelly – Homicide'. The medical officer's report confirms the cause of death – concurring exactly with Murf's assessment. Who would claim the body? Who exactly is Captain Kennedy/Black Donnelly?

Fox had spent the weekend in Tipperary, where he made contact with the Kennedy family. There is no doubt that Daniel Edward Kennedy disappeared after the Great War, and Black Donnelly fits the description of the missing Kennedy, yet Fox is hesitant about informing the Kennedy family in Riverstown prematurely. What if he is wrong? After all, thirty years have passed since any member of the Kennedy family laid eyes on Daniel. Fox sighs. He knows that he is delaying the inevitable. He is obliged to notify the next of kin, who would then conduct an identification of the body. What a nasty revelation this will be to the Kennedys, to learn the ignominious history of the fair-haired boy in such shocking circumstances. Fox decides to wait for confirmation from RIF in Armagh, just a few days more. Then, Fox will have no excuse to delay any longer. The next of kin has the right to physically view the remains, but he will attempt to dissuade them in favour of their accepting the medical officer's report with the supporting photographs. The medical officer has chosen pictures showing the head only. He was sufficiently compassionate to clean the face and hair, and to avoid showing any damaged body. Daniel Edward's nose, a broken nose which had healed, gives a peculiar shape to his face, a unique unmistakable identifying feature. Will they be satisfied with the pictures provided by the medical officer? If agreeable, the body would be released to the next of kin in a closed coffin. Fox sighs again.

Fox goes to his desk, sits down, opens the right-hand drawer for his goldgrain biscuits, sips his tea and stares at the newspaper. O'Reilly had pencilled 'see page 2'. He doesn't want to look. He pushes the paper aside and stares at the floor, irritated at the biscuit crumbs that have lodged in the wood and in the carpeting. He needs Murf to be here. Murf is confident and always knows what is relevant. But Murf is off in Northern Ireland tying up his unconnected dots in the case.

Fox lifts the file. It is a light file. However, it weighs heavily in his hands. He turns the manila file-folder inside out and, reaching into the top drawer, he chooses a black fountain pen. He removes the cap slowly, and writes a new heading: 'Daniel Edward Kennedy'. He takes a rubber stamp from the left-hand drawer and stamps the file 'HOMICIDE'. He then works on entering information on the sheet inside. There are lots of pages torn from Murf's pocket-pad clipped in chronological order. He slowly transcribes this information to the required summary in the permanent file.

"Where is Murf?" he thinks aloud. Murf speculated that the case would be cleared up quickly. Is he making an arrest? Will there actually be an arrest? What did he mean that one suspect will probably give himself up because he has nowhere to go? That would be Mickey Carr. Surely there is not enough evidence to charge Carr – they need to place him at the scene at the time of the murder, not just afterwards on the following morning. Should he be brought in for questioning? He might confess. No. Murf counselled patience. So Carr was placed under observation to ensure that he does not leave the area – like Carr has anywhere to go. That's what Murf said. "Carr has nowhere to go." And why did Murf go to Northern Ireland? To ask about dogs? What have 'dogs' got to do with the case? Fox had told the Divisional HQ that the suspects were under surveillance and that an arrest was imminent. He couldn't see how; not yet. What will he tell O'Neill if he phones? He stands up because of the itch.

A knock at the office door. It's Garda O'Reilly. "Excuse me D.O., but Mickey Motor is outside. He insists on seeing you."

Fox thinks, "What does that amadan Mickey Motor want with me?" It takes a second for Fox's brain to register that amadan Mickey Motor and suspect Mickey Carr are one and the same. He immediately feels guilty. Everyone treats Mickey as an amadan, except Ben Muldoon. Fox always felt that Mickey was actually smart, except that his head worked in a strange way. He remembers too that he is in debt to Mickey. So is this the *'one suspect who will probably give himself up'*? He sighs in resignation to what he must dutifully perform and proceeds to conduct this professionally. "All right, O'Reilly. Send him in." He sits down and hopes that the meeting with Mickey will not be too difficult.

"Mickey Carr, sir." as O'Reilly leads him in.

Mickey looks awful. Then again, Mickey always looks awful. Mickey sits in the chair indicated and, with slow ceremony, takes a cigarette packet from his inside pocket. He removes the sole cigarette, a Will's Wild Woodbine, and lights it in his familiar manner by flicking his thumbnail on a red-headed safety match.

Fox shouts out the doorway, "O'Reilly, bring an ashtray!" And to Mickey Carr, "So Mickey. Have you something to tell me?"

"I wrote a note. It's for you."

Strange, thinks Fox. He never knew Mickey to write anything ever. He knows that Mickey is able to read a little, but with difficulty. Yet he always believed that he was unable to write. If Mickey wrote something, it must have been quite an effort, and must be very important to him. "Well, thank you, Mickey. May I have it?"

Mickey passes him a folded cigarette-pack cover. He sees 'Will's Wild Woodbine' printed on the outside. Fox unfolds the paper cover and reads –

TIMKIL JIꓘMIT

As Fox tries to make sense of the note, Mickey says, "It's all there. It's all you need to know."

Fox is at a loss as to what to say to Mickey. It is no joke, he could see that.

Then Mickey says, "I need to go to the lav."

"Oh sure, Mickey. The lavatory is down the hall, on the left, at the end."

Mickey leaves his cigarette smouldering in the ashtray. Fox notices the strange water stains on the cigarette; he wonders if Mickey had dropped it in the rain and had retrieved it. He rises from his chair, goes to the ashtray and stubs out the cigarette. Then he walks to the window. He looks out at the wet Mayo day. Fox speaks aloud to his reflection in the window. "Being unable to write, how could

Mickey put down his thoughts on paper? And what kind of thoughts does Mickey have? What is the meaning in the note? Murf would know – but Murf is not here."

He shows the note to his reflection in the window and instantly realises that it is a palindrome. Not just a palindrome, it is exactly the same in mirror-fashion. It must mean something – something important. So how does Mickey think? Fox remembers what Mickey said to the North Cork Brigade Captain many years ago –

'I kill – that's what I do best. Some things are meant to be killed. I kill what is meant to be killed. At the right time I too am meant to be killed.'

Fox continues conversing to his reflection. "That's how Mickey thinks." He reads the note again paraphrasing it. "'TIM KILLS' – no, that's not it...

"'TIME (to) KILL' – and the second part is backwards? – 'KILL(ing) TIME'"

Fox is jolted by a sudden flash of understanding. "Dear God! The lavatory! Reynolds! O'Reilly! Caldwell! The lavatory! Hurry!"

"The door's locked, sir!"

"Break it down! Smash the lock! Just get in there!"

Caldwell grabs the fire-axe from above the red bucket, and swings it at the lock. The lock smashes and the door flies open. On the floor lies Mickey, his throat cut, clearly dead; in the pool of blood is a meat knife.

Fox leans on the door jamb and says to Mickey "'*A time to kill, and a time to be killed*'. That's what you told me, Mickey! Isn't it?

"Reynolds! Get Division on the line. We need the County Medical Officer again!"

"D.O.! I know the procedure! I'll handle this!"

It is clear that Fox is taking this badly. Fox goes back to his office and continues to work on the report. He needs order and closure to this mess. He'd better have answers for Divisional HQ when they phone back.

At 16:50 the phone rings. "It's O'Neill," Fox says to himself. He shuts his eyes and grips the report. He is not yet ready to speak to O'Neill. He lifts the phone. "Yes? A call from RUC Belfast? You're sure, O'Reilly? From the inspector general you say? That's the chief constable for Northern Ireland. Are you sure? All right, O'Reilly, put him through." And to himself, "As if I don't have enough on my plate as it is, and now someone claiming to be the chief of the RUC. Wait! Isn't that where Murf went? To the RUC?

"This is District Officer Superintendent David Fox. How may I be of assistance?" Fox hears the police telephone operator connect the call. It is an unmistakable northern accent.

(Pause) "Inspector-General Norton, this is District Officer Superintendent David Fox.

(Pause) "No. I'm sorry, Inspector Murphy is not here at present. He's off working on a case – I thought he was up there with the RUC.

(Pause) "Yesterday? Not yet, anyway.

(Pause) "All right. I'll give him the message," reaching for his pen."

(Pause) Fox repeats the message back to Sir Robert Norton, "*I have located the dog's collar – a person of interest is assisting with our enquiries – contact this office ASAP for the next phase.*" Norton is satisfied that the message is accurately received, and the telephone conversation is concluded.

Fox presses his head into his hands. Why would the

chief of the RUC contact a garda station in Mayo about a dog's collar? This is getting more and more bizarre. And then a flash of realisation dawns upon him. It's a coded message, and it's about the case. It's about Murf and his 'dog' enquiry with Sir Robert. It's about the Kennedy murder. Murf followed a lead to Northern Ireland. Murf's prediction was right; one suspect detained in another jurisdiction, and one surrendered here.

Fox is relieved. The case is progressing satisfactorily and quickly. A suspect is in custody, both suspects if you include Mickey Motor Carr. There is still a lot of work ahead. The next phase is to assemble the evidence to make a solid case. At this point Fox feels that he has surmounted the greatest obstacle, the one he considered impossible just a few hours ago.

17:00 hours. O'Neill phones.

Fox speaks on the phone. "Yes, Chief... No, Chief...

"The case is progressing well. Amassing evidence, and tidying the loose ends – the medical officer's report – family to be notified, or state internment if the bodies are unclaimed...

"Yes. I did say bodies. The homicide victim and one of the suspects…

"Yes, Chief. There are two suspects – one took his own life in the lavatory here before we could intervene – that's why the medical officer was summoned. What a mess. The other suspect is in custody in Belfast…

"Yes, Chief. You heard correctly – 'Belfast' – the other suspect is in custody in Belfast. I just spoke with the chief constable ten minutes ago...

"Yes, the chief constable, the inspector general himself. Sir Robert Norton is taking a personal interest in the case, and has requested Inspector Murphy's assistance. That can only mean that this case is much bigger than a single murder in Mayo. The RUC are treating this as quite serious...

"Yes, Chief. Apply for extradition...

"Yes. I agree. Good detective work in just fourteen days...

"That's right, Gardaí and RUC cooperation...

"Well, I am confident that we can finalise the file and look forward to a speedy and successful 'case closed'...

"Thank you, sir...

"Murf – I mean Inspector Murphy cracked it...

"I agree, the best detective on the force...

"Thank you, Chief. Goodbye."

Talking to himself, "5:30pm – No, 17:30 hours. No sign of Murf yet." Fox is unaware that Murf is sitting in Fox's own living room waiting for him to return home. "I'll phone Mrs. Casey to ask about that discount on Mary's 7/11 sunhat. Then I'll knock off. I need to use the lavatory, and ours is 'engaged' until the M.O. finishes up in there."

CHAPTER THIRTY-ONE

MICHAEL CARR'S FUNERAL

Mícheál Mac Giolla Chathair

1906 – 1947

R.I.P.

Óglach na hÉireann

"Sinne Fianna Fáil"

Michael Carr

1906 – 1947

R.I.P.

Irish Republican Volunteer

"We are the Warriors of Destiny"

Friday 22 August

Superintendent David Fox is walking to St Bawn's Church to visit Father Flanagan. Walking along the side of the Blackwater refreshes his mind. It begins to drizzle. Foxy accepts it. Everyone accepts it in North Mayo. The forecast is for 'scattered periods of light rain between some dry spells', much like yesterday's forecast when it was 'dry spells between periods of light rain'. Two funerals resulting from the recent tragedies need to be arranged. The County Medical Officer has concluded his examinations and has presented his reports. Consequently, the bodies are thereupon ready to be released to their respective families.

Yesterday, the Kennedy remains were released to Donal Kennedy, the deceased's Father. Donal Kennedy and nephew James identified the body of Daniel Edward Kennedy. The identification was quick and without any show of emotion. Clearly, it was an unpleasant duty for Donal. He had already made a satisfactory identification based on the photographic evidence and personal items. He barely glanced at the body and made the obligatory confirmation. "Yes. That's my son, Daniel Edward Kennedy..." and he left. The undertaker representative remained behind to look after the funeral arrangements.

Superintendent David Fox is concerned about the bodily remains of Mickey Carr. The official cause of death was given as 'accidental death resulting from a self-inflicted injury'. The term 'suicide' is avoided wherever possible. Mickey had no known family, so funeral arrangements would fall to the state. Fox believes that the community should undertake the arrangements. Hence, the visit to Father Flanagan to arrange a Requiem Mass and internment in the Church graveyard. Would he agree to a Mass under the circumstances?

As it turns out, Father Flanagan is very understanding. He had long worried about Mickey Carr's state of mind. He regards the 'accidental death' as due to a disturbed state of mind and, as such, would not be treated as 'suicide'. But why is Superintendent Fox inquiring, he asks, since arrangements are already underway? As it turns out the 'Old IRA' had stepped forward as 'family' and had already spoken with him early this morning.

"The IRA was here? To make arrangements?"

"To be precise, I was approached by 'Cumann na mBan' the Irish Republican Women's Paramilitary Organisation. Their spokesperson is 77-year-old Margaret Mary O'Hara, you know 'Maura Rua', mother of Martin O'Hara, the deceased Captain of the North Mayo Brigade IRA."

"Oh, yes. I know Mrs. O'Hara quite well. It's strange that I was not aware of this."

Fox returns to the station and contacts the County Medical Officer. Sure enough, an application to claim the body had arrived today from Margaret Mary O'Hara. The medical officer requires the Gardaí to enquire if this is legitimate 'family' before releasing the body. Fox knows that Carr has no surviving family; the IRA is the only family Mickey ever knew. He goes to visit Mrs. O'Hara in Ballycorry, to satisfy himself. True enough, Maura Rua O'Hara has stepped in as 'family' for Mickey Carr. Actually, this is a relief to Fox. It appears that Carr may not be as neglected in death as he was in life. He reports back to the County Medical Officer and to the County Registrar's office that all is in order to release the remains of the deceased as per the application. The body would be released on Monday 25 August.

Word spreads rapidly throughout the republican community. Mickey's service with the North Cork Flying Column 22 is remembered with added embellishment – the most feared assassin in the country's most feared flying column. Mickey's connection to the murder-assassination of Kennedy adds additional interest. The IRA now knows that Daniel Edward Kennedy, the accurate identity of Black Donnelly, is undeniably the man who was once the most hated auxiliary in the West, known then as Captain Edward Daniel.

David Fox, at first, was concerned that Mickey Carr's funeral would not be attended by anyone, except by Ben Muldoon, Mickey's only friend; and by Fox himself who is indebted to him. On Tuesday night, 23 August, the body of Mickey Carr is brought to St Bawn's. Following the rosary at eight o'clock, the body lies in the church for the vigil wake. The coffin is draped in the green-white-orange tricoloured flag of the Republic. Two IRA volunteers in slouch hats decorated with tricoloured hatbands, and with Lee-Enfield rifles inverted, stand guard at the coffin. This is going to be a funeral befitting an IRA volunteer.

The chief commissioner's office in Dublin is alerted and is concerned about the anticipated large IRA public presence. They contact the Divisional HQ in Castlebar and instruct them to provide security: firstly, because of the political heavyweights expected to attend; secondly, 'just in case of trouble'.

Divisional Chief O'Neill leans on David Fox to sound out the local IRA. Fox pays another visit to Mrs. O'Hara. He needs assurance that there would be 'no trouble' at the funeral. He discloses to Mrs. O'Hara his concerns about the attention the funeral might receive, and consequently the inevitable large garda presence.

She nods. "You'll be there, Daithi."

"Of course, Mrs. O'Hara, I'm the district officer. Of course I'll be there." And why did she address him as 'Daithi'?

"No, not as part of the garda security detail, I mean in the church – at the funeral."

"I'll be there – in the church, at the funeral."

"Daithi, you need to be there – for Mickey."

On Wednesday morning the church is crowded with people arriving for the funeral. Old IRA North Mayo Brigade is regrouped and is in attendance. The North Cork Brigade has a detachment of Old IRA in attendance. Sinn Féin is represented. Fianna Fáil, the 'New Republican Party' that split from Sinn Féin, is represented.

In the church, Fox makes sure to have a seat near the back, close to the main exit doors. Chief Superintendent Ultan O'Neill from Divisional HQ sits beside him. Both are dressed in dark-blue garda uniform. Fox is wearing the old-style high-collared uniform, the uniform of the same cut and style as the RIC (now RUC), the same jacket previously favoured by the Black & Tans. Only the colour is different. In the dark interior of the church all dark colours look black. O'Neill raises an eyebrow at Fox's uniform, but says nothing. He knows that Fox favours the old-style uniform because of its regimental-style smartness.

The coffin is still in place from the vigil of the previous night, befittingly draped in the same tricoloured flag of the Republic of Ireland. The 'family' is seated in the front pew on the left side – Mrs. Slattery, Ben Muldoon, Mrs. O'Hara and a member of the IRA. The IRA volunteer is dressed in the acknowledged military overcoat of the IRA, albeit a size too large for him. Margaret Mary O'Hara is dressed in her long brown equestrian skirt and brown military shirt. Sixteen pallbearers are seated in the front two pews on the right. They are dressed in military winter overcoats, even though it is August. Their slouch hats are turned up on the left for rifle carrying. While in church, the hats are worn off the head hanging by the chin straps. Each hat is decorated with a tricoloured hatband, and the IRA badge – '*Óglaıġ na hÉıreann FF.*'

Fox peers at the IRA volunteer seated beside Mrs.

O'Hara. He is unable to identify him from the back, and wonders who it might be. The man turns to speak to Mrs. O'Hara. Then Fox sees the right side of the man's face. It is badly scarred, one eyelid is permanently shut. Fox exhales loudly. It is Charles 'Joker' Kelly. Inspector Murphy in plain clothes enters the family pew and speaks with Mrs. O'Hara. They both look back to where Fox is seated and spot him. Murf leaves the pew. Mrs. O'Hara whispers to Ben Muldoon who then comes back to Fox and invites him to sit with the family. They move over in the seat to make room for Fox, except for Kelly. So Fox sits between him and Margaret Mary O'Hara. In the front pew and visible to all in attendance, the three uniforms look out of place side by side – the IRA overcoat, the old-style police jacket and the brown shirt seated together.

Mass starts – "et introibo ad altare Dei..."

Fox is confused by the Catholic Latin Mass. He never knows when to stand, or kneel, or sit. He looks to Mrs. O'Hara for guidance. She is crossing herself with a rosary, kissing the crucifix and beating her breast. This is beyond what Fox can execute. He looks to Joker Kelly who just sits immobile staring ahead. Why couldn't he be with Murf at a time like this? And where is Murf? He saw him in the church earlier, and not in uniform. The priest approaches the coffin, followed by the altar boy and Murf. Oh, there he is now. The altar boy is carrying a bucket of holy water, and Murf is expertly swinging a smoking thurible with effortless familiarity. The ceremony is coming to a conclusion. The priest sprinkles holy water on the coffin and incenses it with the thurible. At a signal from the priest the ceremony is concluded, eight pallbearers encircle the coffin and carry it to the front entrance, followed by the family and the remaining pallbearers.

Outside, Mrs. O'Hara speaks with Divisional Chief O'Neill. "Keep your men well back, to respect the dignity of the funeral and the grieving comrades. I want no guards coming to the graveyard."

The procession is set to walk the two miles to Killbawn Abbey. The abbey was sacked by Cromwell in 1650 and never restored, but internment in the graveyard continues. Leading the procession are the national flags of Ireland – the tricolour of the Republic, the green flag of *Erin go Bragh*, the Plough and Stars of the Irish Socialist Republic and the Sunburst of the Irish Republican Brotherhood. The coffin is hoisted onto the shoulders of eight pallbearers. Just then David Fox approaches the coffin followed by Ben Muldoon. Fox takes over the lead position and Muldoon the rear position of pallbearers. There is no objection. The sixteen pallbearers will change places many times on the route to the abbey. Flanking the coffin are three honour guards on each side with reversed Lee-Enfields. One more follows behind. This is followed by a military band, the mourners, and finally by the four provincial flags of Ireland representing the four ancient kingdoms. The band plays in slow-march tempo *'All Around My Hat I'll Wear the Tricoloured Ribbon'*.

Murf, O'Neill and the Gardaí watch the procession leave St Bawn's Church. Mary Fox comes up to stand next to Murf. She is softly singing to the music –

> *'All around my hat I'll wear the tricoloured ribbon.*
> *All around my hat, until death taketh me.*
> *And if anybody's asking why I am wearing it,*
> *It's all for my true love...'*

Mary stops singing. "Murf, nobody ever loved Mickey Carr, not from the day he was born to the day he died."

She falls to silence as she watches the procession wend its slow way to the abbey. The Gardaí follow at a respectful distance, but close enough to provide the required security. Mary and Murf remain at the church, watching the procession wend its way to the abbey.

Mary speaks again. "The flags. The drums and guns. Is that for Mickey? Or is it for the IRA's past glories? Look at them now, marching back into the past." Silence again. The band is fading into the distance. "Murf, we didn't do enough for Mickey Carr. We should have done something when he was alive. Now it's too late." Murf and Mary Fox are now alone by the church. "I don't think he could even sign his name. That's how neglected he was."

Mary was correct. Mickey could provide his signature all right, but he executed it as a drawing rather than writing it as a series of letters.

"Take me home, Murf. My legs are weak under me."

Murf does not speak. Mary is grieving. She leans heavily on his arm for support. They walk slowly homewards to the Fox house. At intervals she stops to quote from Isaiah 53:3. "He was despised." She walks a bit more, and stops. "Rejected." Another step. "A man of sorrow." They reach the house. "Acquainted with grief."

Maggie Larkin the maid opens the door. Murf gently releases Mary's arm and addresses Maggie, "Mrs. Fox needs a hot whiskey. Use Foxy's best, the Crested Ten."

"Oh, right you be, Inspector. Come on Mrs. Fox. I know just the thing for you." Maggie has things well in hand. She shuts the door and Murf leaves. He hurries to catch up with the funeral procession.

At the graveyard, the Gardaí are assembled by the wall. They see the funeral party in the near distance. Murf joins O'Neill. They hear the oration, but not sufficiently to distinguish the words.

"So, Murf. What's up with the other suspect in the case?"

"He has been arrested for 'Trading with the Enemy'."

"Trading with the Enemy? How so?"

"We don't have enough evidence to pin a murder charge yet. This arrest puts him out of circulation with no risk of flight while we continue to work on the case. I'm off to Belfast again after the funeral. I'll be assisting with the interview tomorrow."

"How sure are you...?"

He is interrupted by the sound of shots, the rifle party of seven firing into the air three times. After the shots, the 'Last Post' is sounded by the bugler. All are silenced by the sombreness of the ceremony.

The funeral party is breaking up. There is some security work that demands the divisional chief's attention. O'Neill speaks with the reporter from the Connaught Telegraph. His objective is to discourage any reporting that could cause embarrassment. He is beaten to the post by Sinn Féin. There would be no pictures. Sinn Féin has provided the wording for the obituary – the only reporting that would appear in print. The reporter shows him the prepared obituary. O'Neill looks it over, and is satisfied, and thinks to himself with relief, "Good. No 'sensitive' names mentioned, and no pictures – thanks to Sinn Féin."

Mickey Carr is laid to rest peacefully.

CHAPTER THIRTY-TWO

PRIOR IS INTERVIEWED AT RUC HQ

Thursday 28 August 1947

Royal Ulster Constabulary, Atlantic Buildings, Waring Street, Belfast. Terence (Tracy) Prior is in a holding cell. He has just returned from a pre-trial appearance. Garda Inspector John Patrick Murphy is admitted to the office of the Inspector-General Sir Robert Norton. Murf enters carrying a small thin attaché case in his right hand, and a crumpled butter-stained brown paper bag in his left hand.

"Come in, Murf. I saw you at the pre-trial just now." And indicating to the man seated beside his desk, "This is someone who is also interested in Terence Prior. May I introduce you to umm, umm…?" Murf places both the brown-paper bag and the attaché case on Norton's desk.

"Patrick. You may call me Patrick."

Murf recognises him from the pre-trial earlier that morning. They both had looked at each other for an instant, no doubt each curiously regarding the other as out of place in a Belfast courthouse.

"Yes, Patrick. This is Inspector Murphy who has agreed to assist us." It is clear that 'Patrick' is not his usual name. Patrick is dressed in a charcoal three-piece suit, clearly Savile Row. Matching bowler hat and folded umbrella are on the side credenza. Patrick rises and Murf steps forward to shake hands.

"Pleased to meet you, Patrick. Oh, just call me 'Murf', everyone calls me 'Murf', even Nobbie here. Up from London, then?"

Patrick responds, "Good. All on first-name terms. All the quicker to get into the guts of our situation. Yes, I'm down here from London." He stresses 'down' to correct Murf's 'up', and reinforces it with "Up from the country, I see?"

Norton intervenes. "So much for the introductory detective work. Let's all be seated."

Patrick sits carefully so as to avoid wrinkling the crease in his trousers. He stretches out his legs so that his knees do not broaden or 'bag' the material. This pose also displays his highly-polished black shoes, and reveals wrinkle-free socks, held up by suspenders no doubt.

Murf sits in a similar pose, legs outstretched, crossed at the ankles. In contrast to Patrick, Murf's trousers have a crease only part way; the crease disappears at his baggy knees. In preference to shoes, Murf sports rubber-soled boots, somewhat scuffed and discoloured by country living. His socks are of a comfortable heavy wool, fallen down around his ankles.

Murf executes a quick glance around the inspector general's office. The office is luxurious compared to the Kilbawn Garda Station. Everything is pristine – the desk, the wall paintings, and Norton's well-fitted uniform. Murf looks down at his own scuffed and stained boots, and at the crumpled brown paper bag he has placed on Norton's desk.

Norton glances at both without looking directly at either, but does not waver in his discourse. "Murf, I am not optimistic about this case."

Patrick chimes in. "The case is being transferred to London."

Norton continues, ignoring the interruption. "Did you pick up anything of value from the pre-trial?"

"Well, yes, and no."

Patrick expresses impatience. "Either 'yes' you did, or 'no' you didn't."

"The point of the pre-trial was to determine if the case should go to trial. The charge was laid. The defendant refused to plea; he claimed the 'right to silence'. There was a ruling on how to present evidence protected by 'The Official Secrets Act'. Application to move the trial to London was granted."

"So, Murf? 'Yes' or 'no'?"

"'Yes'. I see that Prior is playing you. That's obvious. And 'no'. There is little value in wasting energy and resources on a case that can only bring embarrassment to the Crown."

Norton is incredulous. "Prior is playing us? How so?"

Patrick is more understanding. "Embarrassment and expense. He's right, Nobbie. Prior knows that we have a weak case. The onus is on us to prove, without a reasonable doubt, that he knowingly traded with the enemy, and that the enemy actually benefitted, and that the benefit occurred subsequent to the declaration of war. The only clear benefit was to us, the Crown's Colonial Police. His silence forces the prosecution to present all the arguments in the case. He expects us to dig ourselves into a hole, all on our own. Even at the very worst for Prior, if found guilty, he would receive a prison sentence of only two years."

Norton leans forward with hands on the desk. "So why did you plead to have the trial moved to London?"

"Time, Nobbie. We need time."

Murf continues, "Nobbie, don't lose sight of our objective. We want him for murder."

Norton thumps his head. "Yet so far, we are unable to bring a successful murder charge against him," and to Patrick, "Isn't that so?"

"Nobbie, for the past while, I've been re-visiting old

suspicious cases in Kenya. I've gone over the files, and over them again. Where evidence had been corrupted or concealed, we cannot connect any wrongdoing to Prior. Even in dirty cases, Prior is as clean as a whistle. He covered his tracks every time. Anything we have is just circumstantial and/or conjectural, despite the overwhelmingly strong suspicion."

Murf realises that 'Patrick' and 'Piper's Son' are one and the same. He's from the Foreign Office.

Norton turns to Murf. "So, Murf, over to you. I'm hopeful that you will obtain some success from the interview with Prior. Do you have anything on him in the Mayo murder? Anything of substance? You went to his flat last night."

"And I was there early this morning too, in daylight. McSorley was with me both times."

"...and?"

"I'm still filling in dots to make a complete picture..."

Patrick interrupts. "What 'dots'?"

"Assembling the information according to relevance. Even small things can have significant impact on putting crucial evidence into context. Identifying, searching for, and accumulating hard evidence..."

Norton is impatient. "And did you...?"

Patrick draws his feet back under his chair to lean forward, wrinkling his trousers behind the knees. "So, Murf? Tell us if you have something."

Murf waves them to silence. "I have a few dots to connect still. I may be able to give you something if..." Murf hesitates. Norton and Patrick anxiously await his conclusion. He continues, "...the interview. Nobbie, you arranged for me to be present at an interview with Prior?"

"Yes, at 12:00 noon."

"If this goes well..."

Norton notes the tone of optimism. "If it goes well? You know that Prior is exercising his right to silence?"

Patrick is also speaking. "If it goes well? So you expect to serve an application for extradition?"

Murf, to Patrick, "Extradition. Perhaps, but not necessarily. I'm looking at the wider case, the multiple unresolved cases."

Patrick opens his mouth to request Murf to clarify, but Murf is already addressing Norton. "Nobbie, I need an interviewer, someone smart, well-dressed, well-groomed, respectful – a by-the-book policeman. Have him engage Prior according to the accepted police interview protocol. And let me observe the interview from the observation room for ten minutes or so."

"Murf, do you understand 'exercising right of silence'? Prior is not communicating."

"And that is why I need to observe him being interviewed. What is his posture? His breathing? His eyes? Mouth, face, hands, feet? Every part of him communicates something."

Norton nods understandingly. "McSorley, that's who. You need a polite by-the-book policeman? You need McSorley."

"Okay. Get McSorley in here. I need to prime him for what is required."

Norton flips the switch on his desk intercom. "McSorley! To my office!"

Patrick is attentive to where this is going. But can Murf get to Prior? Murf has no jurisdiction here, so he is not authorised to conduct a police interview. But to observe? To be present? "Murf?"

"Yes, Patrick?"

"Perhaps I could assist at the interview. I have..."

"Patrick, you are the last person I would bring to the interview. You are the epitome of the empire, the symbol of the very establishment that Prior is committed to discrediting. Your presence would only embolden him to greater resolve of resistance."

"Ah, I see. But you, Murf, have sympathy with his proletariat position and his socialist aspirations. The scuffed boots and the stained brown paper bag. These are interview aids."

Murf gives him a knowing look.

12:00 noon. Murf, Norton and Patrick are seated in the dimly-lit observation room. One wall is one-way glass. Through the one-way glass they are able to observe the interview room. A uniformed officer enters the interview room, followed by Prior, a civilian, and lastly by Sergeant McSorley. The uniformed officer shuts the door, and remains standing with his back to the entrance. McSorley indicates the two others to be seated on one side of the desk, the side facing the one-way mirror. McSorley sits in one of the two chairs on the opposite side. He angles his chair 45° and leans one elbow on the desk so that the observation room can read his face. There is a jug of water and four glasses on the desk. Four chairs, four glasses. Prior must realise that the interview room is prepared for four participants.

The walls are bare, except for the cloth-covered intercom fixed to the wall at the mirror. There is no other furniture in the room, and no window. McSorley places his writing pad flat on the desk, and extracts three pencils from his breast pocket – black, green and red. Using the black pencil, McSorley writes a heading on the pad to record the meeting. He proceeds with the mandatory cautioning and informs the defendant of his rights.

Norton reads Murf's gaze in the direction of the civilian. He enlightens him. "That's John Henry Grafton, Esquire, a pro-bono solicitor. The judge at the pre-trial directed a solicitor to meet with Prior to advise him, to counsel him on the folly of representing himself while invoking the right of silence. He has that right, of course, but in the opinion of the judge, it is a rash decision. Prior, however, appears to be ignoring the solicitor; on the other hand he has not dismissed him either. It's not a problem for you, is it?"

"Hmm. It may be to our advantage," Murf remarks.

"How...?"

Murf is concentrating on the interview, and waves Norton to silence. McSorley is fielding standard prepared questions in a professional manner.

"Observe," says Murf, pointing to Prior. "Note the posture. Sitting straight in the chair, resting back, feet together firmly flat on the floor. Both arms are extended 90°, resting with palms down on the desk."

Patrick remarks, "He is relaxed, confident..."

Norton adds, "...in control. Look how silent and motionless he is."

Murf stands close to the glass wall. "Observe his shoulders, the breathing chest, and particularly the eyelids." Norton comes closer. "Look at him. He is alert, yet relaxed." Patrick joins them at the glass. Now all three are standing, observing Prior.

Patrick remarks, "Prior has the look of a card player with a winning hand. He knows that he is holding the trump cards, waiting for the most opportune moment to play his hand."

Norton, who has worked with Prior for many years,

cannot but admire his stoicism. "Look," he says. "Prior is the only one in the room who appears comfortable. He could be at home. The other three are in professional pose." The police officer is standing to attention, guarding the entrance door; the solicitor has a serious legal look; and McSorley is playing the conscientious police interviewer as directed. Norton looks sideways at Murf. "Prior is impenetrable..."

"No, Nobbie. Not impenetrable. He is steadfast and confident. And that is the chink in his armour."

Patrick quizzes him. "How is his confidence a weakness? Surely his resolve is his strength?"

"Prior has been a police officer for 25 years. He has been to court many times and is familiar with the procedures and etiquette. He knows police practices and interview techniques. Everything we do is predictable, so he is a step ahead. He is playing you, not just with his silence, but by his demeanour and conduct. At some point he may change tactics, and take us by surprise and press his advantage. So..."

Patrick is fully in step. "So, Murf, we undermine his confidence by introducing something unexpected. A dilemma or challenge, to make him change tactics..."

"This is where I visit the prisoner. Pay attention, gentlemen. I may need some assistance at the appropriate time."

Murf enters the interview room. He places the stained brown paper bag on the desk. He removes a manila file from his case. This too he places on the desk. He sits down, placing his case on the floor beside his chair. He assumes his usual relaxed pose, legs stretched out, crossed at the ankles, revealing scuffed stained boots and wrinkled socks. Prior does not look at him.

McSorley notes his arrival and inclusion in his pad, and informs the meeting. "Inspector John Patrick Murphy, Éire

Police, is joining us." Solicitor Grafton raises his finger to inquire. McSorley, however, in anticipation of a protest, continues, "Inspector Murphy has no jurisdiction here. He will not be asking questions. He is here to observe, to inform, and to be of service to Defendant Prior."

Murf does not acknowledge Grafton. He continues as if Grafton is not present. "Hello, Tracy. Maura Rua sends her regards. She has sent you some soda bread with country butter and home-made gooseberry jam." He indicates to the brown paper bag.

"As you can see, there is no rationing in Mayo. But I'm afraid the RUC has sliced up the bread. Procedures, you know. They checked for a concealed weapon in there." Murf opens the bag and peers inside. He nods as if to confirm the efficiency of the police search. He places the open bag on the table and delicately slides it forward at an angle, closer to Prior but to his side.

Norton and Patrick (Piper's Son) peer at Prior. They nudge each other when they see Prior's eyelids rise in puzzlement at the mention of Maura Rua. And he cannot help but turn his head to take a quick glance inside the paper bag.

Murf continues to talk, as he bends down to untie the leather whangs (thongs) of his boots. "The lads in the North Mayo Brigade are all in a flutter about you coming to Mayo next month. 'What will you say?' they ask. 'What will be dug up from the past?' they wonder.

"Well, Tracy, I don't need to tell you. You know the anti-treaty IRA and how sensitive they are about their subversive activities. Even after 25 years they don't want to awaken the old dog; better to let him lie. That's the talk that is going around in Ballycorry. Some of the lads are even talking about preparing a pie."

Prior now has a look of bewilderment. His look says

"What on earth are you talking about?" Yet he remains stoically silent.

Murf grunts as he removes a boot, and exhales loudly in relief as he resumes his usual pose. He is holding one of his soiled boots aloft, which he then thumps indelicately on the desk.

Prior sweeps his palms in an arc on the desktop, and draws his arms away from the boot and back to his chest. The look of confidence is gone. His personal space is shrinking. He glances from McSorley to Grafton for some clue. They appear to be just as bewildered as he. In the observation room, Norton and Patrick continue to nudge each other at every observed change in Prior's posture.

Murf continues to talk. "Just look at my boots, Tracy. The bog has them ruined with indelible stains. Of course, you know that. Like you, I favour rubber-soled boots, but the dirt gets stuck in the grooves." As he is speaking, Murf takes a small penknife from his pocket, swings open the blade, and uses it to point at the dirt-caked grooves. "Bogs are unique, Tracy. Mayo bog is much different from Cork bog. Ah sure, why am I telling you this? You have first-hand knowledge of most of the bogs in the West of Ireland." Murf tears a sheet of paper from the back of McSorley's pad, and pours a glass of water while he is speaking. "Now look at this, Tracy." Using the penknife, Murf scrapes some dirt from a groove in the sole of the boot onto the sheet of paper. "Mayo peat. But not any Mayo bog." Murf appears to be counting the little specks of dirt on the paper.

Everyone – Prior, Grafton and McSorley – is straining to see what Murf is referring to. Murf dips his finger into the glass of water. Then he rubs his wet finger along the blade to moisten it. He presses the blade on the specks of dirt, and smears the wet dirt into a stain on the white paper.

"Observe the discolouration spreading out from the dirt. There is something else mixed in with the peat here. Smell it." Everyone sniffs – an automatic reaction to the suggestion. "Pig. That is the colour and smell of pig manure. There is only one place in Mayo, in the whole world actually, where you get Mayo bog and pig manure in the same place. It's an area of no more than 150 square yards. A peculiar thing about bog. A layer of scraw, mostly moist moss, grows on the surface. To get bog wedged in the sole of the boot, one would need to stomp or jump in the bog, or stand for some time so as to break the surface moss. I got all this stuff wedged in my boots by running through the bog and then skidding to a stop at..." Murf lets his words hang in the air as he folds his knife and places it back in his pocket. He removes a folded sheet of white paper from his manila folder. "...the old RIC barracks in Ballycorry."

Prior is now visibly disturbed. He is pressing the heels of his hands against the edge of the desk, and drumming his fingers in agitation.

"But you know, Tracy, I found the same composition of dirt in your flat last night, wedged in the grooves of your rubber-soled boots." At this, Murf unfolds the paper from his folder and places it alongside the first sheet. Both sheets exhibit identical stains.

Sweat appears on Prior's upper lip. He rubs it off. His hand is unsteady. He audibly scrapes the floor with his feet as he shifts position.

Murf bends down. He opens his case and takes out a little hinged box. His head is partly under the table when he says "Mickey Carr." He resurfaces and resumes his familiar pose. He places the little box in front of Prior, and removes his boot from the desk, dropping it on the floor beside his chair. In other circumstances it might be amusing to see a policeman sitting with legs outstretched, feet crossed at the ankles, one loose boot on and one boot off. In spite of this, the atmosphere in the interview room is tense. Grafton is so taken with Murf's performance that he does not inquire as to the relevance of the information. He does not even question if the search of Prior's flat was conducted with proper authorisation. "Mickey Carr has an interesting abode. It's filled with junk. Now, here's a piece of interesting junk from Mickey's place." Murf flips open the box to reveal the timing device that had been on Mickey's workbench. "There is a fingerprint other than Mickey's on this." He pauses for a second and looks at Prior's drumming fingers. In a defensive reflex, Prior stiffens his hands and curls his fingers into a fist. "We have a match." Murf snaps the box shut and quickly places it back in his case like a conjurer performing an act – now you see it, now you don't.

Prior is opening and closing his mouth. It is not clear if he is attempting to speak, or if he is suppressing his desire to speak, or if he is struggling to breathe. He clenches his fists to regain his former bearing and maintain strength of will. Sweat smarts his eyes. He blinks rapidly to focus.

Murf is drawing more papers from his folder. He places two sheets of paper side by side. Both contain dog hairs secured by cellotape. Murf points to each in turn. "Dog hairs from Ballycorry RIC Barracks. Dog hairs from your clothes." Murf places both sheets of paper back into the folder. Prior is blinking, struggling to focus. Things are appearing and disappearing rapidly before him. "If I'm going too fast, Tracy, let me know. Or if you want to examine any of this more closely, you only need to ask. I brought all this to show you, to give you advance warning of what is in store for you in Killbawn next month."

Prior makes a sound, which turns into a cough. He rubs

his mouth and rubs his eyes. His shoulders have drooped significantly in the past few minutes.

Murf continues, "A large dog, fitting the description of an English mastiff, was seen in Ballycorry." He slides a picture from his folder. It is a picture of Rex Secundus. "...a big dog fitting this description. You know, Tracy, this kind of dog was very common 100 years ago. Every big house had a mastiff back then. Fifty years ago it was still quite common. Even ten years ago there were quite a number of mastiffs in Ireland. I consulted the dog-licence records to see how many dark-coloured mastiffs are currently in the country. Well, would you believe it? There is not a single brindled mastiff in all Ireland, not in the Free State, not in Northern Ireland," Murf taps the picture of Rex, "...except this one."

Murf removes a slim green book from the folder. It is Old Moore's Almanac. "Tracy, you take a few days off. You visit your old friend, the other half of the IRA's most competent assassination team in the West during 'the Troubles'. And you visit old haunts. There is no harm in that at all. Now, here's the thing..."

Murf thumbs through the almanac and stops at a page. "Pig-market day in Killbawn, Tuesday 05 August 1947." He turns to another page, "time of sunset..."

He gazes up at the ceiling as he makes calculations, "The cart passed the creamery and turned the bend onto the straight mile to Ballycorry as the sun was setting. Now the straight mile is really only seven furlongs – I measured it. A jennet walking at four miles per hour would reach the old barracks at...hmm. Now that was when the mastiff was observed entering the building. Yes. That's the date and time that a dog fitting the description of Rex here, was observed entering the old RIC barracks in Ballycorry. The next morning, the sole occupant of the house, Captain Daniel

Edward Kennedy, the same Captain Kennedy you knew in the trenches during the Great War, was found dead. Savagely murdered he was. And here's a strange detail: every clock in the old barracks was stopped at the same time – twenty past ten."

Prior is now slumped in the chair. His head is down. He looks spent. McSorley is moved at his appearance. He fills a glass with water and passes it to Prior. Prior takes it and drinks. He drains the glass. This revives him a little. He looks weary, but not defeated. He remains bravely defiant.

"Mickey Carr would not talk to me about the incident. Instead, he hand-delivered a note to District Officer Fox."

There is an audible 'Ah' as Prior inhales sharply, and his eyes register disbelief.

Murf continues, "Carr is illiterate. He is unable to read or write. But his inability is not absolute. Despite his many disabilities, Carr is very intelligent. You must know that, Tracy. You worked closely with him for two years. You must also know that Mickey can recognise some words, and can draw some words, and that he is able to render images in writing."

The brightness that briefly flashed is fading from Prior's eyes.

Murf extracts a flattened cigarette carton sleeve from his folder. Prior can see that it is Will's Wild Woodbine, Mickey's choice of cigarette. Murf taps the edge of the carton sleeve on the desk. "Mickey wrote a note. A very brief note. He wrote it on the inside of the sleeve of a cigarette pack. If you want to see it..."

Prior shakes his head, and turns away. His eyes exhibit a dull tired gloom.

From the observation room, Norton and Patrick watch Murf place his items back into the folder, and return the folder back inside the thin attaché case. Prior appears exhausted, but far from defeated. He still has the look of dogged determination.

Patrick nudges Norton. "What do you think?"

"We are not there yet. We need a confession."

"Look. Murf is not finished yet."

Murf assumes a different posture. He pulls his chair close to the table and sits squarely in front of Prior. This is as close as he can come. He lowers his voice and speaks softly to Prior. "Tracy, you will be tried for murder. You will be found guilty. You will hang. That's the reality of your situation. That's the best you can expect. The IRA may try to reach you, but that is unlikely. We know how to keep you secure. The Department of External Affairs will contact the Foreign Office to execute the extradition order. That will take two weeks. In the meantime, you will remain in custody."

Murf reaches down to retrieve his missing boot. He struggles to put it on. Then he stands up and places one foot on the seat of his chair. He pulls the boot whang tight with a grunt and secures a knot. He tugs the loop and is satisfied that the knot is fast. "You know, Tracy, there IS an alternative."

Prior looks at him with sudden interest. Murf puts his foot back on the floor and proceeds to tackle the second boot. With his other foot on the chair, Murf leans forward on his knee and addresses Prior. "James Connolly. He was executed by the British in 1916. Yet he continues to be an inspiration to socialists to this day. People don't just remember him — they bear witness to him. They speak of him. They fly the Plough and Stars at Bodenstown every year. Every time he is spoken of, his story is validated and the events of his life are given meaning."

Murf fastens his remaining boot whang and places his foot on the ground. Prior is looking at him with renewed interest. Grafton and McSorley are looking at him in curious disbelief. This is not a sentiment one expects to hear in the RUC Headquarters in Belfast.

In the observation room, Patrick is smiling broadly in understanding. Even though he cannot be heard by Murf, he exclaims, "That's it, Murf. Go for it!"

Murf is now ready to leave the room. He walks to the door, hesitates, and turns back to Prior. "Don't go to Mayo to face a death of shame. Why be remembered for the murder of a forgotten old recluse in a forgotten old building? Choose to be an inspiration to your comrades. Give them something glorious by which to remember you. How you rattled the mighty British Empire..." Murf trails off. Prior's mouth is moving as he mentally details his activities in the cause of communism. "Go out in glory, like James Connolly."

Murf slides McSorley's writing pad and the three pencils over to Prior. McSorley quickly tears off the top pages to retrieve his notes on the interview. Murf says softly, "Tracy, a historical account on your service to communism. How you served the cause. This is your chance. This may be your only chance." Murf leaves the interview room.

Murf joins Norton and Patrick in the observation room. McSorley follows him in. Prior and Grafton remain seated in the interview room. The police officer is still standing at the entrance. Prior looks around. He looks at the pad. And then he looks away again. Five minutes lapse.

Aloud, Norton says to himself, "Give him five more minutes..."

As if on cue, Prior lifts a pencil, and positions the pad to write on it. He commences writing, but after the first word, he stops. He looks at the pencil and places it back on the desktop.

Norton throws up his hands and exclaims, "Oh No! He

has changed his mind.”

“No, he hasn’t,” Patrick interjects. “Look. He has changed pencils.”

Sure enough, Prior is writing at a furious rate. He has chosen to write in red pencil. An hour goes by. He is still writing furiously. After 25 pages or so, he stops. He places the pencil on the desk and slides the pad over towards Grafton. He leans back in his chair and rubs his tired eyes. Grafton is flipping through the statement pages.

Norton turns to McSorley. “McSorley, get in there and recommence the interview. Make sure that Prior is aware that the caution is still in place, and remind him of his rights.”

McSorley re-enters the interview room, resumes his place and reminds the defendant of his rights. He concludes with the caution, “You do not have to say anything but anything you do say will be taken down and may be given in evidence. Do you understand?”

Prior mumbles a barely audible “I do.” He then leans towards Grafton and whispers to him. Grafton raises his eyebrows questioningly. Prior gives him no further communication. He leans back in his chair with face tilted up and closes his eyes.

Grafton clears his throat and relays the defendant’s message. “The defendant, Terence Prior, has made a statement which he presents herewith with conditions. A copy of the statement is to be retained by the defendant. The defendant may present the statement in full at trial. The defendant may make public the entire statement as and where he chooses.”

McSorley momentarily looks to the mirror for guidance and realises that he cannot see through it from his side. In the observation room, Norton sends word to him to remain fast and await a decision. Norton and Patrick embark on an argument as to how to respond to Prior. Is it a trick, a new tactic? Is Prior attempting to present unverifiable facts? Or present a fanciful version of events? Or is he attempting to discomfit the establishment?

Norton thumps his fist to his head and remarks, "We don't know if his statement is accurate or if it's far-fetched. Prior may take credit for a lot more than he was involved in."

"So agree, but with a counter-condition," interjects Murf. "Tracy Prior knows that all information must be checked against facts and be confirmed. True, Tracy might be seeking an inflated reputation. And yes, false confessions are common. So, Nobbie, agree; but subject to substantiating the contents."

Patrick is unconvinced. "What about sensitive information? Some of the information may be confidential police information or come under the 'Official Secrets Act' or other relevant legislation. And we can't expose ourselves to egg-on-the-face and public humiliation."

"Really, Patrick?" Murf is not impressed with Patrick's line of argument. "You would restrict justice in favour of face-saving?"

Norton intervenes into what is getting them hot under the collar. "Gentlemen, please!"

Meanwhile in the interview room, the uniformed officer relays the message to McSorley to hold fast and wait for a decision. McSorley looks to the mirror in a vain attempt to elicit a sign. Prior appears to be asleep.

Norton makes a decision. "We will accept Prior's condition with the proviso that the facts check out, and that we comply with, and adhere to, legislative requirements on the disclosure of information. The risk of embarrassment must defer to the pre-eminence of justice. And God help us." Norton goes to the door, opens it and barks instructions. "Get me a stenographer and typewriter!"

Almost immediately, a typist from the pool arrives carrying the tools of her trade – bond paper, onionskins and carbon paper. She is accompanied by a constable carrying a typewriter. Norton grabs a sheet of paper and writes a note. "Go to the interview room. Give this note to McSorley. And be prepared to type." Norton waves them off before either one can say 'Jack Robinson'.

Norton, Patrick and Murf resume their place standing at the one-way mirror. Norton nudges Murf. "Lord, Murf, I could do with some of your 'Three Swallows' right now."

Patrick sighs "Amen."

In the interview room, the stenographer seats herself in Murf's chair and positions the typewriter to her penchant. She feeds in the paper for execution in triplicate, as per the usual police requirement. McSorley reads the note from Norton and informs Prior of the counter-condition.

Prior opens his eyes and says, "Agreed." Then turning to Grafton he says, "Note that."

Whereas Grafton had regarded the pro-bono court directive as a necessary unpleasant task, this engagement with Prior has the makings of a high-profile case. It could turn out to be a feather in his cap. Grafton throws himself into the case with newfound interest and responsibility. McSorley continues to record the details of the interview, duly noting the conditions and counter-conditions in his pad.

Prior looks at Grafton and nods. Grafton coughs to clear his throat and to sound important, and proceeds to read Prior's statement slowly and deliberately. He is cognisant of the need for clarity and the stenographer's typing speed as she types an entire transcript of Prior's statement at the speed of his utterance.

In the observation room, all three refrain from

unnecessary noise and distraction as they strain to hear every detail of the statement. Norton actually smiles for an instant as Grafton attunes his voice to emulate a high-court judge, sounding more like a temperance preacher.

Every now and then Patrick or Norton exclaim a "yes" or a "that's it" in recognition of the facts as they unfold. When it relates to the Humberland case, Patrick almost shouts, "That's it! That's what I believed all along. I just did not know who to pin it on, or how. This ties in exactly."

"Hush!" Norton waves him to silence.

At the account of the high commissioner's driver's demise 'accidental death resulting from blood poisoning from treading on a contaminated nail', Prior describes how he conducted periodic security sweeps of the high commissioner's residence, inside and out, with sniffer dogs. In so doing, he observed the household routines. This gave him opportunity to access the polished shoes. He planted a poisoned nail in the sole of a shoe. The intended victim was the high commissioner. On this one occasion the driver's shoes were on the shelf alongside the high commissioner's. Prior planted the nail in the driver's shoe by mistake. 'An innocent and regrettable error.'

Norton and Patrick punch each other in congratulatory passion. They listen to the entire statement. The interview is concluded with the required acknowledgement, signature and attestation of Prior. There is more to be done, but it's just the formality and paperwork.

Norton considers the next matter to be undertaken. "We will need to inform the authorities in Kenya, so that we can make an arrest pending extradition. For crimes committed in Kenya, Prior will need to stand trial there."

Patrick responds, "Not so. Prior, a British citizen, killed a British diplomat. For the murder of Lord Humberland, we can invoke '*aut dedere aut judicare*'. Prior can be charged and tried here. Of course, Kenya may request extradition and if so we will comply. It is more likely that Kenya would request extradition for some of Prior's other crimes."

"Yes. There are twelve deaths listed in Prior's statement. We may not be able to verify all of them, or be able to make a strong enough case for a conviction in some of them. But the Humberland case is solid. The confession fits the facts exactly."

"Yes. Thanks to Murf, we succeeded in nailing Prior."

Norton turns to speak to Murf. "It's interesting, Murf, Prior makes no mention of the Kennedy killing in Mayo..." Norton stops short. He realises that Murf is not in the room. He enquires in the main office. Where is Inspector Murphy? The front desk informs him that Inspector Murphy had left a short time earlier. Norton instructs the desk sergeant "Send Murf a bottle of Powers Gold Label. We owe him an enormous debt of gratitude."

"Yes, sir!" The desk sergeant is faced with a huge challenge. How is he to obtain a bottle of Powers Gold Label in Belfast? And how is he to deliver it to Inspector Murphy in Mayo, in the Free State?

"I'll look after that," Patrick informs a much-relieved desk sergeant.

EPILOGUE

CASE CLOSED

Terence Prior was transferred to London to stand trial. He was tried for the murder of Lord Humberland, pleaded guilty, and was sentenced. He was executed by hanging. The 'Daily Worker' ran an obituary. The request for the extradition of Terence Prior to Ireland for the murder of Daniel Edward Kennedy was rendered redundant.

Inspector John Patrick Murphy had unravelled the mystery of the 'Black Pig' killing; the case was solved; the perpetrators were detained successfully, albeit never actually arrested for the crime; and the case was officially closed.

A week after Murf's visit to Belfast, on Friday 05 September, an unmarked van delivered a wrapped box to the garda station in Killbawn to the attention of Inspector Murphy. It was a crate of Powers Gold Label. No note, no message. The only clue was a page torn from 'Mother Goose'. It was a picture of a cheeky little boy running down the road with a pig under his arm.

The caption was '*Tom, Tom, the Piper's son, stole a pig and away did run.* The first word was curiously underlined.

POSTSCRIPT

They are all dead now, mostly forgotten – the RIC constables, the Irregulars, Fox, Murf, Daniel E. Kennedy, Joker, Ben, Mickey Carr, Tracy Prior.

The 'Free State' is gone – now a republic.

The border is still there; not actually settled, but no longer actively disputed.

The RUC is gone – replaced by the PSNI, Police Service of Northern Ireland – and it has an excellent K-9 unit. In 2002 an Inter-Governmental Agreement on Policing Cooperation established a programme of long-term personnel exchanges between the PSNI and the Garda Síochána.

The RIC barracks in Ballycorry is now an upscale inn – a picturesque 19th-century stone building. It is situated on a busy highway, the Killbawn by-pass on an 'E-class' road. By contrast, Killbawn, once a busy market town, is now a remote town off the beaten track.

The 'Ballycorry Inn' has a high wall bordering the car park sporting slogans for beer. Does anyone realise that this is the back wall of the handball alley where the RIC once exercised, and where four Cork IRA volunteers were killed during 'the Troubles'? Or that the stylish dining room inside is where six auxiliaries were assassinated? Or that this is where 'Black Donnelly' once killed rats and pigs?

Murtagh Muldoon
12 January 2018

ACKNOWLEDGEMENTS

Confessions: Psychological and Forensic Aspects, By S. M. Kassin and others –
International Encyclopedia of the Social & Behavioral Sciences

History of Royal Irish Constabulary (RIC) and An Garda Síochána – www.garda.ie

Royal Ulster Constabulary (RUC) – Wikipedia

The Second Battle of the Somme, Irish War of Independence and Irish Civil War historical data – Wikipedia

The 'Black Pig': a figure from Irish popular folklore; a variation on the 'Black Dog' and 'Black Hound' myths common throughout Western Europe and Britain. A sighting of the 'Black Pig' is an omen of impending death.

ABOUT THE AUTHOR

Fergus Patrick Egan was born in 1945 in Donegal in the northwest of Ireland. His childhood home was a small village at the Donegal / Fermanagh border between the Irish Free State (later the Republic of Ireland) and Northern Ireland. He spent summers with his paternal grandparents in Mayo. While employed as a banker he lived in ten different areas, where he observed and absorbed the cultural peculiarities of urban and rural communities in the Republic of Ireland and in Northern Ireland. He currently resides in Ontario, Canada.

Books Written by Fergus P Egan:

Black Donnelly, Rats and Pigs
The Coin and the Key
The Famine Field
Dorinda Trapper of Red Rapids
Field of Endeavour and Death
Lanta: Song of the Sea

9 781999 394103